I0546814

Cop House Stories

Seven Allegories

By

WALLACE SHIELDS

Cop House Stories: Seven Allegories is a work of fiction. Names, characters, places, and incidents are the product of the author's imagination or are used fictitiously. Any resemblance to actual events, locals, or persons, living or dead, is entirely coincidental.

Copyright © 2019 by Wallace Shields

Published in the United States by Wallace Shields

Poems "Life's a Bear," "I's as Human as You," and "I Didn't Float Away" are all by Wallace Shields

All rights reserved.

Paper Back ISBN: 978-1-7347561-0-4

eBook ISBN: 978-1-7347561-1-1

FIRST EDITION

Book design by Wallace Shields

with photos by Wallace Shields

DEDICATION

TO MY FAMILY DEBORAH, ERIN, AND CHAD;
LIVE MANY LIVES
AND
ENJOY THEM ALL!
ALSO, THANKS KAREN!

CONTENTS

ACKNOWLEDGMENTS

I would like to gratefully acknowledge my gratitude to the All Mighty, the Great I Am, the Son of Man, for allowing me the people I have met, the places I have seen, and the experiences I have had. I am truly grateful for each because without them my work would not be possible.

THE BEAR HUNT

Life is a bear hunt,

But who's kidding who?

Sometimes you get the bear,

Or sometimes life gets you!

Up the slope, ash-colored clouds with white tops were just starting to set in. And Margret, or Tapeesa as she preferred, thought of a mother and two small redheaded children she had seen earlier playing in a small park near the southern end of her district. She decided to give that area one more look before meeting a friend. Another shift complete.

Better yet, the park where she had seen the family

was at a trailhead leading along slopes and beautiful vistas of the White Mountains. It gave her the urge to signoff up there, call her friend and they could walk. The fact that bears had been breaking into cars in that area was no cause for her to worry. Her patrol area had mainly tame bears, so to speak, bears that rummaged for food in cars with windows left open or trash bins they could get into.

Tapeesa had waved at the family around noon and the woman had not only waved back but also had instructed her kids on how do the same. She even took one child by his little arm to demonstrate waving by flopping his hand up and down. Tapeesa had smiled, but also noted that the woman's minivan appeared secure, and all the area trash bins were locked.

It was a four-season day in northern Alaska, and when Tapeesa had beamed to see the waving toddlers, the sun was shining in a partly cloudy sky. Now, three hours later, she thought how different her day had started. Indeed, there was heavy fog and some freezing rain at first light; sleet and wind came later in the morning; light snow flurries showed by afternoon; and, now sunshine appeared near the end of her shift.

She turned her patrol truck onto Steese Highway, and just as she completed the turn and the road started to allow for cruising at speed, off to her left, she saw a raven flying and flapping as hard as possible to keep up with her. She had a sense of deja vu as she watched the bird struggle to keep up. It hit her then that she had seen a raven the day her father died. That raven had raced her home to receive the bad news from her grandfather. He had told her the bird was most likely her spirit animal and her messenger of trouble ahead. Now, she smiled at that thought because she was not the religious the person her grandfather was. Then, her cruiser's radio cracked and broke a squelch.

"Margret," a male voice called. It was Frank, the Natural Resources Ranger dispatcher.

"Go ahead Frank."

"FPD just put out a report on a missing female and her two kids. Said they might be up near one of your trailheads."

"Okay, I might have seen them earlier this afternoon. I'm headed down that way now to do my last check anyway. I'll let you know if I see anything suspicious. I'll call you on the callbox down there if I've got anything." The raven peeled off to the west.

The radio repeater that serviced that area for the trailheads where the family was last sighted had been in and out of service, but mostly out, for months. However, Tapeesa knew the callboxes at the trailheads were always reliable.

A different Frank—state trooper Frank Ducey, sometimes just called "Ducey," but most often tagged, "Double Nickel"—had heard the original call from the Fairbanks Police Department on the troopers' frequency and decided to make his own sweep through the area since he was close by. He was just coming on shift and was on his way to his patrol area much further north.

When Double Nickel arrived at the trailhead, he was somewhat surprised to see a ranger's truck sitting empty, next to a pale-blue, Odyssey minivan, also empty. No one was in sight. An overturned baby stroller next to the van, and a torn diaper bag, its contents strewn across the lot, were prominent in the scene. Naturally, this sight was disturbing, but with over fifteen years of experience on the Alaska State Highway Patrol, Trooper Ducey didn't jump to conclusions or lose his composure.

Even by Alaskan standards, Double Nickel was a pale man, a natural condition caused by the lack of sunshine most of the year and all that. He had silver-white hair that he combed to the back. He opted for a cap, which he was wearing at the time, instead of the traditional trooper's hat.

He stopped next to the ranger's truck, but before he could get out, a Fairbanks Police Department cruiser pulled next to his. It was driven by Officer Charles Newsome, whom everybody called "Chance." He was a four-year veteran of the Fairbanks police and an early self-reject from the Houston Police Department of the Lower Forty-Eight. Chance was medium—that is, medium brown skin, medium brown eyes, medium build that hid the muscles of an untrained body builder, medium height, medium shaved head, medium wisp of goateed hair in the groove under his medium bottom lip, and finally a medium temperament. He was in plain cloths: dark utility pants, brown hiking boots, and a dark muscle shirt. A waist length, light brown, light weight, utility jacket that matched his shoes completed his attire.

"What you got, Double Nickel?"

"Don't know," Double Nickel replied in his deep Georgia accent. "Just got here myself. How you doin', Chance?"

Double Nickel was six feet two inches tall, but he usually slumped his shoulders and stooped to about five feet eleven. He was wearing the light blue top and dark blue bottom of the AHP standard uniform.

The two men reflexively shook hands before the verbal greetings were done. Taking care not to step on any possible evidence, they walked over to the Odyssey and looked through the windows. A small smudge of gray mud was on the outside of the front passenger-side door. Double Nickel instinctively put his palm on the hood and noted the metal was cold. Then, he and Chance went over to the overturned stroller and diaper bag that had its contents strewn over the gravel. They immediately noticed a very small, but obvious, smear of blood and several droplets that seemed to lead towards an upper dirt parking lot, terraced, about ten feet up hill from them.

Considering this area was not FPD jurisdiction, Double Nickel casually asked, "You on a call out here?"

"No," Chance said, "but when they described the vehicle, it sounded like it might be someone I know, and I know she likes to come up here."

Knowing he had been lied to, Double Nickel took the time to straighten to his full height, rubbed his chin, lifted his cap, and stroked his hair front to back. He had heard a slight hesitation as Chance's very first word escaped his lips. The trooper didn't know why the FPD officer had lied, but he decided to let the deception pass for the moment. He let the subject drop.

"This don't look so good," Chance thought out loud.

"This *don't* look so good," Double Nickel replied not intending to mimic the local officer.

Chance also felt the hood of Tapeesa's truck, noting it was warm. Then he subconsciously rubbed his wisp, something he did when he was in wonder or worry. "You seen the ranger?" he asked.

"Naw, just got here, like you."

"I'm calling for a rescue team to head this way just in case."

"Good luck wit' that. The repeater's bad up here. This look like your friend's vehicle? You'd be better off calling in at the callbox at the trail head." Double Nickel pointed toward the upper parking lot.

"It does, but I'm not really sure." Chance lied again in response to the trooper's question about the minivan.

Chance went to his cruiser, hunched inside, and put a fist around the radio mike. Hearing nothing but hoping to break squelch, he stood outside the vehicle and stretched the cord tight and tried again. It was as though he thought a taut cord would allow a connection to be made. It didn't.

"Nothing," he said to Double Nickel. "I guess the repeater *is* out."

Double Nickel shrugged and looked towards the tree

line along the upper lot, as though the repeater was up there where he could see it.

Just then, Tapeesa's feminine, but loud, voice boomed from some distance away. She was above the upper lot and on a slight ridge at the edge of the woods. She was waving her rifle over her head. They could clearly make out the gray top and green trousers of her duty uniform. Her top was partially covered by a non-regulation, green utility vest.

"C'mon!" she shouted. "And—bring—long—guns!" She clearly enunciated.

Police have this strange habit of engaging in macho banter and actions when situations get tense, and repartee is just what Chance and Double Nickel reverted to at Tapeesa's call to action.

She didn't have to ask Double Nickel twice. His preferred *long gun* was an AR-15 with a scope and fifty-round drum. It wasn't exactly regulation or light, but it was what he preferred in a fight. He was always happy to "bring the long gun," and an eager, odd, happiness showed on his elongated face, even though, he had no idea what was going on.

Chance, on the other hand, liked to think he chose something with proven stopping power against man or beast. Reaching into his cruiser, he came out with a regulation Remington, eight-seventy, pump shotgun and a bandolier full of double-aught buckshot cartridges and slugs. He slung the ammo belt over his head to rest on his shoulder and told Double Nickel, "This is Old Fateful, and yes I meant F-a-t-e-f-u-l."

This raillery was the epitome of breaking stress for the two men. This kind of cowboy banter fed their courage.

"Okay, I'll bite. Why is that?" asked Double Nickel "'Faithful' too hard to spell?"

By then, the two men were walking fast towards Tapeesa. Their mission seemed urgent, but their pace was calm, quick, and steady.

"The dictionary says 'fateful' is to have far-reaching and disastrous implications. That's what I'm all about when I carry this thing."

"How long you been waitin' to spring that little nugget?"

Both men laughed, and the "little nugget," as Double Nickel called it, helped break the tension of the moment even more. They were also both relieved to know the ranger was okay and it showed on their faces.

Tapeesa planned to meet the other two officers nearer the edge of the field on the edge of the upper parking area. This was a spot not visible from where the two men first saw her.

As they came back in sight of Tapeesa, Double Nickel said, "I don't believe I've ever seen her before, but she looks familiar. You know her?"

"Yeah. She's been here for 'bout six months or so. Moved from the North Slope country. Nice girl. She's Inuit."

"That's strange. I didn't know any Inuit women were in law enforcement up here."

"I can tell you she is one of a kind. They say her granddaddy was a legend up there in the north. Said he could talk to bears."

Tapeesa was small compared to the other officers. Her straight, black hair was pulled back behind her ears into a ponytail that extended down her back. She wore a DNR cap and bore the traditional facial tattoos rarely seen on modern Inuit women: a faint, double-line V tattoo that extended up from the bridge of her nose with extensions that continued in parallel lines, one above each eyebrow. Another group of tattooed lines, two thin and one thick, started under her bottom lip and went straight down, curving under the cleft of her chin. She had not had the tribal markings when Double Nickel had last seen her as a young girl, a child really, and he felt reluctant to mention them, but he was sure she was a young girl he knew well.

Apart from the tattoos, her eyes and cheeks were sharp and could have belonged equally to a Russian Cossack or a Dakota Sioux, a nod to her ancestors probably crossing the Bering Straits from Europe to Alaska long before either place existed on a map. Her body, though petite, was wide in a sexy kind of way, at least that's what Chance thought, and his raw carnal desires peaked through his straight face.

She carried a rifle almost as tall as her, which she draped over the fold in her left arm, barrel up, in the manner of an Inuit hunter. That practice left her right hand free to shake hands, pull her Glock 228 pistol, holstered on her right hip, or cross-draw the large Atlas knife she kept on the other side at her core. On this occasion, she wanted to shake hands.

Double Nickel exclaimed, "Tapeesa?"

She smiled. "Most people call me 'Margret' down here, but you called it right. I'm surprised you recognize me, Mr. Ducey."

"I didn't, at first. And other police officers just call me Ducey or Double Nickel."

"My guardian mother found it hard to call me by my real name, so she asked me to choose another one from the Bible. I chose 'Martha,' but she insisted on calling me Margret most of the time. I didn't mind 'cause neither one was my name anyway. But I kinda liked the one she called me, so I keep it as a nickname, and that's how most people down here know me. Too much information, right? Especially under the circumstances.

"Hi, Chance!" Tapeesa said in a flirty tone as she focused her sharp eyes squarely on the square-jawed Fairbanks officer with the bandolier draped over his shoulder. She smiled and asked, "Who you, Pancho Villa?"

"Hi Margret, I mean Ta-pee-sa," said Chance. "I guess you two know each other," he added, speaking of Double Nickel in hopes of diverting attention from himself and the awkward struggle with her name.

Tapeesa looked at Double Nickel and said, "See what you started? That's why."

Double Nickel rub his chin as he started to put pieces together in his head.

The men shook hands with Tapeesa, but the smile

had faded from her small face. The jovial greetings and cordial, if brief, conversation between the three may have seemed out of place to some, but the true nature of their business was not far from their minds. The sense of urgency, which was sparked by the call for long guns from Tapeesa and had moved the men into action, faded to a sense of disappointment once they arrived at her location and saw nothing to fight, nothing to fear. The pace of their mission was like moving from rescue to recovery, if either of those option even existed regarding the missing family. Only Tapeesa could explain their situation. Maybe?

Tapeesa squatted and pointed to a place where the grass was bent and twisted. For her, this bit of muddle showed that someone—or something—had been pulled or dragged across the thawing soil. She also pointed to two divots about an inch apart that might have indicated someone resisting that dragging motion.

Chance stroked his wisp and asked, "You think she was pulled off in the woods?" He was referring to the mother of the family.

"Yes," said Tapeesa. "But..."

Double Nickel interrupted, "I guess you've told us if you saw sign of the kids."

"But I think it was a bear." Tapeesa continued. "And no, there is no sign of the mother or her kids so far. I would have gone after them on my own had I seen anything obvious. I went up in the wood line and saw some bear sign, and I believe I found a place just over there ..." she pointed to a field at the end of the lot, back towards the cars, "…where a bear has been staging."

"Staging?" Chance asked.

"Yeah," said Double Nickel. "If they huntin', bears stage on high ground sometimes before they attack." He looked at Tapeesa. "Your granddaddy taught me that."

Tapeesa didn't respond directly to Double Nickel but said, "I've been looking for where he killed the family. Thought it might be close by, but there's no sign, so far, just the blood droplets in the parking lot. I guess you saw 'em."

"How do you know it was a 'he'? Not that it matters," said Chance.

"I saw fresh tracks over there and it's a big one, maybe nine hundred pounds, and a grizzly. Too big to be a girl. I think we need to get on the trail as soon as possible, find the kill site, and then track it from there. I've already called for a search team, by the way. Used the callbox. They're sending dogs, too."

Chance said, "I figured you might. You believe the kids run off?"

Double Nickel said, "First, I want to see them tracks you talkin' about."

"Them kids probably followed they mama if she was dragged off," Tapeesa said. "We're losing time, but you two go ahead and look. You can read tracks just like me. I'm going ahead and see if I can catch a sign while we can. You guys can catch up. You see them clouds." She looked towards the west. "We could get snow anytime. And you know how fast the weather can change."

Double Nickel stood taller again. He removed his cap, looked at the sky, sniffed the air, and rubbed his fingers through his hair again before putting it back on and heading off towards the spot where Tapeesa had pointed. Chance followed the trooper. Tapeesa turned, went back into the wood line, and slipped from view within seconds.

The sky was suddenly grayer, and the breeze picked up, making the uncut sedge grass, mix weeds, and bushes move like green waves of seaweed in a current of emerald water. The men found the spot where the vegetation was packed and saw signs of where the bear—if that's what it was—had actually crawled to the edge of the parking lot, several times probably, looking over to where the cars were parked.

"I think she's right," Double Nickel said. "This is staging." He was looking at dotted depressions in the grass and a sparse patch that revealed a partial paw print in the mud.

He whistled low to himself and said, "This thing is huge. And I'm pretty sure it's what got the woman. The mud matches that what was on the car so that could mean she caught it while it was trying to break in, or it startled her. It could've knocked her to the ground, maybe even knocked her out, or killed her, and then pulled her across the parking lot. That's why there is so little blood or signs of a struggle. But I still think there should be more blood and even some remains if a bear got 'em. But on the other hand, what I see could have been man or beast. Bears don't have table manners, especially males. They kill, then they eat."

Cops were doing what cops do, discussing the theory of the crime. Chance looked back towards where Tapeesa had gone into the wood.

"She seemed pretty confident," said Chance.

"Her granddaddy was the same way, cocksure about everything. Saved a lot of lives up on the slope though, including mine, before he took one too many chances. Now, I think I better do him a solid and take care of his granddaughter."

With the idea of saving her from herself, Chance and Double Nickel headed through the cottonwood forest to find Tapeesa.

Chance, as nonchalantly as possible, asked, "Why do you call her Tapeesa?"

"I don't just call her that. That's her name. It means 'Arctic Flower.' By the way, you can drop the act. You doin' her, ain't you?"

Chanced grinned and didn't bother to answer.

The two men followed general protocol when hiking in bear country by talking and making noise. The wind was in their faces and they hoped this wind direction would give them the advantage over whatever—whoever—they were tracking.

They simultaneously spotted Tapeesa ahead in a clearing in the wood. She was staring at an old aspen tree. The growth around it split the faint trail they were on. She put a clinched fist in the air, as though she was signaling a possible ambush to her combat patrol. Double Nickel had seen her grandfather, Johnn Bayer, do this many times to prevent attacks on pipeline workers when they were on the lookout for polar bears and wolves. At least, that's what Bayer had been hired to do back then. Tapeesa continued to stand in that spot for another quarter-minute, and then her hand came down.

"What've you got?" asked Double Nickel. He thought about the many times he had seen Bayer "talk," as he called it, to trees, rocks, rivers, wide places in the road, and even whole mountains. On some occasions, Bayer had even talked to the moon, stars, and sun. What may have seemed strange, even alarming, to relative newcomers like Chance, was completely familiar to Double Nickel.

Double Nickel thought he understood the Inuit people as animists in its purest form. As a state trooper, he had taken a course on the native populations of Alaska and learned the Inuit believed all objects had something to say if one had the patience to listen. But he had learned an even deeper understanding during his work with Johnn Bayer, more than he would ever learn in any course or could explain to any non-Inuit.

At the moment he saw Tapeesa with her fist up on the trail, Double Nickel also felt his life had suddenly boiled down to this time and place. He recollected how Johnn, who was a drunkard and profane man, could talk to bears, especially what he called the king of all bears,

"Nanuqs," or polar bears. Ducey smiled to himself when he thought about how Johnn Bayer did his best *talking* when he was drunk and about how he also cursed these same creatures and objects in English, French, and Inuit. Many people had told Double Nickel that Johnn also had this gift with "Taqukaq," or grizzly bears, but he had not seen this gift for himself. As for the polar bears, Johnn could get them to stay away, and if they didn't listen to him, they ran toward him in hope of being killed by a "great hunter," Johnn claimed. At least, that's how he had described his methodology.

Johnn would say, "This Nanuq is going to charge. He wants to hang on my wall and have me bring him gifts of my best beer and knives."

The Mainland Pipeline Company had hired men like Johnn to provide fresh meat to the camps and keep the bears away. Sometimes, those two tasks coincided, as some of the workers put it, and the camp had fresh bear meat stew as a result. Many of the pipeline workers came from the southern and western lower United States and had grown up rough, to say the least. They agreed with the description of themselves as "exiles in their own country." Some had come to Alaska as criminals and misfits, often running to evade punishment for one crime or another. Others considered themselves nonconformists who wanted the freedom they thought Alaska would offer. These men often clashed with their bosses, the native populations, and the police. But their superiors overlooked these transgressions if they showed up for work mostly on time and mostly sober or if they could at least work safely while drunk.

As for their problems with the native populations, that was one of the reasons men like Johnn had been brought on the pipeline as well. These were Inuit men who didn't necessarily agree with the pipeline or the oil fields, but they garnered respect from the lower forty-eighters by taking them hunting and fishing in their off hours. The two groups got along on this basis of mutual interest, but a few workers had come back to camp with bumps and bruises for insulting their guide or Inuit women. Some men on those crews hadn't come back at all, but not much mention was made of their absences, and no reports to the police were ever filed. It was best to assume these errant men had run off to other adventures.

Of all the Inuit men working for the pipeline, Johnn was by far the most respected. Yes, he'd lost men, as in they were killed, who'd chosen not to listen, as many misfits and criminals were prone to do, but he never purposely lost anyone.

When the company hired Frank Ducey, he had a bad reputation. He was considered a misfit and a mean drunk, but he was not disrespectful to Johnn but once. Johnn took Frank Ducey under his wing and made him into Double Nickel.

Johnn took Frank on many hunting trips in the far north. As Frank often told the story, it was one of these times when a big Nanuq threatened to charge him from no more than twenty-five feet away. Johnn stepped into the path of the great white beast. He showed no fear and even smiled; his gun draped across his arm. He stood perfectly still with a hand out to Frank, signaling him to do the same, to stand perfectly still. Bayer stared at the animal for about three minutes that seemed like three hours to Frank. Then the bear sniffed the air and made as if to charge more than once but stopped each time and pawed at the ice instead. Finally, the huge animal backed away of his own accord. It was then that Frank started to understand the true nature of Johnn Bayer.

Relieved to have escaped a bloody death and yet angry Johnn had stepped in the path of the creature to save him, an odd, but common, phenonium among the Alaska misfits, Frank shouted at Johnn, "I thought you were paid to kill bears!" His anger made him tremble.

"Nanuq said he wasn't ready to die today. Besides, I'm not paid to kill bears, I'm paid to keep them from killing you," Johnn replied in a calm voice. "This is his home, where he is king. He decides who lives and dies here, even if it's its own death he achieves."

"You learned all that in a stare-down contest. He blinked, and now you understand him?" Frank had said at the time.

Johnn had replied, "No, but I understand life. Are you just going to wish for a gun and a kill as a way to solve all your life's problems? The bear hunt that is life requires lots of solutions and most of them start with just being still."

Frank Duccy was no more than twenty-one years old

back when the incident with the bear occurred. Only a few people knew his first name. In fact, the suspicion among his coworkers on the pipeline was that he was wanted in Georgia. The truth was he'd left Georgia on a freight train heading to Texas when he was fourteen. Why the Lone Star State? He said it was his idea of western adventure with cowboys, roughnecks, oil fields, and fortunes waiting to be made. When talking to his fellow workers on the pipeline about his previous life, something he seldom did, he laughed about stealing cans of potted meat and packs of cheese cracker from convenience stores unfortunate enough to be located near the railroad tracks.

Years later, after he became a state trooper, he said to his police buddies, "But for the grace of God go I. If they had caught me doing half the shit I did back in those days, they'd have put me on some prison farm and called it a good day. But a man's gotta eat!"

And Frank did eat. He survived but he never, ever talked about the home he left in Georgia or why he left. His friends and coworkers knew little about his life before he moved west.

After arriving in Texas, Frank eventually got a job with a subcontractor in Port Arthur, while living rough, sleeping in homeless shelters, and on the streets, and doing every low paying job he could find around the railyards for a time. He had to lie about his age, which meant a stable job was out of the question. He lived strictly on the gig economy.

He even picked cantaloupes when the farmers paid

well. But Port Arthur was an oil a gas refinery town, so it wasn't too long before he was hired by a subcontractor to scrub out the big oil and gas storage tanks for the refiners. By then, he looked like a man, so his employer asked no questions about his age. It was some of the most dangerous work around, but it got him in the door and paid better than fruit picking or minimum wage.

About two years into that job, the newspapers reported how, one after another, four of Frank's close friends and coworkers crawled into one of those giant storage tanks they were supposed to clean and promptly died. Each was trying to save the other from carbon monoxide that had built up in the huge structures without warning. What the news didn't report was that Frank was the fifth man on the crew. He didn't go down into the tank after he saw what was happening to the four who went before him. He went for help instead.

After that tragedy, no matter the reassuring words from the other workers that it was "not his fault," he felt the other workers blamed him for not crawling into the same tank to a certain death, in a symbolic effort to save his friends.

By age nineteen, Frank had hired on with a rigging crew to do roughneck work in the oil fields of Alaska, one of the few places left where ruffian men could make legal fortunes.

A lot of people in the Alaska oil fields went by last names or nicknames, so people started calling Frank "Ducey." That was okay with him, until he nearly beat a coworker to death for trying to nickname him "Dukey." Frank thought this sounded a little too close to another name for baby shit. He decided to put an end to it before it started. Of course, he was drunk. They were all drunk. And drunken fights were just everyday living in the oil fields.

Frank was fired after that incident, mainly because the other guy was a better worker. Then, Frank went to work with Bayer, who was working for the pipeline as a hunter and guide. Bayer hired Frank as a favor to the foreman who had just fired him.

Frank told Bayer at the time of his *interview*, "You know how it is in the oil fields. We're like a dysfunctional family, but we close. We hate each other half the time and loan money to each other or shared our whisky, the other half. Hell, me and the guy I beat were drinking buddies again a week after he got out of the hospital." Of course, Bayer couldn't have cared less as long as Frank was a good worker.

Johnn was already famous as a hunter and tracker long before Frank arrived, and it was a good thing Johnn was a patient man. He and Frank didn't hit it off for a long time because Frank didn't like working for a native. Johnn saw this relationship as a challenge. The other men were hunting for meat and keeping the bears and wolves away from the pipeline and oilfield workers, but Frank's job was to help cook, wash clothes, and generally keep campfires going. This was really just Johnn's way of soliciting humility from his newest employee.

In that deep Georgia drawl, Frank once recollected

to his state patrol coworkers: "Bear attacks really never happened, but the bears were all around because back in those days, the food scraps and trash in the work camps was not strictly policed. Johnn was one of the first ones to point this connection out and his observation eventually made the camps change their ways. It didn't occur to the workers at the time, but Johnn never killed any man-killer bears. Deadly bear attacks just didn't happen 'cause he kept 'em away. However, they did sometimes hunt 'em for meat, just like they hunted caribou, elk, ducks, and rabbits. Nothing tastes better than roasted, artic rabbits."

After Frank's almost-fatal encounter with the polar bear, he went to Anchorage to buy a handgun for personal protection. When he came back up to the camps, he was wearing two nickel-plated, Smith & Wesson, Model 19 revolvers on a two-gun shoulder rig.

"He got them on a package deal from a pawnshop," Johnn told his work crew at the camp. "After two days of me and everyone else laughing at Frank behind his back, I let him have one of my old hunting rifles and insisted he take them damn fool gadgets off."

But that wasn't the end of Johnn's chiding. He also started to call Frank "Double Nickel." But Frank didn't like the name either, so he bowed up at Johnn.

"But Johnn pulled his second-best hunting knife," as Frank later described. "Then, he started lookin' at the blade, then into my eyes, and threatened to mark me up good if I raised a hand to 'im. Said it in kind of a fatherly way. And for me, that look ended that. I was no longer interested in challenging Johnn Bayer."

Frank later reflected on how Bayer had also saved him in another way, by truly saving him from himself. Frank described himself as a dangerous drunk with a bad temper back in those days. While Bayer never talked directly about Frank's drinking, Frank said Johnn often led him deep into the woods where they created sweat lodges that they shared. Sometimes, they just sat and talked for hours.

"Keep in mind, Bayer could drink most men into unconsciousness and out cuss a cowboy herding cattle for branding," Frank often recalled. "But something about that experience in the lodges seemed to change me."

Bayer also taught him to read signs, track anything, and understand the noises that others described as the "quiet outdoors."

After a couple of months, Frank had quit drinking. He explained to his coworkers at the camps, "I just lost the taste for it." After the transformation, Bayer took Frank hunting and tracking and even tried to teach him how to talk to the trees, but for Frank, that ability didn't take.

By all accounts, after Frank calmed down, he was reborn as Double Nickel. The Inuit men called him "Nutara," loosely meaning "new child" of Johnn Bayer. But Johnn and Frank's misfit friends still called him Double Nickel, a name he eventually came to love.

Double Nickel was remembering those past times, not to distraction but more a whisper of contemplation, when he came back to the hunt and saw Tapeesa standing in the fork of the trail in front of that aspen thicket, with her fist up.

"What you got?" he asked, as he and Chance slowly advanced.

"Not sure. Strange, though. I was reading the area, and something was just out of place. I can't quiet put my finger on it."

Double Nickel said, "Your granddad was always good at that. Tried to teach me but… Don't tell me you have the gift?"

"My only gifts from him included his second-best knife—the one he carried every day—knowledge of where to hunt caribou this time of year, and where the king salmon spawn." She smiled with nostalgias before continuing, "He said I would never go hungry. No. My granddaddy just taught me to pay attention and to understand what my senses tell me. And right now, my senses are telling me to go right, up the slope, even though a wild animal will usually go downhill towards water. The instinct of most bears is to make the kill and eat their fill. That's not what this bear, or whatever it is, is doing. And something else is out of place but not unexpected."

Tapeesa suddenly focused on the ground to the right side of the main tree. She saw something struggling in the thick. It was a blackbird, a raven, attempting to fly, but it was stopped by the thickness of the brush. She watched as it freed itself and flew off up the hill, to the surprise of the two men. Tapeesa cautiously walked up through the dense scrubs and plucked out a toddler's white shoe. "I suspect we might find them up there," she said, pointing further up the slope in the direction of the bird's flight.

"If it's a bear, why wouldn't it have killed them by now?" Chance wondered aloud.

"No reason to. I believe you know what I mean, Tapeesa," said Double Nickel.

Tapeesa heard him, but she was already headed up the slope, and in her mind, her spirit animal was already preparing her to find a bloody mess of clothing, human skin, hair, and gnawed and cracked bones. This gory vision, more than any hope of saving the mother and two children from harm, was behind her urgency. The sense of déjà vu was strong, powerful. She had seen places where bears had made kills, and she could only imagine what a human kill would look like. She wanted to put her expectations in the deepest place in her mind and leave it there so she could function. Then, she would be filled with relief when the kill sight was not quite as bad as she imagined. But believing the family was already dead didn't lessen her desire to take care of them. That aspiration of helping them was where her sense of reliving something she knew had never happened met her hope that she could do something useful in the real world.

Many people, coworkers and friends of Johnn Bayer, said he had been a harsh taskmaster to Tapeesa's father, Johnn Jr. These same people said it was because Johnn Jr. had chosen to abandon the Inuit subsistence traditions of hunting, trapping, fishing, and guiding hunters in favor of working with the survey crews marking the route for the pipelines. The contravening deed is that Johnn Jr. was eventually killed on a trip to the Far North, while showing some coworkers the Inuit way of fishing with nets on the ice. He and two other men were accidentally dragged under the ice through a hole they had made and extended a net through. It was believed a whale got caught in the net and dragged them under the ice.

Part of Bayer's job was to track missing workers, so it was only a matter of hours, after arriving in the area where his only male descendent had gone missing, that he found his son in the shadows of a sound. Tapeesa was ten years old when the accident that took her father happened and she continued to live with her grandfather for four more years, until his death in 1982.

"You was born, and your mother died," her grandfather had said when Tapeesa was old enough to understand. He didn't sugarcoat his message or over dress it. He simply answered her question about why she didn't have a mother. Few words with his granddaughter was Johnn's way unless he was teaching or explaining, and neither he nor her father said that much more about the death of her mother. There were no other siblings, so Tapeesa had occasionally bounced around relatives' homes and lodges, hunting villages, and workcamps from the time she was a born until her grandfather died. But she was always under the old man's watchful eye. She would miss him much more than she missed her father.

Though her father was around on and off, she considered the time with her grandfather as her best. During those years, he showed her the ways of the Inuit, much as he had done for her father. He took her out on the ice and into the trees on bear and moose hunts. They collected geese and wild duck eggs. They shot caribou and elk with rifles and bow and arrows. They built snow caves and camped out on the ice to see the Aurora Borealis at special times of the year. He taught her where to hunt in all seasons, when and where to go and always find fish, and how to track anything, but he did it with a silent gentleness he'd never shown his son. She learned to thrive in nature under his guiding hand.

Tapeesa recalled one of best times she ever had was a year before her father died when her father and grandfather drove her to Canada for the Calgary Stampede. She was so excited. "I thought they were going to stampede horses through the town," she said to her grandfather at the time. Then, she finally realized it was a just big rodeo, not that she understood what that was either. But the main reason they went was to be part of a pow wow of thousands of native peoples from all over the Great North.

Her grandfather wanted her to see this gathering. They walked among different clans and relations, talked with distant cousins, and traded skins and knives. They attended cultural dances, sampled foods, participated in ceremonies, and generally enjoyed the fair-like atmosphere.

They camped on the edge of Calgary with hundreds of others. It was July and no need for a fire, but they always had a small one anyway because that's how they cooked their food and heated their wash water.

As they sat cross-legged on skins covering the ground around the embers one night, her grandfather, always a man of few words to her, looked into the wispy smoke and said, "Always remember this. You belong to this wild country up here just as your mother and grandmother did, just as I and your father do. These places will take care of you. Don't let borders stop you. You must take care of it all. Talk to it. Hear it when it speaks back. Know its languages. Carry this burden with you, always, and it *is* a burden.

"Life is like a great hunt, a bear hunt. If a problem charges towards you, stare it down and, if need be, take it on. If it runs a way, leave it alone. Little bears bring little troubles. Big bears bring killing troubles but don't turn your back on either. Never turn your back on either. Just be prepared.

"I have done my best to prepare you for the hunt, and the hunt will always find you. When you find your big bear, look it in the eye, and both you and it will know what to do. Some trouble you just can't run from. Trust yourself. And after the successful hunt, you will feel a peace like you never felt, but remember, there are always bears ahead."

She nodded but had no idea from where this locution had erupted. But she always remembered what he had told her.

With her father and grandfather dead, she decided to go into foster care as a ward of the State of Alaska. She had an aunt and two great uncles who asked her to come and stay with them, but they had big extended families already, and she didn't want to be a burden or to get lost in their big clans. Besides, she knew she would probably go into a foster home in Anchorage, and she always like it there when her grandfather took her to the dogsled races. She also knew she could get her college paid for as a ward of the State.

Tapeesa was placed with a strict foster mother, Genene Swanson, who had one of the few homes that would take in an Inuit teenager. She had a decent experience in foster care, despite being forced to pick a new name.

Swanson was a single mother of two boys who fostered children for a living, so she looked upon her young charges as more business than personal propositions. That meant the foster kids were adequately clothed and fed, but there was nothing extra, including affection. It was a cold house in many ways. Although Mrs. Swanson was a no-nonsense foster mom, Tapeesa loved the environment.

Like her grandfather, Tapeesa found herself to be an introvert when it came to people, though she had a way with nature.

She went straight from foster care at age seventeen to the University of Alaska at Fairbanks where she graduated in three years with major in Alaska Native Studies and a reputation for being a loner. She spent a year hiking, living off the land, and immersing herself into her

Inuit culture. That year was also when and she got her native tattoos.

Straight out of her immersion, she began her career with the Department of Natural Resources on the North Slope where she excelled as a sworn DNR officer. She had a disarming way that said, *I'm cool with you and your hang-ups, but don't play me for stupid.* After four years, she was transferred to the Fairbanks district. A year later, she started a tentative relationship Chance Newsome.

They met at an elk supper put on by the Paramount Gas Company. "In appreciation of local law enforcement," the flyer read. The place was an old, one-room, log cabin rented out by the Elks. Tapeesa had expected to find her usual place at events like this, on the wall and in the shadows. But this bronze, Fairbanks cop, who also looked out of place, would not leave her along. He spent the whole night asking her questions and getting one-word answers. She suspected it got to be a game to him to try and get more than one word out of her at a time, but she never relented. Then, the next day, he tracked her down and left a phone message for her at work. She didn't call back.

Six weeks later, they met again on the scene of a logging truck accident. It was night, windy, and light snow was falling. She was using a flashlight to direct a tow truck into position to do its work.

Chance walked up behind her and said, "You don't give a brother a break, do you?"

She turned, smiled for the first time, and said, "Fine."

The tow truck continued to move backwards at her directions.

"Fine? What does that mean?"

Her attention was still focused on what she was doing. "That means I'm off as soon as I'm done here, and I would love a cup of hot tea in a warm place."

Hot tea and warm places lead to hikes at Denali and fishing on the Chena River. They finally sheared a tent at Birch Lake on an ice fishing weekend. Tapeesa still kept to herself when it came to everyone else, but she loved trying to show Chance all the activities her grandfather had shown her.

Double Nickel had heard that when Tapeesa was about fourteen years old her grandfather had gone out onto the ice alone on a far-north hunt for Nanuqs. Local legend had it that he "lived with them ever since," meaning he died on the hunt.

The word of Johnn Bayer's death came to Double Nickel about two years after he had walked into a state trooper post on his mentor, Johnn Bayer's advice and applied for a job. At the time, a grizzled old corporal had looked at his younger sergeant and said, "If he can learn to stand up straight, put on a few pounds, he might do." They were in the regulation of hiring tall men back then so Ducey fit the bill on that account.

What Double Nickel didn't know was the sergeant was holding a letter of recommendation from Johnn Bayer. He was well acquainted with Bayer. As a boy, he and his father were guided on many fishing and hunting trips by the Inuit legend. Of course, the young sergeant ignored the playful chiding of his older subordinate and helped bring Double Nickel onto the job, and he never told of their connection.

Back on the hunt, the Aspin forest had opened up to true bear habitat. Tapeesa crested the top of the rise and saw a lake in the next valley, she was thinking the bear had to be close by. There were outcroppings of rocks, low bushes, and a good water supply flowing down the hill. There were ample brushes where a bear could hide a den. Double Nickel walked directly behind Tapeesa as she moved more cautiously, and Chance was on her left. Some deep instinct nudged her. Her grandfather's words came to her: *Life is a bear hunt. Be ready for a fight.*

She froze, sensing she may have made a terrible mistake. In an adrenalin laced flash, her eyes caught a rising of brown fur and wild eyes to her left. There was no mistaking the face of a grizzly, big and imposing. It charged them, galloping more like a rhinoceros than a bear. But before Tapeesa could say or do anything, she went flying. She landed on her side at the feet of the two men but came around much like a snake uncoiling. Still on the ground but sitting, she held her knife in her right hand as she would to cut with an ulu blade, the metal extending outward from the bottom of her hand and facing out from her body. She had the choice of slashing or stabbing. In an instant, she slashed out and came within a sock's thread of cutting

Chance's Achilles tendon before abruptly drawing back.

She had not realized it, but Chance had swept to his right and knocked her aside, hitting her with his entire body and bringing his gun into a standing, firing position.

Tapeesa yelled, "No!" *I'm okay with your hang-ups but don't play me for a fool.*

But it was too late, or just in time from Chance's point of view. Firing into the mass of fur with a slug, a hard wad of lead, he knocked the animal back two feet with a stunning blow to its shoulder. Chance knew if he held the trigger pulled and racked the shotgun, the weapon would fire automatically each time he pushed the action forward, and that was what he did. But in the excitement, he missed his two subsequent shots.

It was clear the battle was not over, for the thing shook his huge head, and its eyes showed anger more than pain. Chance was racking Old Fateful for another shot, but Double Nickel had already moved past him, putting three quick rounds in the beast from a different angle. A three round burst was his training. The bear fell back on its haunches in a seated position, held his head high, and flopped over on its side much the same as a giant teddy bear might fall from a chair. Its huge frame rolled several feet backwards down the hill.

Tapeesa shouted, "Stop! Stop!" and jumped to her feet at the same time. "Stop! Stop! Stop! You had no right! This is not right!"

She pushed Chance. Anger flashed in her eyes much the same as it did in the bear's. She rushed down to the bear without considering it could still be alive. She punched it with a fist. It grunted, and she stabbed it in the throat with her big knife and then made a deep cut across the hide, veins, and muscles of its neck and windpipe. The bear's still-pumping heart did its work as blood gushed out six feet from its neck into the bush. The two men were frozen, not believing what they had just done and seen. Light snow started to fall, barely touching the bear's fur before disappearing into thin air.

Double Nickel shouted, "What are you doing!"

Tapeesa said something in Inuit.

"Is that some foolishness you learned from Bayer!" Double Nickel yelled. "You could've been killed, gotten us all killed! You don't have the right to go 10-96 on us in the middle of a bear fight."

"I'm not crazy, and neither was my grandfather!" the young woman shouted back. "He knew more about bears than anybody, and you should know that. He understood Taqukaq's and Nanuq's spirits better than any of you. He was the best hunter because he understood how to communicate with the bear spirits."

Now wasn't the time but it was the place, and Tapeesa let her thoughts pour out like her grandfather sometimes did—in a story. "When I was a little girl, I wondered why he always hung the hides of Nanuqs, polar bears to you Chance, in places of honor in our igloos." She was speaking rapidly and forcefully to Double Nickel. "He would offer them his best knife, the one with an elk bone handle, and even beer. I asked him one time why he did that, and he explained that if he showed the bears he killed great respect, the others would willingly come to him to be honored in the same way. This action also told the spirit world what a great hunter he was. That's why he was so successful in both hunting for food and protecting the pipeline workers! You!"

Double Nickel scoffed. "Well, if he was so successful, why did he get killed by polar bears? I heard what happened!"

"I don't know what you heard, but my grandfather was sick! He never told us what was wrong, but he was coughin' up blood near the end. One Saturday afternoon, we had a party, and all our family and friends brought his favorite foods. We all ate, and he even let me have some beer. He said he was sorry for leaving me alone, but he knew I could take care of myself. He reminded me of where I belonged, some words he had spoken years earlier that I still didn't understand. I was young, but I felt so proud. At that moment, I knew he was going to die, but the surprise was that he took his elk-handled knife, his best one, and headed out alone to a place on the ice where he knew the Nanuqs would gather. He was taking them his best in hope they would accept him as a gift and spare me and the other hunters from harm. I've never told it before, but this is the real story of how my grandfather went to his peace. Less than a day later, there were reports by bush pilots that there was blood smeared on the ice, and bears were nearby. Grandfather went the way he wanted to go.

"And you, Chance! I don't know what you think you

were doing! I came within a hair of slicing your ankle. Don't you ever put your hands on me again with that macho bullshit! My grandfather told me how to deal with bears and trouble!"

Just then a wolf howled long and low, and everything—the anger, the excitement, the threating weather—all seemed to melt back to places they hid when they weren't needed. The wolves were almost invisible in the distance across the valley.

All three hunters looked up from their kill and out onto the scene of a shimmering blue-green lake nestled about a quarter of a mile down in an open valley. They had each seen this place, or a place just like it, but never together. The scene brought them closer. They felt the crisp, clear air for the first time since the bear hunt had started. They saw a tranquil scene, with green trees and some snow left over from the last storm. The sun light was bright on the far side ridge of the valley. It became beautiful blue-yellow light as it broke through the clouds in shafts, leaving spotty shadows gliding across the lake and valley below them.

A majestic herd of a hundred or more elk was trotting, crossing the far hillside in the sunlight, probably because of the wolf's call. Even at their distance the hunters' the elks' buff rumps were as prominent as their antlers. A big bull had tucked himself in amongst the cows to possess them; or maybe he somehow knew it wasn't cow-hunting season, and they were his cover from hunters.

A small group of younger bulls followed, daring not to get close to the females.

The small pack of wolves, like flees on a green and white carpet, trailed the herd from a less than a quarter of a mile behind. They were in a diamond formation. Three wolves had broken from the pack into a single line and were flanking the elk along the bushy edge of the lake, planning to ambush them if they came down to drink or cross to the other side.

The sounds and scene that caught the three bear hunters' attention had equally caught them off guard. They slowed their breathing and let the adrenaline of their kill drop in favor of the scene they viewed. They could have been hunters from a thousand years ago operating on primal instincts. They could have been, but they were not. They were in the moment, in the hunt.

Chance said, "This is beautiful. That's why I came up here to Alaska."

Double Nickel said to Tapeesa, "This's what your grandfather showed me a hundred times, and it still gets me. He told me, 'This 's the chain of life, each animal depending on the other for its existence. It's been like this for thousands of years.'"

For all three hunters, the thoughts of mission and urgency faded. The recovery of the mother and children would have to wait. This moment became theirs alone, and it was all they had to die for, to live for, to love for, to find peace in, to find joy in.

Tapeesa wanted to touch Chance, just rub his arm or

hold his hand, but she held steady where she stood. She knew at this moment there would never be a better part of the day, a better time, or a better place. She understood she could never have better companions. It was at this moment Tapeesa understood exactly what her grandfather meant when she was around the embers in Calgary. She knew she was as much a part of this place as the elk, the bear, the trees, and the wolves. And she remembered: *And after the successful bear hunt, you will feel a peace like you never felt, but remember, there are always bears ahead.*

At the moment, Chance remembered this feeling was truly why he had come up to Alaska, not that he had just said the words, but that he had actually done the deed. His estranged mother had described him to her friends as her "wandering child." She would explain how at age six he often crossed the highway in front of the trailer park trying to follow his father to work at the refineries, not realizing his father was just meeting the carpool. His mother feared he would get hit by one of the gasoline haulers or oil trucks that ran at highspeed between Port Arthur and Beaumont, Texas.

Now, here he was gazing across this valley at a lake of blue-green water, surrounded by green meadows and patches of white snow. Gray elk with white butts, hunted by wolves, inhabited the forest. He realized he had crossed the highway again, and he was safely on the other side for now. But his road to this place had been much more dangerous than any busy four-lane throughway.

Chance stood there, soaking in the scene yet considering how he had *wandered* to this place. He thought about how his mother had moved them to Houston against his will and how his real father, a man he worshiped, had drifted from his life. He blamed his mother for the drift. He was in the ninth grade at the time and hated the man his mother had taken up with. His name was Dal—short for Dallas—Copeland, and he was an overweight, drug dealing, loan shark, bully, and former bouncer—not necessarily in that order.

Chance's mother worked as a bookkeeper in a gentlemen's club in the Uptown section of Houston, and Dal was a partner in the place. He had a reputation of being a dangerous man with many assaults on his record, and Chance was afraid of him. But menace and risk were what Chance's mother loved about Dal. When a Houston cop tried to warn her away from Dal, she just said, "Yeah, he's quite a man and he takes care of me." His warning only served to make her want Dal even more, but Chance had to live there, too. He was caught in the middle.

Chance thought about the time when he was sixteen and showed up at school with bandages running the length of his left arm. His friends thought Dal was the reason and teased him about it. They thought Dal had beat him like some men in their neighborhoods did, just to show their kids who was boss. His friends were right about the bandages being Dal's fault but not for the reason they thought. Chance often considered if his friends had only known the truth, they would have believed he was the toughest kid at school. But Dal threatened to kill Chance if he ever told them or anybody else how he got injured.

The truth was that Dal thought Chance was soft, so on some weekends, he took Chance down to Old Mexico to teach him the ins and outs of doing drug deals. Chance still had his baby fat.

Dal intended to toughen him up. "I need for you to be able to make this run to Mexico by yourself," he told Chance, "and free me up to keep an eye on my other businesses. Them other fools is robbin' me blind. You need to step up, you know, be a man."

Chance always subconsciously shook his head when he thought about those days and that was what he did as he looked out on the valley scene with the other two hunters. The bandages and his injuries became fresh in his mind. It was like yesterday, as he bit his bottom lip and considered all that had happened to him in Mexico. It was on one of those weekends when Dal took him to a little no-name bar in Reynosa to meet up with some drug contacts.

Dal had described the place to Chance as a "little shithole full of tough talkers, knife fighters, and drug dealers. But they won't hurt you 'cause a me." Then Chance remembered how the adventure had gone so bad so quickly, and he stroked his wisp at the thought.

Dal was talking to these guys in the bar about turning his drug run over to Chance. They were rubbing their chins like they were considering the deal when a fight broke out right in front of them.

One old guy had a knife, and the other, about ten

years younger, had brass knuckles. The one with the knuckles was stocky, brutal, and getting in his licks, but he was also getting all sliced up. Sweat and blood were everywhere, even on Dal and Chance. Everyone was cheering the fight on. Then, the situation got all weird for Chance because everybody started looking at him. And the more they looked, the quieter the place got. The mood went from fiesta to suspicion just like that. And, Chance was the object of their wariness. Even the fighters paused and stared at him as though he was caught trying to be manly when he was only a boy.

The older man said to Chance, "What the fuck you looking at? You come down here for a show?" The words were all in broken English, but that was the gist of it.

Then, it was like supernatural skill or something, Chance remembered. A knife flew all the way from the back of the bar, whirling in the air, end over end, and stuck in a post next to their table. The thrower was small man, dressed like a peasant, but he was clearly in charge. He was a man cooked in the Mexican sun with deep lines in his face. He had a thick black mustache and matching head of hair. His eyes were dark, cold and dead. Thick sweat clung to his hair, face, and arms.

"You Americanos come here to buy my dope," the thrower said, "but you don't understand us. You have so little respect. You bring your pudgy boy in here to sit with men and expect us to do business with him on your say-so, based on your reputation. Well, no my friend, not so easy. If your boy wants to do business with men, he's got to take the knife. He's got to prove he can take a little pain. He's got to prove he's man enough that he won't let our product get taken away from him. He's got t' prove he's brave, that he's a man!"

Dal, thinking better of the situation, started to get up so he and Chance could leave, but as soon as he made a move, three or four knives and a pistol told him he had to keep his seat. Chance was on his own.

Chance remembered the little man, the leader, looked directly at him and calmly said, "We know Dal. Now, we need to get to know you. C'mon Chance. By the way, I like your name. It's just a knife, not a machete. No one here wants to kill you. C'mon take a chance, Chance. It's time. I tell you what, if I accidentally kill you, I'll take your name and you can go on living through me." The man grinned and it was then that Chance noticed he had gold teeth.

Dal leaned back in his chair, helpless, virtually abandoning his common-law son to his own fate, and everybody started to hoot and holler again. Fiesta!

In an odd way, Chance was proud of himself after that trip to Mexico. His friends had teased him about his bandaged arm, but he knew they would never understand what a gift Dal had been forced to give him. He had passed a real test of manhood, something his friends probably could not understand or do.

When Chance looked up at this valley and thought about his life after Houston and Mexico and Dal, he knew he had made the right choice. He had wandered across the highway all the way to Alaska and remained his mother's "wandering child."

Dal picked up a parole violation shortly after that trip, and Chance never had to go back to Mexico, but he knew he could. He remembered the last time he had seen his common-law father was on the occasion of visiting day at Hutchins State Jail in Fort Worth. Dal had gone full gangbanger by then. He had facial tattoos and half an ear missing to prove it.

"I heard you gonna be a cop," Dal said at the end of the visit, "Well, remember who made you a man." Then, he winked. Chance had not seen him since and heard he was stabbed to death about a year later.

Chance came back to himself when Tapeesa gave in and touched his arm. She used the hold as an excuse to steady herself while she crouched in front of him on the uneven ground, on the balls of her feet, and examined their kill. Her rifle was cradled in the fold of her waist, and with her left hand still held the knife as she poked and examined the bear that lay before them.

Tapeesa said to Chance, "What are you shaking your head at? You broke its shoulder with the first shot."

Then, to Double Nickel, she said, "And you only increased its pain. I don't believe any of your shots hit anything vital, the head or heart."

Finally, she stood and sighed. "This isn't our bear."

"Bullshit!" Chance shouted, more loudly than he

meant.

She continued calmly after an obvious eyeroll and smirk. "This bear is too small, and you see that slash under his jaw? That's fresh. We didn't do that. It was made by another, bigger bear, probably the one we're after."

Double Nickel stood tall and said. "I agree. This ain't our bear. If this one got his ass kicked by ours and got fired up, that explains why it came chargin' at us the way it did."

By then, they could hear the faint, low barking of dogs. They were probably back at the trail head parking lot. The wind was coming from that direction but constantly changing.

"If our family isn't dead, they will be if they bring them dogs up here. Nothing like a panicked bear to kill." Tapeesa said.

"I don't know what you mean," said Double Nickel.

"I mean, I think the family may still be alive. I believe we've got one smart bear. He's been breaking into cars for weeks up here. Never been caught; never even been seen. He staged over the parking lot, and we see signs of him dragging the woman. I think we've got a bear that knows he can eat today and then tomorrow if he gets those two kids to follow they mama back to its den. He's ready to go into torpor, maybe. He wants to fatten up. But the minute he knows them dogs are on the way; he won't be a smart bear. It'll just be a bear. He'll probably kill, eat his fill, and run off. Let's get moving."

The group, led by Tapeesa, walked further along the

slope. The signs were clearer then, and the wind had changed again, in their favor. The beast was like a person who had pulled off the big caper and now was free to enjoy the spoils, so being cagy just didn't seem to matter anymore. His tracks were present and clear.

Snow came, and it seemed to blow up as much as down, whirling around them but still not sticking. Shadows from clouds quickly moved over the valley below and shaded the hillside where the three hunters trekked. Cold came with the shade but warmth stayed with the sun.

Still, the sounds of barking dogs, barely perceptible to an untrained ear, rode the wind. Double Nickel and Tapeesa inclined an ear farther up along the slope. Before Double Nickel could fully form the words, "I hear a baby cryin,'" Tapeesa was ten steps out in front of the men and moving fast towards that whisper of a cry on the currents.

Double Nickel yelled, "Stop, Tapeesa! You'll get 'em killed."

It was only with this last bit of advice from Double Nickel that the only grandchild of Johnn Bayer stilled herself and turned to face the two men. "We don't have time to plan a grand rescue," she said, firm but calm. "We know a child is on this trail. I say let's go get 'im. The bear will come to us or run away. It will make itself a gift to us or we to it."

"I agree," said Double Nickel, his voice soft, somber.

Chance took off his jacket and threw it to the side of the trail, revealing long-ago-healed blade marks on his left arm, left there when he had picked up a knife at a shithole bar in Mexico. He had neither won nor lost the fight, but he had proven he could take a little pain and keep going.

He had told Tapeesa, on one of their trips, how he had brought back packets of heroin from Mexico in gauze bandages wrapped around his forearm. He explained how the border crossing agent had looked at his bruised face and smiled, felt the bandage, and saw him wince. "I see you had a good time in Old Mexico," the agent had said. "Welcome back to the U-S-of-A."

And so, as Tapeesa suggested, they continued along the trail. She was up front, and the two men fanned out behind her. All three were ready for a bear fight and to save a life if they could. They heard sounds of a child's cries louder on the wind and cautiously speeded up. As they reached the start of a gully that stretched out below them, but cut perpendicular to the trail, they saw a little redheaded boy with wet cheeks and dirty hands just ahead on the path. He wore a toddler's blue T-shirt, a filthy diaper, and white socks. The child was in shock—cold and shivering—but not crying. The three hunters approached slowly, wary of a possible ambush by a smart bear.

Tapeesa realized right away the crying they heard was not coming from a place they could see, but rather a place further down the hill. This was where the gully opened out to form a vee, with the narrow part cutting back into the hillside. It was a good place for a bear's den.

The men subconsciously assumed, of the three of them, Tapeesa would be the one to stop and take up the orphaned redhead. But they were mistaken because she sprinted on past the small child they could see, headed for the sound of the other crying baby they couldn't see. Added to the sound of crying, came the almost playful growl of a bear. Double Nickel, last to approach the first child, picked him up with one hand, smelled the toddler's diaper and almost put him back down. Then, he fanned his AR-15 to his rear as though he expected a rear attack.

Tapeesa ran down the hill, and as soon as she could, walked up the crevasse, moving slowly. She saw the second crying child right away. This one was shirtless and standing, looking out towards her.

A huge, silver-gray, grizzly gnawed at something about ten yards to the child's rear. Tapeesa wanted to fire immediately, but she had to consider the youngster's safety. The toddler could get hit if her aim was off. And, even if she missed the child and hit the bear, the beast could rampage towards them, killing the child in the process. One swipe of the bear's claw, in anger, and the child could be torn in half.

Chance didn't think about any of those possibilities as he raised his shotgun while standing next to Tapeesa and preparing to shoot down range. She instinctively put her fist up, and he froze. She pursed her lips while in deep concentration and, without making a sound, pointed at Chance and then down to the ground where he stood. She meant for him to stay there. He did as she indicated. Then, she walked calmly to a place about fifteen feet up the draw, got down on one knee, and motioned for the child, who was about fifteen yards away, to come to her. The kid stopped crying, put one finger into his mouth, and pointed back towards the bear with his other hand, at the same time looking in her direction. He had a runny nose, and he was dirty, bloody, and scraped, but not bleeding.

Tapeesa calmly whispered, "I know, I'll get your mama."

The child walked towards Tapeesa, and she noticed his hair was browner than red. He was shivering.

Tapeesa carefully walked to a point where she could place herself between the boy and the bear. She stood at her full height to discourage the animal from charging, but the bear was preoccupied.

It seemed even larger than she imagined. He was focused on the remains of his victim, the boys' mother. The woman was there under its feet. She seemed small, but intact, and curled in the fetal position. Most of her clothing was torn away, and cuts and scratches spanned her tiny contorted frame. Her head, a mass of matted red hair and not-so-fresh blood, was the worst of what Tapeesa saw. It was as if the bear had been gnawing on her skull, maybe playing with its food.

By then, Chance had taken the second boy by the hand and slowly walked backward from the scene. The boy was still pointing towards his mother. Double Nickel stood on the bank of the draw, about fifteen feet above them, holding the first kid to keep him from crying. He was also aiming his rifle down toward the bear.

The bear tossed the woman's small frame by the

head, then trying but not really trying to get his nose and teeth into her underbelly, it licked and nipped at her arms. It wasn't trying very hard and the woman was resisting.

She is resisting! Thought Tapeesa. She could see the woman was clearly resisting the bear. *She's alive!* Tapeesa stood still.

Twenty seconds went by before the huge beast became self-conscious and realized he was being watched. He looked towards Tapeesa. He stood on his hind legs and sniffed the air. He had a huge deep cut near his nose that was probably a result of his earlier fight with the other bear.

Tapeesa and her *trouble* locked eyes. It came down on all fours and started to charge but stopped just in front of her. Tapeesa, as small as she was, stood her ground. The bear pounded the ground with his front paws like a gorilla and again faked a charge. The ground shook, and rocks on the walls of the crevasse trembled and fell. Tapeesa held her ground. She was considering the possibility of attempting to back away from her foe, but she realized it had no place to go except through her. *Some trouble you just can't run from.*

Her two hunting partners, one behind her and the other above, seemed to sense she was in charge of the situation. But just then, the dogs came howling into the site. They positioned themselves at the upper edge of the crevasse next to Double Nickel.

Double Nickel yelled, "Hush dog! Hush!" But it was too late for that. The dogs, ten or more, tore down the rim of the crevasse, yelping as they ran, bent on attacking the bear. Not far behind them was their handler, a young native man. He was shouting, also calling off the dogs.

Tapeesa knew her options were gone. Now, the dogs would control the situation. As they rushed down towards the bear, it stood to his full glory, baring his teeth and claws. It charged her in earnest. Tapeesa swung her rifle from its perch. She knew she had less than three seconds to pull the trigger and hit her mark.

II EBENEZER

INTRODUCTION OF MANUSCRIPT

I found my grandma's manuscript when I was cleaning out an Airstream trailer that sat behind our home in Jacksonville, Florida. We were clearing out the house and adjacent structures—the trailer and sheds—due to the pending sale of the property after the death of our mother, who was preceded in death by our father, three years earlier.

For as long as I can remember, the trailer accumulated our family's trash and treasures, so I was not very surprised when I found the manuscript tucked away. I was surprised, however, at how well it had been preserved from the rats by being sealed in Visqueen plastic. Along with some pages of notes, it had survived in pristine condition.

I suspected it was a treasure.

The manuscript belonged to our grandpa's second wife. We called her Grandma Mae, and I will go no further in identifying her here because she made it a point not to identify herself in the manuscript. I will say she died in 2003 while living with her stepdaughter near Savannah, Georgia. She had never made mention of this writing to me or anyone else in the family that we are aware of.

Grandma Mae partially identified several people in her notes. They included her best friend in life, Miss. Patricia Kathern, last name not used, and an African American mortician whom she called Moses Hardrick III in the manuscript, but that was not his real name. I spoke to Miss. Patricia and, with her help, I also found the black mortician, as well as several others who helped authenticate this account.

Parts of this material we—my brothers, sisters and me—could not interpret as to intent. For example, the first line of the first page begins with, "Bury me with Ol' Mose so I can skip with Tweetie." We were unable to determine if this opening line was a request, a title, or the beginning of a poem. So, I decided to present the manuscript here, in its entirety, and let it speak for itself:

Bury me with Ol' Mose so I can skip with Tweetie:

Then Samuel took a stone and set it up...
He named it Ebenezer, saying,
"Thus far the LORD has helped us."

--I Samuel 7:12

I don't believe in ghosts, never have, or in what the colored people—that's what I used to call them—along Ebenezer Creek called "Haints." But I have to admit my certainty was shaken to its core a few years ago when I was confronted with real proof that such things exist. The proof came in the form of what I saw with my own two eyes, smelled with my own nose, and even tasted with my own buds. A real corpse and the stories of real people are all part of my evidence, and this is the first time I have told this story in its entirety.

At the same time, to this day, I'm not absolutely certain what I experienced was real and not just a dream or something just real crazy, as some people claimed. My best friend, Pattie Kay, says I'm a little crazy anyway, but she couldn't be impartial because we've been crazy together for over sixty years. I do know that a real person's remains, my Uncle Duke's, were found along the creek in a place that had been searched many times, and that was the same place where this, what I'm about to tell you, all started and finished. It's all real.

First, let me say you're gonna have to be patient with me. I write a lot like I talk and it's only with the help of Pattie Kay, who also helped me edit, that I'm able to put all this down on paper in the first place. Let me explain that I was a deputy sheriff in Effingham, County, Georgia—one of the first female deputies—for over twenty years, but that job was mainly filling out forms, not narrating stories.

I want to thank Pattie Kay—yes, the same Pattie Kay—the Rincon city librarian, for helping to get me through this story. I took a "writing-as-therapy" class in the library put on by the local state college. When Pattie Kay saw how emotional I got while I was writing this account, she wanted to read what little I had. I couldn't say no because she was in a little bit of it, too. I later figured it was a good decision because I couldn't have done it without her. She encouraged me to stay with the story and say it in my words.

She said, "I want to leave enough of you in it so people will know who you are, and how you grew and changed, so they can make sense of you." I understood what she meant. She was always a good writer and even worked for a couple newspapers around Savannah before becoming a librarian because, as she told me, "the papers didn't pay so good." She also suggested I not use real last names or, in some cases, not even first names so as not to embarrass the people we know.

The last thing I want you to know is this experience has been real therapy for me because writing about what happened has lifted a huge responsibility from my shoulders. I think, I almost know, why this happened to me now.

Where to start? "Start at the beginning for me," said

Pattie Kay, though the whole story started much earlier.

Me and Pattie Kay had been going to spots along the different creeks in our area for as long as I could remember. But ever since I was nine years old, we'd favored a place everybody called the "Crossing" on Ebenezer Creek. We often went with assorted friends, relatives, or whoever, and stayed for the afternoon. This place is just outside the little town of Rincon, Georgia.

At the time, I never knew or cared why they called it the Crossing. I only know we churned ice cream, played in the water, fished in the creek, and occasionally played baseball or some other games like Hide and Seek on the level ground that was close by. We explored the ruins of an old settlement and church graveyard, too, but they were barely visible in the tall bushes and weeds at the time. Only recently, at the time of this writing, has the State cleaned out some of the debris and made it a historical location.

I only know those times we spent at the Crossing were the best, especially for little girls like me and Patty Kay, who happened to be in love with my uncle.

Uncle Duke, that wasn't his name but was what everybody called him, was usually around, down on the creek. "For your own protection," he would say. Not that we expected trouble, but our parents always felt better, and were more likely to let us go there if Duke was around.

He was my mama's brother and our transportation, too, most of the time. I didn't know his real name until I was grown, and by then, he was long dead. I just knew he was tall, sunburned, sandy blond, and handsome in our eyes. But before you get the wrong idea, he didn't have eyes for me or for Pattie Kay. Though she denied it, Pattie Kay had a huge crush on him, but he treated her the same as me, like a little sister. I could tell she liked him because she always wore a hint of makeup when she knew he would be around, and her mother, just like mine, didn't allow that. We both came from strict Lutheran congregations, which were plentiful in that area. When I confronted Pattie Kay with my suspicions about her makeup, she just giggled but never denied it.

I believe we would've done anything for Uncle Duke, but fortunately he never asked. He liked older women, juke joints, and white liquor, and he didn't mind saying so.

I mention Uncle Duke now because other people started calling me Ghost Girl, mainly because of his and Pattie Kay's teasing me about what happened along Ebenezer Creek at the Crossing one of those Sunday afternoons when just the three of us were down there. He had to be nineteen or twenty by then. I was twelve.

Me and Pattie Kay was kicking around a beach ball, you know, like it was a kickball or maybe even a soccer ball, not that we knew what soccer was back then. I accidentally kicked the ball over Pattie Kay's head for the second time, and she had to go back in the woods to get it. Out of spite, she kicked the ball over my head and the dang thing flew in the creek that was flowing about twenty feet behind me. Pattie Kay insisted I had to get hers, since she had got mine. We could see the ball in the edge of the creek as it started to float down towards the Savannah River. The river was about a quarter mile away, but we knew if the ball got to the currents it was gone for good. So, I went after it pretty hard.

If you don't know Ebenezer Creek, then you wouldn't know there are giant cypress and other trees along its banks, and it's almost swampy at the edge. There were better places along the banks for swimming, but the Crossing was the best place for playing games and even fishing. Huge tree roots snaked into the water, and they could be dangerous if you didn't know the area. As I was climbing along the bank, trying not to fall in, or get tangled in the roots, or drown, or get snake bit, I lost sight of the ball. My foot slipped and got my shoe wet, and I gave up pretty fast after that. I decided to go back to where Pattie Kay was waiting and blame her for losing the ball.

I was calling her name, and she was calling mine. All of a sudden, it was like night in the trees. Everything slowed down—the current, the air, everything—and I got cold. I started getting confused, and shadows were closing in. The surroundings were like the sun was gone down, but it wasn't. The season was like it was winter, but it wasn't.

As I turned to my right, starting to climb out of the creekbank, there was an old black man and a little girl, also black, sitting there on the bank. He wore an immaculate black suit, crisp white shirt, and a flawlessly tied black necktie. He was rigid-like and straight. His back was against a big pine tree, and he was holding a fishing pole across his lap. The little girl sitting next to him was dressed in a very clean, white flour-sack-of-a-dress. She was holding my ball on her lap and looking at me with the prettiest, light-brown eyes I'd ever seen on anybody black or white. I would swear, and have several times, those two had not been sitting there three seconds earlier when I passed that spot. It was not unusual to see the "river folks," we called them, fishing along the creek from time to time, especially on Sunday afternoons, but these two just seemed to be dressed more for church than fishing, the man anyway.

As I said, it was almost dark, but it seemed darker than dusk, and the mosquitoes were coming out. In fact, the lightning bugs were starting to flicker, and there were a lot of them. They were like sparks from a distant fire just floating on the strangely still air.

I looked at the little girl. "Can I have my ball?" I asked.

The girl, maybe three or four years old, just giggled the way kids that age do, while showing she still had her baby teeth.

Then, the old man spoke or maybe shouted, I couldn't tell, but he said, "You can't be here!" He said it with such firmness in his voice, he scared me.

As I think back on that day, firm didn't really fit the expression on his face. It was more like formal serenity. His voice and eyes expressed frustration, but he was tranquil and, dare I say, dead-like.

The little girl giggled louder and handed me my ball. I thanked her and took it, but the moment I touched the ball, I got a chill I can't describe, but I remember it to this day. It was like when someone startles you from behind and your hair stands on end. You jump and get goosebumps.

Irregardless, Pattie Kay was still calling me, so I threw the ball out to her and followed right after it.

Pattie Kay asked, "Who was you talkin' to down there?" And she started to pat my hair with both hands and say, "An' what's goin' on with your hair, girl?" Then, she started rubbing my exposed arms like I was cold. I didn't realize at the time that my hair was a mess, and I had visible goosebumps.

I said, "Stop it, Pattie Kay! What's wrong with you?"

"What's wrong with you? Did you fall in?" she asked me back.

"Nothin'! Some old colored man and his little girl... Leave my hair alone," I said because she was still fussing with it. "And where is the ball I throwed up here?"

"Ain't seen no ball."

By then, Uncle Duke was walking up saying we had to go before it got too dark. I realized the light had changed back to normal.

He looked at me and asked, "Where the ball, little girl?" So, I told him what had happened, and he got all mad.

"Where they at!" he demanded. "Did that colored man touch you? He had no business scarin' you!"

I pointed to the spot, and he asked again, "Did he touch you? Ain't nobody got the right to talk to you like that, especially one o' them. I'll show 'im who ain't got the right to be here!"

Then he stormed off towards the spot where I pointed mumbling, "One of them can't tell a white man nothing, especially where he can or can't be in his own country."

At the time, his words didn't seem unusual because Uncle Duke made sure the "coloreds," as we most often referred to them, knew which way was up when it came to them respecting white people. That was Uncle Duke, through and through. He loved to be called a "redneck," wear white socks, and drink Dixie beer. He thought he was the toughest man in the county, and maybe he was.

He later became an Effingham, County sheriff's deputy and turned out to be a real terror to everyone. But I'll get to that later.

I thought there was going to be trouble, but after a few minutes, it was completely dark by then with just a three-quarter moon and lightning bugs providing any light, Uncle Duke came back and asked, "Did they come up by yawl?"

"Naw," I said, looking confused I'm sure.

Pattie Kay said, "Ain't nobody come by us, and we ain't seen nobody."

Uncle Duke looked at me and asked, "Did they have a boat?"

I said, "I didn't see no boat, but I didn't see them either, at first."

Uncle Duke then patted me on the head, started to fix my hair like I was a little girl and said, "Don't tell me you done seen one of them ol' Haints everybody says floatin' around down here." He let out a big laugh.

I knocked his hand away, forgot all about our ball, and pouted all the way home in the back seat of Uncle Duke's red Fairlane. He and Pattie Kay were laughing with each other about me, but I didn't want to hear it.

They made fun of me for a good year after that. I also had nightmares for years about seeing the old man and girl at the creek, being cold and wet, and just a jumble of nonsense. I always woke up when the little girl handed me the ball.

It took a year for the kids around Rincon to stop teasing me about that day, and that only happened because Mama made a stink about it at church. The only times I went back to that part of the creek were for family funerals and graveyard cleanup days.

My mom and dad are buried down there in well-tended graves where a remodeled Lutheran church now sits. It's about a quarter mile from the Crossing. Both sides of my family are down there: uncles, cousins, and oh yeah, Mama's granddaddy, too. They were all a part of the Lutheran congregation.

Most lately, Uncle Duke went missing down there. Of course, he wasn't part of any congregation unless they met while huntin' and fishin' or raisin' hell at certain pool halls in Springfield, the county seat. When he went missing, everybody just thought he met the wrong man's wife and probably ended up in the swamps around the creek. The sheriff's office searched the area for weeks but never found him. About six months later, some fishermen found his patrol car, submerged in the swamp muck, about a half mile away from the place he went missing.

As I said, I'm not scared of the dead. My first husband was a fulltime deputy at the sheriff's office, and he always made it a point to get me out on all the murder scenes. I've seen them—corpses I mean—fried, chopped, marinated, and just plain dead for no visible reason. I believe he felt more manly having the special privilege of showing me, his then girlfriend, around a ghastly scene. I also think he kind of got off on that. Of course, that wore off after we got married, and I became a deputy, too. This's when the marriage started to fall apart.

Notwithstanding, my second husband was an axillary deputy and fulltime mortician's assistant at Cobb Funeral Home in Rincon. I was a fulltime road deputy by then, and I took a special course in cosmetology just so I could make extra money at Cobb's by helping out with hair and makeup on the bodies. I don't mind telling you I got so good other funeral homes started calling me to help out. Even some of the black morticians would call when they had a really light-skinned black to get made up.

Helping with the makeup is what led me to Hardrick's Funeral Parlor, an old red brick house in the heart of the black section in Springfield. This is when my childhood experience at the Crossing came back to me, full throttle, for the first time.

I walked in Hardrick's front door on my first day, and on the wall in the front parlor, staring me in the face, was a picture of the old gentleman I'd seen at the creek years earlier. I'm sure I must have been dumbfounded because, though I didn't realize it, my mouth was open. The reason I know this is because this younger, light-skinned black man—he was probably forty-something—who owned the place, tapped me on the shoulder. When he tapped me, my vision changed from the picture of the old man to my own reflection in the glass protecting the portrait. My mouth was open.

The young black man standing next to me had gray eyes and almost sandy but processed wavy hair that went perfectly with his flawless white teeth. He was slightly shorter than me, and he stood with his hands behind his back as though we were admiring the same photo.

"I see you're awestruck by my grandfather," he said.

I thought he was trying to be funny. He stuck out his hand and seemed a little put off when I didn't take it right away.

He spoke in perfect English and said, "I see you are admiring my grandfather."

This was obviously a dumbed-down version of what he said the first time. I suspected he may have thought I didn't know the meaning of *awestruck*. He wasn't right, but he was the first person I'd ever heard use it in a sentence. He was right the first time about my impression. I was awestruck.

In that same frame of mind, I said to him, "Is he about? I'd kinda like to see him a minute."

Moses Hardrick III, that was my new client's name,

just laughed and said, "He's my grandpa, the original Moses Hardrick. He started this place in 1953 and died back in '68." Pausing a minute, he asked, "Aren't you the deputy that does the hair and makeup? We've been expecting you."

His hands folded at his waist, he quietly and calmly led me to his client. She was a grand old lady—must have been ninety—with only a few strands of hair left on her head. She was naked but partially covered with a grey sheet. A silver-grey wig stood on a mannequin head placed next to her. A picture of her as a younger lady also lay there. She looked just as white as me but was pale as the sheet that covered her.

"Is there another one of your relatives that took after your grandpa?" I asked after I got busy. "I mean, is there anybody else around here now that looks like him?" I was trying to be nonchalant with my questions, but I could tell my inflection wasn't natural and so could he.

"No. As you can see," he smiled, "I take after my mother's side. Why do you ask?"

By the look of his body language, I considered he was getting a little perturbed, so I thought I would cut off any ugliness by confessing my thoughts. "I saw somebody down at Ebenezer Creek that looked just like your grandpa, same suit and everything."

He got quiet then, the kind of quiet that goes with reluctance. "When was that?" he asked calmly, but I could tell I had hit a nerve. His vocal inflections were not natural.

I was fluffing out the wig, which I thought was a little too light for the kind of makeup I intended to put on her. I took a can of gray spray paint from my kit and toned the strands down just a bit.

He snapped at me, "I can't have that smell in here like that!" He was rather abrupt and uppity when he said it. I thought about how times had really changed from my days with Uncle Duke. Hardrick would have found himself on hard times if my Uncle Duke had heard him speak like that to any white person, especially me or any other woman. He wouldn't have taken that tone from Hardrick for a second. But business was business, so with their new civil rights and everything, I just let his remark pass.

"It's water-based," I said as calmly as I could. "The smell 'll be gone in a few seconds." And, it was.

Surprisingly, when I finished, the younger Mr. Hardrick had not forgotten my earlier questions about his grandfather.

With some quiet reflection, he said, "My granddaddy 's buried out there at the Crossing where the old church used to be. It's the only well-kept grave at the old graveyard there. It's marked with a wooden cross but with no name, at his request. That's the way he wanted it. He used to take my daddy out there fishing when Daddy was a boy. He made my daddy promise to bury him out there. Daddy died two years ago. But as for looks, there was only one Moses Hardrick." He chuckled. "I barely remember him, but he was a straight-backed and stern old man. I don't know who you saw, but it wasn't my father or grandfather."

After a few more seconds of introspection, he said, "I'm sorry, but I thought you were trying to be funny out there. There are stories among the river people that on some nights ol' Mose Hardrick, that's what they call him, 'goes walking around out there looking for business.'"

He smiled to himself and got busy sewing the back of a dress he had ripped to get it on the grand lady. She was turned up on her side, and he had just slipped the dress up into place.

True. Our business relationship started our shaky, but it started. I let any thoughts of unpleasantness pass in the hope that me and Mr. Moses Hardrick III would have many satisfied clients in the future. And, over time, we did get more relaxed with each other.

I went back to the Crossing and walked the old, overgrown, places he had described, the places where I had played as a kid. Just as he said, the only well-kept grave was that of his grandfather. It was marked with a simple wooden cross.

When I told him about my visit, a little over a year later, he gave me a puzzled look again. We were working in his prep room, putting the final touch on a retired postal worker out of Savannah, Georgia. She was already in the coffin, and I was putting the last touches on her face with an air brush. He was expecting her family at any moment, and he wanted to be able to offer them a private viewing.

"You know," he said, "my grandfather taught my father this business, and he taught me. They both went to Howard University up in Washington, D.C., and so did I, for that matter. It's mostly a black university, and I don't expect you would have heard of it."

He was right about that. I knew about Savannah State College and Florida A & M. As a rule, I didn't travel in circles that found knowledge about black schools a topic of discussion unless it had to do with crime or the use of my tax dollars. At that time, I had not had an awakening of sympathy or empathy of anyone's plight beyond my own narrow world view.

"Well," he continued, "it has a direct link to the Crossing—"

Before he could tell me the connection and expand my view of his world, his parlor bell rang, and he was off chasing money, I suppose, like any other businessman. I packed up and took the side door out.

I didn't get to finish that conversation until a month later when I saw him at a morticians' convention in Jacksonville, Florida. When we saw each other, he was examining some Atlas chemicals they use in his end of the business, and I was looking for some foundation putty, also by Atlas, to make my job easier.

This may sound funny, but I probably never would have sat down with him around Springfield or Rincon. I would have been too self-conscious. But in a big city, away from friends and relatives, it seemed the most natural happening in the world to have a cup of coffee with one of my clients when he invited me to join him.

He broke the ice by telling me how surprised he was that the same company that made makeup also made embalming chemicals. We both laughed nervously at first. I think he felt the same liberation from small-town eyes and, what I now know as, small-town prejudices. Not just racial prejudice necessarily, but the prejudices of those people believing you're getting above yourself because you want to learn or experience something new and different.

We were sitting in the middle of the exhibit hall, laughing, talking, and drinking coffee, and people from all over the country were walking by and not giving us a second look. This, too, would have never happened where we grew up, and the feeling was truly liberating.

He said, "You know … I mean … do you remember when you first mentioned seeing my grandfather—I mean somebody you thought was my grandpa—down on the creek? I really thought you were just messing with me. I think I told you about what the river people would say about him. I mean, they claim ol' Mose gets up and walks around down there." He laughed nervously. "And while I didn't really know him, I didn't know you either. So, I'm sorry if I turned a little cold."

"No offense taken, but you were the first colored I ever worked for. I hadn't been around colored people much before, except my Auntie Lucille, the lady that helped to raise me. She cleaned up, cooked, and took care of me when I was kid. She was just like a second mother. She's dead now."

"So, she was your aunt, then." He smiled as he spoke, and I knew he was poking fun at me for calling her that.

"God no!" I blurted out. "That's just what we called her. She was like family though. And so that's what we called her."

Then he got serious, though he was still smiling. "Just out of curiosity, do you know her last name? Did she have children, and do you know their names? And you don't have to answer that."

I was glad he let me off the hook on that one because, for the life of me, I couldn't recall Auntie Lucille's last name. We enjoyed our coffees, talked about business, our experiences with the dead, and we really got comfortable with each other.

Then he said, "Can I tell you something without offending you?" He asked as gingerly as possible, but it was my sense he wasn't afraid of offending me. He just didn't want me to get up and leave after he said what he had to say. So I nodded.

"The word 'colored' is offensive to me, and most black people in America, when used by Anglo people, and especially in the way you use it. It's almost like calling me that other degrading word people sometimes use. We are people of color but not colored people."

"But I hear ya'll calling each other that all the time—not colored—but that other word. Not that I would," I added quickly.

"Yeah, I know, but that doesn't make it any less degrading for Anglo people to use it. Some people would say it's like sending your Auntie Lucille to the back door if she doesn't go there on her own. And if she goes on her own, you can be sure she knows what happens if she starts to use the front door. I mean the word; it just puts her in her place. That's all. You using those words like 'colored' tells me you're putting me in my place."

I'm sure I gave him a puzzled look after that because I had no idea what he meant. I hadn't called him anything. I had no idea how he knew Auntie Lucille used the back door of our house. I used the back door of my house, growing up, all the time. Naturally, Auntie used it. I never really understood the big deal around that. Auntie started her day in the kitchen, so naturally she came in the back door.

He continued, "My daddy told me a long time ago that we black people represent an unsolvable problem for Anglo America. Not because of the ill-informed, racists, perceptions that we are uneducated, and are poor, or lazy; but simply because we are a visual reminder from America's past of people that never received a fair shot at the American dream, and they knew it. And that was okay as long as we represented an invisible, humble, and obedient work force in society.

"Only when we began to bring attention to ourselves—to our plight—did Anglos' really notice us. If we get too smart, too famous, too wealthy, too familiar, too integrated, or too use the front door, then bad things start to happen. Doors start to slam shut. The rules change. And these bad events are reasons for some whites to want to push us back to that invisible place where the back door is located."

I didn't understand him. What he was saying was actually quite confusing and uncomfortable. On top of everything else, I wondered why he was calling me Anglo and not white. I knew he was venting. But I stuck in there because he was an interesting person to talk to. He sounded really passionate about what he was going on about, and I wanted to know more about his grandfather.

"My grandfather went to Howard University in Washington, D.C., and on to Meharry Medical School up in Tennessee," he said, right on cue with my thinking and without my prompting. "He came back to Springfield with the intention of starting a medical practice to provide good medical care to the black people in the county. But some of the local Anglo men, men who organized themselves as the White Citizens League, wanted to keep us invisible. They told him he would not be practicing medicine in Springfield or anywhere else in the county because they would never give him a minute's peace if he tried. He understood them to mean they thought he would undercut the existing medical practices and draw black and some poor Anglo patients from the Anglo doctors, doctors that had 'colored' waiting rooms and upheld the social order while charging whatever they wanted. So, Granddaddy decided to not fight that battle and chose to use his medical degree, his knowledge of the human body, to open the funeral parlor and go into one of the few professions open to him in the area. He also saw a need for his services."

I thought to myself, that that can't be right. He's making this story up. But then I thought how Uncle Duke would have been one to do something like threaten black people to keep them from rising above what he thought was their station, even though the incident the undertaker told me about was before his time. I tried to justify in my own mind why anyone would have done something like that but eventually I just scratched my head and let the maddening thoughts drop away.

"Ol' Mose Hardrick decided to teach himself how to embalm bodies, and that's the life he made for us. He taught my father, and my father taught me," the youngest Hardrick said. "Now, I'm going to tell you a secret, and you can't tell anybody. Okay?"

I nodded cautiously, and he said, "My granddaddy was never embalmed." And then he smiled as though he had been waiting a long time to disclose his *top secret*. "He detested the practice, but it is Georgia state law. That was a request he made of my father. He asked not to be embalmed and to be placed in a plain pine box."

I don't, to this day, know why he told me that, but he seemed relieved after he said it.

"So, what about the other graves down there and the old church?" I asked. "We used to explore around the old stone foundations you mentioned and an old well, but where did they come from?" I was hoping to keep him talking. "There are also a lot of old broken dishes and even an old grinding wheel back in there. I guess they were all part of the old settlement?"

I kind of knew there was something down there because my Uncle Duke used to tell us not to play in certain areas. He was afraid we might fall in a well or get hurt. Of course, we ignored him.

After a few seconds of silence, I said, "I've never known but one church and graveyard out there. You're talking about Ebenezer Crossing, right?"

"Yeah. Back right after the Civil War, there was a little black church out there everybody called Second Ebenezer," he said. "It was on land granted by General Sherman himself to former enslaved people that settled in that area. Back then the people called him 'Uncle Billy.'"

The young undertaker took a note pad from his coat pocket and wrote "II Ebenezer" on it. As he showed the name to me. He told me this was how the old people around there used to write it.

"The original Lutheran church," he continued, "was part of a town call Ebenezer that sat up the hill from where your parents are buried. Their church, the black people I mean, was the second one on Ebenezer Creek so that's why they called there's 'Second Ebenezer.' There's also a biblical reference, something about 'the Lord helping us thus far.'" He was lecturing me then.

I never knew that history. I guess I just assumed the graves near the creek were just more old graves from what I thought was the original Lutheran church.

I don't think my family ever owned slaves. We worked hard to get everything we got, so I didn't want to hear nothing about the downtrodden slaves and all that old stuff. I just let all that subject drop because, at the time, I believed all that kind of talk just led to black people believing we, white people, owed them something. I thought they just need to get over it. Just like my people did when they got here from Germany. Then, it occurred to me what he meant about making people invisible to keep them in their place, and I regretted my earlier confusion.

When my ancestors arrived from Germany, they were never invisible. They blended in as being white, so I guess there was a difference. That term *Anglo*, Mr. Hardrick had used, also came to mind but I couldn't quite place the reason why. *Was that term a better description of me and my family, a better description than white? Did he think he was taking power away from the term white by calling us Anglo?*

He said there is much more to the story, but he explained he had a meeting to attend and left without me having the opportunity, in our frank discussion, to ask him why he continually referred to my race as Anglo.

I left the sheriff's office because I was sick. They took my ovaries, and I had chemo that year. After a few years, when I was doing better and cancer-free, Cle retired, too. He suggested we move to Jacksonville, Florida, to be closer to his grandchildren.

At first, I resisted. But then, at Cle's suggestion, I counted up my real connections to the Rincon area and there weren't many. Other than Pattie Kay and my dead parents, the ties equaled one ex-husband, whom I hated and never should've married in the first place, and his one estranged daughter, Janie. Though she is my stepdaughter, I love her like my own. She was grown by then, though, and making her way in the world without me or her father.

Janie once asked me why I would marry a man such

as her daddy, and I told her, "He was just like my Uncle Duke, tall and handsome, a sheriff's deputy, and I thought he was the perfect man. But just like my uncle, he was far from perfect. He was a wife-beater, a drunkard, and a drug abuser. And he only got worse when he added in the authority of being a deputy. Privilege had made him toxic to be around. By the time we divorced, every bad thing that happened to him was someone else's fault, especially minorities."

My marriage to him was the worst six years of my life. It only ended when the high sheriff came out after one of our battles and told us we were an embarrassment to the badge. He said to me the department was having to respond to our house too much. I was standing there with a busted lip, and the sheriff was saying, "It's either your badge or him."

For a brief time, I thought it was going to be him because I just thought sticking by their husbands was what good women did. By the way, my then husband was never asked to quit. I didn't quit, but I did get the courage to leave the marriage.

On the other hand, my next husband, Cle, was a dream. I met him while he was an auxiliary deputy, but we actually got together after a killing out in the county where these two young black boys started fighting over a TV channel or some other nonsense. There were only three TV channels back then, so I guess the point was that one kid felt he owned the TV, and the other objected. One kid cut the other's throat in his sleep with a straight razor. Blood was all over the sofa, but amid this grisly scene, this guy, Deputy Cleophas, kept giving me the eye.

Cle, what everybody called him, was a tall, thin man, ten years my junior, who chain-smoked and had gray hair since his late thirties. We dated only six months before we were married. We couldn't have children, so he pampered me, especially when I got sick.

After he retired, he bought me an old Airstream Land Yacht, and we fixed it up. To pull it, he bought himself a new, power-blue, Chevy Suburban and called it the "Stallion." We rented us a parking spot two blocks from the beach near Jacksonville, Florida, and we were set for the retired life. But we didn't just sit there.

We loved to travel. We went up to Maine for the fall leaves and out to New Mexico for the annual balloon festival. Those were two of our, almost, yearly trips. One year, we trailer-camped all along the Appalachian Trail and day-hiked until we'd done the whole exploit. It was this adventurous spirit that led to my last encounter with Moses Hardrick—the original—at Ebenezer Crossing.

Cle got it in his head to visit all the Civil War, or the War of Northern Aggression, as he called it, battlefields, even the ones up north. So, one midsummer morning, we hitched up the Stallion to the Land Yacht and, with maps in hand, we headed down to the Tampa area for our first visit. We had no idea there were so many battlefield sites in America. There were six in Florida alone. But we faithfully stuck with the desire, at least, to drive by all ten thousand-plus locations. Cle was more of a Civil War buff than I knew, but none of this war history really interested me. I just went along for his sake.

In some places, like Gettysburg and Petersburg, we spent days. Cle walked the battlefield of Picket's Charge from the wood line to the stonewall. The City of Gettysburg had a temporary exhibit of women's Civil War–era dresses while we were there, and I really loved that.

In Petersburg, Virginia, where over 70,000 men died. I took one tour and heard how the Yankees, besieging the city, ended a stalemate by digging a tunnel under the South's lines and blew a hole in their earthworks. Then, the Union soldiers were stupid enough to march down in the hole and be slaughtered by the southerners when they couldn't climb out. The funny thing is a troop of colored soldiers—their words not mine—that had been trained to march around the crater were ordered to follow the white soldiers into the hole. I suppose they would have been called cowards had they not followed the orders, so in they went knowing what would happen. An old black gentleman there said he had read that some of the Southerners helped pull some of the white Yankees out the hole, and then those same Yankees turned around and started killing the black troops down in the hole. That was crazy, right? But "That event was the rumor at the time," he said.

After spending half a lifetime with Uncle Duke and my first husband, I tried to grasp if they had a hatred of black people that equaled what happened in that battle at Petersburg. I also tried to grasp if my own compliancy with the way we treated some black people when I was growing. Did some of my actions appear to equal that level of hatred?

Multiply these visits by twenty or thirty and I would say we were battle-fielded-out. By late November of that same year, there were plenty of sites left to visit, but we decided to go back home and winter in Florida. More key to this story, we decided to stop on our way through Springfield, see Janie and Pattie Kay, and perhaps, if they needed, clean around my parents' graves. Cleaning their graves was something we did a least once a year irregardless. Even though we were only two hours from Jacksonville, we decided to camp near Ebenezer Creek the night we arrived and get our visits and work done the next day.

This point is where my memory gets a little iffy. It was late when we arrived, but Cle took the time to unhitch from the Stallion and level-up. I know I was awake, but I can't discount the possibility that I was also half asleep. I also can't discount the idea that maybe it was all the death and destruction I had heard and read about over the past four months that caused this experience. No matter, I would swear these events I'm about to tell you happened.

We arrived in the Rincon area about half past midnight on the morning of December the 9th. It was a clear night, and the moon was up. Cle parked closer to the creek than the cemetery. It was crisp for the Savannah area but in lieu of some sort of heat, I told Cle I would make some hot tea to help us both relax. It became obvious that

Cle didn't need any help because he was snoring before I got the kettle un-stowed.

Our Land Yacht was laid out the same as any other Airstream because there was not much you could do to change one. It was a tube covered in aluminum with walnut veneer paneling lining the interior. It was long but not quite as wide as a lane of highway. The main eating and cooking areas were up front, and a front door on the side led directly outside. A bathroom and a utility area were in the middle. The sleeping quarters were at the back end, which also had an outer door. Each exterior door had a porthole just like a ship. An inside, pocket door separated the sleeping quarters from the bathroom/utility section.

Occasionally, one or the other of us would sleep on a built-in bench sofa across from the front door located next to the kitchen. The sofa extended from a small prep area on the right side and ended at a U-shaped dining booth that curved neatly across the front end. That night, Cle and I shared the bed, so I could clearly hear that he was enjoying his sleep. The pitches of his snoring could be heard all over our small trailer and probably outside. He even almost drowned out the noises of nature—crickets, frogs, and other night creatures—just outside our back door.

My mother had a term she used when she was paralyzed with sleep but half awake. She was a big woman and had a hearty voice. She would stretch some mornings and announce, "I must have been tired 'cause the witch rode me all night."

I had no idea what she meant until the night I'm about to describe. I lay in bed feeling awake and listless but not able to respond to my senses. Intermittent with the Cle's snoring, I could hear a grinding sound, like metal against stone. The noises of the creek and nature seemed to have fallen silent. I wanted to get up and look out the bedroom porthole, but my body wouldn't respond to the commands of my brain.

The grinding sounds got louder and louder, closer and closer. I imagined somebody was sharpening metal against one of the tombstones up the hill. Then I remembered the grinding stone I had found. I wanted so much to get up and just look out, but I felt as though I was pinned to the bed. I would believe I had gotten up to look out, only to find myself still in bed. All the time, the grinding sound seemed to move until it was just outside the back door. And then, from the bed, I swear I could see the backdoor handle slightly move as though someone or something was trying to get in. I wanted to elbow Cle, but my body couldn't move. So, I lay there paralyzed and being ridden by my mamma's witch.

I decided to have some tea and do a little reading to relax. And just like that, with that logical thought, I was fully awake and could move. I got up and looked out the bedroom porthole, but I couldn't see anything outside. It was pitch black, and I could hear the creek again.

I made tea on the butane burner and sat down on the bench sofa intending to sip and listen to the sounds of the creek. I was hopeful I could get back to a dreamless sleep, but then I heard noises outside. It was as if cows or horses were moving through the area. I thought maybe someone's livestock had broken out and was grazing the graveyard. I looked out the front porthole this time and again saw nothing. Maybe it's the wind, I thought. Then, I realized there was a three-quarter moon that seemed low and bright in the night sky. It seemed to reflect itself, making it look as if there were two of them in the sky. One was slightly offset from the other.

I heard the grinding noise again, and it got louder and louder and louder, but I didn't see anything making the sounds in the double moonlight. I drew my head back from the window and felt in full control of my senses. So much so, I could smell and taste the graveyard, the old dirt, and the dampness of the creek. I smelled rotting harness and old horse leather. The taste and smells started making me sick. I looked out the porthole again. The light of the moon was gone and had been replaced by a void, a darkness so deep it made me dizzy. I felt sucked towards it.

I've had dreams before, but I've never dreamed about black people, not even the ones I worked on at the funeral homes. I've had nightmares before, but I've always recognized them for what they were and awakened myself. This event was neither dream nor nightmare. It was something different. The darkness replacing the moon outside the porthole seemed to be devoid of air, water, sound, touch, smell, or taste. It was nothingness so deep I could find no reference points. It seemed to pull me into the middle of it with no way out. I felt as though it vacuumed out my stomach and flushed my veins, replacing red blood with some inhuman vile concoction of organic pus and rotted secretions that infused me with pure knowledge of some kind.

I realize now that I was being prepared for what was to come. That concoction would become a preservative of this experience. Even now, when I think about that night so many years ago, I get that taste in me, and I can remember every detail, every word, of what happened, and I shiver.

When you light charcoal soaked in lighter fluid, or when a gas flame on a stove comes to life immediately from only air and a spark, it makes a sound that is hard to describe. There is an audible and angry "buff!" Flame finds existence where none existed before. That's the sound I heard in the room behind me that night. It changed the color of entire room to a brownish hue. I thought for a second I had left the butane stove's burner on without lighting it. When I turned, a cold and sudden shock hit me inside out, and I was frozen. It was as though a picture was dropped into a stereoscope attached to my eyes. Everything was still three-dimensional but not quite real to my human eye.

There on my sofa, no doubt where the heat of my own body was still rising, sat ol' Mose Hardrick, the man I had met on the creek so many years earlier. And next to him sat the same little girl I'd seen with him. They were both the same as I remembered. He was prim and proper. She had her hand on his arm, as a child might when looking for security. But now the fishing pole was replaced by a woodchopper's ax lying across the old man's lap.

He said to me in a clear firm voice, "You can't be here!" And the little girl giggled just as she had all those years earlier.

He looked at her and said, "Now, now, Tweetie," and she pointed at me.

At that moment, I felt sure I would vomit but, strangely, I was not afraid. When I was a kid playing with Pattie Kay, the grownups would say, "If you see a ghost, ask them: 'What in this world do you want?' So, I said, "What in this world do you want?"

Moses Hardrick's solemn stern expression changed as he looked directly at me for the first time. I realized I couldn't see his eyes as I had all those many years ago when I was a little girl. Now, his eyes were in dark shadows. He said again in a calm clear voice, "You can't be here. This is their night to go over. You are in the way."

"Buff!" The atmosphere belched again, and another type of light dropped in. This light was brighter but still tinged, this time with yellow.

"What do you mean?" I asked. I could hear my own frustration, and it was starting to scare me.

"Step away from the door, please," he said in a much softer voice. His eyes were coming into view and they directed me to the curved nook, and to sit. This man with an ax wants me to step away from my best way out the room, was all I could consider.

I did as his eyes directed, though I was

dumbfounded by my own compliance.

The front door flew open as though sucked outward by the void, or by a strong wind, but nothing in our small sitting area was disturbed. I heard the whinny of a horse, but I saw endless darkness outside. The blackness abruptly stopped at the door and lurked.

A few seconds later, a man with blond, flowing, hair and wearing an immaculate gray Confederate Army uniform walked in from the darkness. His clothing had all the markings of an officer but not the shoulder braids of a general. I had learned that much from my travels with Cle. This soldier wore a golden sash at his waist that was partially covered by a brown leather belt where his pistol was holstered on one side, and his sword hung in its sheath on the other.

Moses Hardrick, without expression, said, "Good evening, Captain Best."

Without a word, the officer repositioned his sword sheath in order to make a small bow towards Moses Hardrick. He then looked at Tweetie and removed his hat, and with hat in hand, he made a large sweeping motion with it out into the room, bent a knee, and brought the hat sweeping across his waist in an exaggerated bow.

"May I have your permission to sit, madam?" he asked her. She nodded, and he sat.

Captain Best seemed to ignore my presence, and in a strong Mississippi accent he asked the dead undertaker, "Are we having tea tonight, Mr. Hardrick?"

Moses Hardrick asked his own question in response,

"Are they all going over tonight?"

"Maybe, but I doubt it. But you know they never make it, sir. We always get them. They never have time."

Much like something from a wonderland book I had once read, in a blink of an eye, they were drinking tea from fine china with silver spoons. I could even hear the clinking of the spoons against the sides of the cups and the tinkle of the cups as they were placed on the saucers. The mood in the room had changed to one of dainty formality. Tweetie just sat there looking straight ahead until Moses Hardrick handed her a small biscuit that appeared from a dish perfectly balanced on his knee. It was all quite fancy for my taste—the captain sitting all formal and straight, Mr. Hardrick doing the same with his teacup formally raised and the small dish of biscuits on his knee.

It was then I realized the ax Moses Hardrick held on his lap was gone. Tweetie was now wearing a beautiful lace, embroidered, yellow dress, and her hair was done up in curls with yellow, blue, and red bows. I could even hear the two men sipping tea and Tweetie munching small nibbles of biscuit.

I thought this was weird enough, but it got much worse. In the middle of this silent tea party, Uncle Duke—yes! my long lost relative and deputy—walked through the front door, in from the void. I almost didn't recognize him because he had an awful, jagged scar across his neck, and maggots, among other slime, were attempting to pry their way out of the scar and his mouth. He glanced at me with not even faint recognition. Then, he sidestepped towards me to get out of the doorway, much as I had done earlier. He didn't sit. He kept his back to the wall. His eyes darted from the void to the three people on the sofa in front of him.

Captain Best continued to drink his tea without the slightest hint of acknowledgment of this new ghost in the room. He seemed oblivious to anything but his own specter. He was enjoying the moment.

Suddenly the little girl, back to her earlier appearance, pulled closer to Moses Hardrick, whose tea and cakes had been replaced by the reappearance of the axe.

Moses said, "So he is after you again, Daniel?"

Few people in his life knew Uncle Duke's real name was Daniel—Daniel Nobles. Even I hadn't known this Christian name until I was full grown, so I was surprised to hear this apparent apparition from the 1960s know the name of my uncle, who'd gone missing in the seventies.

Uncle Duke opened his mouth to speak, but a puddle of black worms and putrefied green bile spewed out instead. It splattered on the floor in a living, squirming mass. Tweetie held on to Moses Hardrick slightly tighter. I then realized she, an apparition herself, was afraid of Uncle Duke.

The deformed creature that was Uncle Duke managed to choke back the rest of the filth in his mouth and pleaded, "Not tonight, Mr. Hardrick. I'm begging you! They listen to you. Please! Not tonight! If you only knew this torment!" Then, he screamed a sound of agony I'll never forget. It was as if he was roasting alive, but more intense. I had heard a car wreck victim burn alive when I was on the job. I knew that sound, and this was much worse.

In the next moment, his excruciating sound abruptly stopped, and a big black man walked in from the blackness and stood in the doorway. Uncle Duke cowered and looked down at his shoes as though he dared not look at the new visitor. I got the impression that Uncle Duke believed, assuming the dead can believe, if he stood still and averted his eyes, the big black man would not realize he was there. He would be invisible.

This new black figure looked at me or at least towards me. It was then I was surprised to see he was not the semblance of a man at all, but only a boy with the face of a young teenager. His features were innocent in many ways. His ears were big, and his eyes were large and white with dark centers. He was over six feet, five inches tall, and his body was that of a man used to hard work. His arms were long but muscular. They reached to midthigh probably because he had to stoop in the small space we occupied. The tendons that held his massive and callused hands to his forearms and upper arms to his shoulders seemed elongated and unnaturally stretched due to many years of heavy work. He wore no shirt. His pants were of homemade fabric: yellowish, cheap, cotton and stained with sweat. His chest bore a bloodless gash that showed no sign of healing. He was barefoot, and his feet were long, hardened, and blacker than the rest of his body. His hands and fingers were perpetually curled as though they were ready to make a fist or pick up the axe.

I heard the tinkle of the teacup, and the captain asked, "What, sir, is that doing here!" It was a question, but he shouted it as if it was a command.

"Captain Best, please," said Moses Hardrick, not pleading but perturbed. "You know why he is here."

The teacup tinkled with the sound of the stirring silver spoon for the last time, and the captain once more turned his attention to the void outside the front door.

Moses Hardrick said, "Shoe. Do you have to do it tonight?" This time he was pleading.

Shoe nodded in the affirmative.

"But if you do it tonight, you may not make it over the creek. There may not be time." Hardrick's voice was measured, controlled, and convincing.

Shoe looked at Moses Hardrick with such intensity that I could feel words in my head emanating from the shoeless apparition without him saying anything: *And if I don't make it over, it'll be his fault. He and those like him are the reason of this place we inhabit.*

Moses Hardrick gave me a strange look, but said to Shoe, "No, he's not the reason for this," Understanding Shoe just as I did. "Daniel is trapped here just like everybody else! Both the living and the dead are trapped by their pasts."

Can't we let go? Can't we pull together to come out this here place?

"No," answered the undertaker. "Not as long as you

forever chase Daniel, and people like Captain Best forever chase the world they left behind. I would love to believe you could end this stalemate, but as long as the living cling to the past, and we the dead relive the past, we are all doomed."

But can't you git out this here place?

"You always ask that, and you know I can—but who would stay with Tweetie?"

Shoe looked at me with a hard intensity. *Can't she do it?*

"No. Not yet. She cannot. She is only a temporary visitor here."

Then, I may as well go to work.

Shoe, as though compelled and with his hands held shoulder-width apart, reached into Moses Hardrick's lap and took the handle of the axe with both hands. Moses Hardrick held on, but the tug-of-war lasted only fractions of a second before Shoe was holding the sharp instrument.

Uncle Duke, knowing his presence was apparent, let out another scream that would have curdled everyone's blood that had any, mine included.

He said, "Please, Mr. Shoe, not tonight! Please! It hurts! It hurts so bad! So bad! Have mercy!"

Shoe turned on Uncle Duke with a fury I'm sure he reserved for the largest pine trees. And with the axe blade held as high as possible in the confining space, and already in a downward striking position, the big Negro nearly took Uncle Duke's head off in one quick, but powerful, chopping motion. The axe sliced perfectly into the side of

Uncle Duke's neck where the festering scar waited to be reopened.

Shoe took a deep satisfying breath, as though he was actually breathing in real air. His shoulders lifted and fell back in a circular motion. Sweat streamed from his face and chest as though he was at the satisfying end of a hard chore. He rotated his shoulders again in a backward motion while still holding the axe with his left hand near its cutting head and the other hand near the end of the handle. He walked out the door and into the abysmal blackness of the void. Uncle Duke's head was lying over on his shoulder, held there only by part of a neck muscle. The wound looked fresh as the day it was first made. He just stood there, contorted as a scarecrow might. I had the sense that there was no longer any humanness left in him. He stood in place, shuddering in the throes of silent agony. Its torment seemed to envelop the room, me included, yet he never acknowledged my presence. There was pure anguish and suffering on his face. With his head barely attached in that odd position, he asked Moses Hardrick: "Do I have to go back?"

"Yes, Daniel, you know you have to."

I started to stand to get away from the horror before me, but Moses Hardrick raised a hand and gestured for me to stay seated. Uncle Duke walked to the door and was ready to step out, but he turned to face the dead undertaker as though to plead his case just one more time, something he had probably done a thousand nights.

As Uncle Duke's palms reached out into the room,

he started to scream in agony once more as a large cluster of black people's hands connected to black arms reached in through the door like blind people searching for their precious possessions. They grabbed everything that was attached to Duke or Daniel or whatever he was or had been him including the bile and maggots on the floor and sucked it all out into the void.

"Buff!" The sitting room of the Land Yacht was clear again, save for Moses Hardrick, Tweetie, and Captain Best all sitting on the couch. They looked disappointed for some reason, and the captain's tea set was gone. They stood simultaneously to walked out into a beautiful night. Moses Hardrick went first, still holding Tweetie's little hand. Captain Best went next, walking formal and proud with one hand on the hilt of his sword and the other carrying his hat like it was a bouquet of flowers. I followed last.

The real world was bleeding back in, but the void remained around Captain Best's beautiful gray horse. The three-quarter moon was shrouded by bright clouds, but it still illuminated the ghostly animal.

Instead of mounting the horse in the normal way, the officer laid himself on the ground, lifted his booted foot, and placed it dutifully in the saddle stirrup. As soon as he did, the horse transformed into standing bones held together with scraps of gray hide, crawling larva and vile things.

The captain had changed, too. His uniform was in shreds, his head and body were a mass of thick multicolored gore, and exposed bones, rotting organs, and putrefied flesh fell into place. He was just like Uncle Duke in that there was no semblance of humanity left in him. The horse bayed a loud shrill sound, the captain let go a continuous, agonized scream, and off they went. The horse was dragging the soldier along the rough terrain at a gallop before running full speed into the darkness.

"Mr. Hardrick," I gasped, "what was that all about? Was that thing really my uncle, and was that really a Confederate officer?"

"Shhhh," Moses Hardrick urged while placing his fingers to his perfectly positioned lips. "This is the wrong time and place for that question. You will no doubt consider, at some later time, we are mere eidetic imagery, but that would be a mistake. These souls can hurt you or make you hurt yourself, and that bit of information is important to know."

He looked at the moon and its reflection was gone. Then he looked back at me and explained, "It's all right now. That is what's left of Daniel Nobles and Captain Charles R. Best. If Daniel was your uncle, then—"

"But who is Shoe, and what's he doing here?" I interrupted.

"When I lived, I came here to this place quite often. On one of my quiet evening visits fishing along the creek, I met Tweetie as she was skipping along the graves and all the time speaking in poems. I knew right away she was not of the living. Something drew us together, and I came back often just to keep her company. I think I was troubled by the idea of a lonely child sprite always playing by herself.

"On one of my visits, she brought Shoe along, and yes, he was frightening. He was carrying a fishing pole in one hand and an axe in the other. I think he had to decide which was for me.

"Some evenings I would come out here after supper, and Shoe would be fishing in the Ebenezer. He would invite me to join him. And on other nights, I could hear him back in the trees there sharpening his tool, the axe, on a stone grinding wheel. I went back there one time and found the grinding wheel. Tilted in the ground, it had been overgrown and half-buried for years. I would somehow still hear Shoe out there just grinding away. I suppose a sharp axe was important to Shoe's existence when he lived.

"I also know that the living families of the black people buried out here, often brought old cups and saucers to put on their ancestors' graves in the old days. Those items are scattered all over out there now. Those were important artifacts to them, the spirits I mean, and they let Captain Best, Tweetie, and me use them for our teas."

Then Moses Hardrick looked hard at me and asked, "What will be important to your existence when you are gone from the living? Will it be property or eternal bliss and solitude? What will you drag into your next existence? Who will put your favorite items on your grave?

"Tweetie became very important to me. She was my secret. She became attached to me, but what could I, the living, do for a lonely sprite? I thought of her of more sprite than spirit. Nevertheless, we bonded, she in this place and time and me still with the living. I asked that my remains not be embalmed and they be buried out here, just over there, because I knew Tweetie would be waiting for me after my death. I wanted no stiff, old body moldering away out here. I knew my body, just as my spirit, had to stay natural." He spoke in such a mollifying way that I lost all apprehension.

I continued with my question: "What have Uncle Duke and Shoe and Captain Best got to do with what I've seen tonight? And who is Shoe? What kind of name is that?"

Moses Hardrick smiled the way the living do when the answer is only obvious to them. This spirit had not smiled before.

"Shoe," he answered, "is the name given an enslaved boy whose master was not very clever. He was called 'Shoe' simply because his owner said, 'He was as brown as a brogan when he come outta his mammy.' At least, that's what Tweetie told me. It was in a poem she recited.

"She always speaks in poems. It took me a long time to understand what she was talking about, but then I started to communicate with Shoe and Tweetie in other ways, to understand them by other mediums."

Though Moses Hardrick was not embalmed, he was a stiff old man and a very formal man, but there seemed to be thought in his lifeless head. He posed his face the way thinking people do and asked, "Could you understand what Shoe meant to convey back inside the room?"

"Could you?"

He ignored my question and continued. "If so, that is a good sign that Shoe and the confused spirits that follow him for protection will never hurt you. Shoe can't speak as I did, and you do because his tongue was sliced out."

"What!" I said, startled.

"Once his mistress called him stupid for dropping bark on the parlor floor while bringing in firewood, and he talked back to her. He was eight years old. His owner made an example of him and set him to work at hard labor—after taking his tongue."

"And they let his master get away with that?"

"Who would be the *they* to stop him? Remember, Shoe was his master's property, 'lock, stock, and barrel,' as they say."

"So, what's Uncle Duke got to do with all this activity?" I insisted while willing myself not to care what had happened to a slave boy called Shoe.

"Sometimes the good, as well as the bad or indifferent, pay for past evils and not necessarily their own. Sometimes, there is so much pent-up anger that it spills from one generation to the next, from one time to another, and it plays out over and over, year after year, and century after century. Daniel is that kind of pathetic victim of a cruel master, too, though he is a victim of a master of his own making. Racism and hate of anyone not like him were his master.

"Daniel came out here on a night very much like this one. He was searching for a Negro man who escaped from the county work farm. He'd been sent there to serve twenty years of hard labor for stealing a hog. The escaped convict ran into Shoe and his axe. And not knowing Shoe was an apparition, he pleaded his case to him and asked for help. Shoe heard him out then silently hefted his sharp chopper.

"I was standing over there where the earthworms ate my corpse." He said this as though earthworms eating corpse was part of the natural condition of his world.

The whole thing played out in front of me: Daniel stopped his car at the top of the hill up there and bolted out. I stepped forward, trying to get his attention, for the past spirits were upon us, but Daniel walked on by me, very much like he walked by black people all his life because to him I was invisible unless my existence suited him. Daniel's master was calling. Hate.

"He never saw Shoe but as certain as my soul stands here now, Shoe was standing just over there where your trailer home is parked. Shoe drew back the axe and cut Daniel down in your world with one blow from his world, and Daniel never saw it coming. At the same time, he brought Daniel to my place of existence.

"Daniel could see Shoe and me then, and I could see the confusion in his face as his new reality registered. He was standing, looking at us, but he was also seeing himself lying on the ground, in front of himself, with his head nearly severed. We were all surprised but Daniel, of course, seemed the most amazed. Shoe looked at his tool, also apparently amazed at its effect.

"The runaway man dragged Daniel over to the creek and pushed his remains down under the cypress roots where they stay today. He drove Daniel's patrol car into the swamp about a half-mile from here.

"Shoe has been finding Daniel every night since. And every morning Daniel's head comes upright on his body, held in place by the rotted gore, and his agony goes away. Every day, I have to find Shoe's axe to keep him from killing another wayward person from your world. Every night, Daniel begs me to stop Shoe from killing him with the axe. Every night, I fail. It's like Prometheus when it comes to Daniel. He is destined to die the same death every night for the sin of bringing his eternal hate to this world.

"Who?" I asked, speaking of Prometheus.

"Never mind," Moses Hardrick said impatiently. "Your uncle is lost. He is between two worlds, not the living and the dead, but the recent dead and the long-ago dead. When his neck is chopped by Shoe, he rots and feels the agony of a miserable life of hate ended by an axe-wielding, vengeful, Negro spirit."

I considered what Mr. Hardrick said, but I couldn't feel sorry for Uncle Duke because the undertaker was right. Uncle Duke had been a miserable human being. By the time he disappeared, most people in the county, both black and white, hated him and his group of friends. There were only three of them, but they picked on everybody. They ruled the county with fear and intimidation. Most whites put up with it because, at least, they were treated better than the blacks.

Everyone also knew they singled out poor black

people the most. They made them pay made-up and excessive fines, and they put the young'uns in the county camps to work off fines they couldn't pay. Then, they rented those poor folks out to the farmers for hard labor, building ponds, and clearing land. I never thought that much about it until I saw Shoe swing his axe. Then, it became clear to me how hate can flow in the good and the bad just like sweet rain falls on the righteous and the unrighteous.

The strangest thing was that Uncle Duke and his friends often acted against their own best interests just to keep themselves in power. "To hold down the coloreds," they called it, meant they had to hold down everyone, every freethinking person who didn't agree with them, their families included. And they had to hold down any idea that lifted up black people even if it would have been good for the poorer whites, too. They controlled the actions of an entire community. I now see how unreasonable racism, bigotry, and the hate that goes with them are.

"So, what's Tweetie doing here?" I asked my knowledgeable apparition while he was in a talkative mood. "Where'd she come from?"

"It is very difficult to communicate with Tweetie, so it has taken me tremendous effort to understand her story. Tweetie came from a different plantation than Shoe. Her real name is not Tweetie, by the way. She told me her mama secretly called her 'Maua Yangu.' That means 'My Flower', but it was forbidden for anyone to call her that because it is a language spoken where her mother came from, in Africa."

By then, Tweetie knew she was the topic of our conversation, and she started skipping in a circle with Moses Hardrick and me in the middle. She was reciting a poem as she came high on one leg, then scraping that foot on the ground before repeating the same motion on the other leg. She said:

> I's as human as you, and
> What lies within me is just as true.
> Speak to us in our places
> And disdain us not. Or leave us be,
> But not in this day. Our campaign's
> Within ourselves you see.
>
> I's as human as you, and
> What lies within me is just as true.
> Captives without causes
> Let us go! Not the dead,
> Silly, but the ones here and now.
> Best on all sides, not to dread.
>
> I's as human as you, and
> What lies within me is just as true.
> Hooded demons riding high
> ol' nightriders come,
> And bring their fear.
> On morning come, we still here.
>
> I's as human as you, and

What lies within me just as true.
Oh creek, let us pass,
Give me mine and me.
I'll know my place then,
And in this place be ever free!

I asked Mr. Hardrick what she was talking about?

He put his right hand to his chin in a humanly pose of consideration and said, "I told you it's difficult to communicate with Tweetie but try this. This took me years to find out." Then he instructed, "Put out your hand and see if she will come to you."

I did as instructed by reaching out my hand as a mother might to her child.

The little girl skipped over to me and timidly placed her left hand into my right one. I could see her hand but could not feel its weight. I became cold and felt wet. A depressive sadness bogged me down, and I felt so tired I could hardly stand. Tweetie smiled a sweet smile with perfect white baby teeth as she looked up at me, and I began to warm up, to dry out.

As a sheriff's deputy, I had considered people only in terms of "black/male" or "white/male and nothing in between. And black people came in shades of light, medium, or dark complexions. But when I looked down at Tweetie, I saw the most perfect, dark chocolate, brown tones that appeared as though they belonged on a brand-new baby doll. She was only about two and a half feet tall. And while I routinely described most eyes on most blacks as brown or black, it would have been a disservice to humans to describe hers that way. Her eyes were light brown with hints of yellow and red and perfect in every way. They were beyond human.

Mr. Hardrick told her to give me her other hand, too, but she hesitated. Her incredibly large eyes shone in the quarter moon as she looked back at the soul she obviously considered her eternal caretaker.

"Go on, child," Mr. Hardrick urged her, as a grandfather might coax a granddaughter to go with another person. "Give her your other hand. She needs to know."

I put out my other hand, and Tweetie touched it. The feel of that touch was like a circuit closing, but this current was not electrical. I shivered. The energy was less shocking than electricity and smoother like a slipstream and more vivid. Everything went dark. For a moment, it was like the quarter-moon never existed, but I was being pulled along in a void by a slipstream. Then, instantly, the moon came back bigger and brighter than before.

Suddenly, I was walking towards Ebenezer Creek. No! I was held shoulder high in the arms of a woman, a beautiful, slender, black woman. She was carrying me.

Someone shouted, "They 's burning the bridge!"

The woman carrying me murmured, "It will be all right, Maua Yangu," but her lip was trembling uncontrollably.

She ran towards the creek and looked back. And stepping high to keep the water from slowing her down, she attempted to get away. I was looking back over her shoulder.

The ground was shaking. No! Thundering. There was smoke moving along the face of the water. It was blowing over us. Embers glowed and descended like fireflies on us all. People, black people, prayed on their knees in rows on the banks of the creek, but in the smoke and embers, they looked like they were lined up for Hell.

Sounds of distant bugles called men to charge forward on horseback and kill. Great herds of huge horses, carrying Confederate soldiers, thundered at a gallop towards us. Captain Best, oddly elegant on his grey horse, was near the front. His sword was pushed out in front of him as he charged forward and occasionally used it to make a slashing motion on one side of his horse or the other. As he slashed, men, women, and children fell with each pass of the weapon.

The Captain had his sights on us, but just as he was about to run us through, Shoe stepped in with his ax already swinging forward. Captain Best slashed him with the sword, but Shoe had enough life left in his body and enough force left in the swing of his axe to knock the captain from his horse. With his foot still caught in his stirrup, the officer let out a terrible scream, and his animal dragged him away at a full gallop, while being chased by other Confederate men on horseback.

Hundreds, maybe thousands, of black women, children, and men panicked and ran all around us. There was nowhere for us to go. Some people prayed: "God, save your chil'rin." And others cursed or just begged each other for help. I heard shouts of "Jesus!" and "ha' mercy!" all around us.

The Confederates caught us in the shallows. The cracks of gunshots were loud, and I turned trying to bury my head in my mama's bosom. Yes! She felt like my mama, but she was lying in the water with a bloody gash across her beautiful face. I stood in the water for a time, not knowing what else to do. Then the leg of a big horse knocked me down. The blow took my breath away and hurt me all over.

I had just lived through the beginning of the end of Tweetie's life. I was swiftly pulled under water and tried to breathe, but I couldn't. There were other people with me in the water, and they were also thrashing about and trying to get away or just fighting for air—just a breath of air. I wanted to breathe, too, but I couldn't. I saw someone I recognized as my Auntie Mary, but she didn't help me. Her not helping me seemed so strange because she had always helped take care of me. In the panic, Auntie Mary looked all around but she couldn't help me.

The water was so cold, so cold. I saw a horse step on another woman's head, and it flattened then almost returned to its proper shape, but she was dead. Her eyes were popping from their sockets. I realized Mama was dead too, but she held my hand. I laid there on my back, floating with Mama holding my hand, until she released me to the currents of the creek, and they took me away. Slowly and gently, they carried me away as I lay there on my back. The bright three-quarter moon pulled me from the cold and held me close.

My nightmare within a dream—if that's what this event was—was suddenly over. I was once again standing with a dead undertaker and the spirit of a little girl.

Tweetie looked up at me as I held her fading hand. She started to cry and chanted:

> I can't float away
> Cold water refresh me.
> Wit' my mama, I must stay
> 'Cause Jesus knows
> I can't float away.

> Creek done got me, so here I stay,
> Cold water done take me.
> Can I go, Mama? You love me? Say!
> Only Jesus knows
> I won't float away.

> Big moon hold me, so now I stay.
> Cold water gonna bathe me?
> Mama say, yeah I say!
> Yes, Jesus knows
> I didn't float away.

"She's wanting to cross the Ebenezer," Moses Hardrick said to me. So did Shoe and hundreds more freed souls, contraband souls. Not just from here, but from all over the South and all over the world. They want to get to the other side where they can be free."

"How do you know these things?" I asked. "You died so long ago, and they've been dead even longer." My confusion and frustration were visible, palpable, and raw.

Moses Hardrick was unfeeling and cold, as I am sure the dead must be. "I don't know how I know," he said. "I don't even know how I communicate with you. I just know that I do know, Madam. It's maybe the same way you have determined how Tweetie passed from your good earth to where she is now. Maybe, I just know because I am supposed to know. You see, I came to play with Tweetie long before I made this my resting place. Just like Shoe asked if I could leave, my answer has always been, 'Yes.' My light, the light I follow, is just over there, over that ridge, but I cannot leave Tweetie as she is. Don't you see? Don't you now know? She has the answers you seek."

Again, he pointed to his grave marker, his wooden cross, in the distance. "Tweetie was skipping around these unmarked graves and this creek long before I was born. The truth about Tweetie is that she can skip among the living, in this place where we are now, and at the place and time she died and every time and place in between. She has the knowledge.

"On the night Tweetie left the living, she and thousands of other newly liberated Negro people were following the army of General Sherman as they marched from Atlanta to the sea. The people were called 'war contraband.' Shoe was actually freed from a large plantation at Wrightsville, Georgia. Once freed by Sherman's army, he was hired to help clear the path as the army moved towards Savannah. Shoe was chopping down trees so the heavy wagons and big guns could pass. This was the first time Shoe had been promised pay for doing anything in his short life. I am sure he was excited and did his job very well.

"After moving across Georgia and destroying all they couldn't eat, this part of Sherman's army found itself here at Ebenezer Creek with a Confederate cavalry on its heels. They had built a bridge across the creek with the help of men and boys like Shoe. But coincidental to some of those men and boys going back to check on their families, one of the Union officers ordered the bridge removed and burned to stop the Confederate cavalry from attacking their flank. Shoe, Tweetie, and thousands more souls like them were trapped. The bridge was gone. Many could not swim. They tried to cross the creek anyway, and many drowned. Others were caught in the shallows and died in the terrible panic, trampled by horses and killed by soldiers.

"Those that lived faced a terrible, angry Confederate army, Southern soldiers who had seen their families, lands, and homes decimated by 'Uncle Billy.' Some of the people were killed outright. Others were savaged, beaten, and returned to enslavement. Many of them, like Tweetie, were left in the creek, dead and unburied."

In frustration, I asked the ghost again, "How can you, being dead, know these things about the living?"

Mr. Hardrick simply said, "We only know what we knew, what we experienced, and what we learned and desired while we lived. We are no more than the residue of lives, feelings, and passion in the atmosphere, held in place by memories and frustrations.

"Captain Best desires only the chivalry and honor he received when he lived. I suspect that was most important to him. Now, he only has the opportunity to practice that chivalry on Tweetie. I often wonder if his twisted sense of chivalry was the reason he chose to side with people whose guiding measure of success was just the opportunity to own other people. Best was no remnant of a noble lost cause, states' rights, and all that. He was the residue of a lost and detestable way of life.

"Those souls are still trying with all their might to get across Ebenezer Creek. On nights like this, they try over and over, and the ones left here die over and over. That is why you cannot be here! It is not your time to be here, but your time will come."

I understood perfectly at that moment, and my sadness was even greater because of that understanding.

Until that night, the death of a black person represented fifty-five dollars to me at Hardrick's Funeral Parlor. That's if they were bright-skinned. But after what I experienced, to say I understood was not enough.

Then Moses Hardrick looked deeply at me and said, "Tweetie shows herself only to people she trusts to come and take care of her and help her cross over. I didn't understand that until I stayed with her in this place. Shoe only shows himself if evil is afoot, and evil had been afoot since long before Daniel arrived."

Then Cle opened the back door to the Land Yacht, stuck his head out, and asked, "Who you talkin' to out there?" Then he paused and cocked his head before adding, "And you're soakin' wet!"

I looked at him and realized I was soaking wet and breathing hard. I thought for a second that Cle was in extreme danger and looked back towards Moses Hardrick and Tweetie, but they were both were gone.

Cle asked me again who I was talking to, but I just coughed and labored to breathe.

"We can't be here!" is all I said, all I could say.

Cle came to my aid, putting a quilt over my shoulders and rubbing my arms. But knowing me and what he called my "funny ways," he pulled some jeans over his pajama bottom and immediately prepared to move the Land Yacht. Once it was hitched to the Stallion, it was only a matter of removing some wheel blocks and raising the hitch jack. I was sitting in the front seat of the Stallion before he even asked where we were going.

"Let's just move to the Wal-Mart lot in Rincon," I said.

After we set up at our new location, Cle finally asked me what was going on. I hesitated to tell him, so he said, "You saw some things you didn't want to see, right?"

"How'd you know?"

"I know 'cause I had a pretty rough night myself."

"You did? How's that?"

"I thought I heard you tossing and turning all night,

but every time I looked, you were just layin' there sound asleep. But then I thought I heard you in the kitchen, and for a time I couldn't move. It was like I was dreamin' of movin,' but I wasn't actually doin' anything. Then, I could finally feel you layin' next to me. You were ice cold. I remember you gettin' up one time and puttin' the extra blanket on the bed. So, I went back into a comfortable sleep. Finally, I heard you talkin' out there. And when I looked, you were just standin' there and lookin' over at the graveyard. Scared the hell outta me." Then, he laughed.

I laughed, too, but I didn't know how to tell him I never put the extra blanket on him. And I never did.

Historical notes—

Nobody knows how many people actually died at Ebenezer Creek in the early morning of December 9, 1864, but it is estimated to have been in the thousands.

The events at Ebenezer Creek are commemorated on a marker erected for the Civil War's 150-year remembrance by the Georgia Historical Society and the Georgia Department of Economic Development and placed at the spot where the original town of New Ebenezer was, established in 1734. This location is about a quarter of a mile from Ebenezer Crossing. The actual crossing is on private land and can be viewed only by boat.

Major General Oliver O. Howard, one of General Sherman's commanders and a Medal of Honor recipient, was over the Army division at Ebenezer Creek but was with Sherman in Savannah, Georgia, when the events at the

Crossing occurred.

General Howard later became commissioner of the Freedmen's Bureau. This bureau was set up to help former slaves, or freedmen, after the Civil War. Many believe he promoted the promise made by General Sherman (Uncle Bill) to provide freedmen families with forty acres of land and a mule as reparation for their enslavement and as a result of the massacre at Ebenezer Creek.

President Andrew Johnson abandoned General Sherman's promise after the assassination of President Abraham Lincoln.

General Howard also went on to help found nationally prominent, historically black, Howard University, in Washington, D.C.

THE DEAD DETECTIVE

As I look in front of me and see myself falling, but at the same time suspended in the midair, —I know I am dead. I mean literally dead—without life. However, I find myself remarkably calm in knowing my situation. Not calm in a living way—as in, steady pulses, resting mind, and controlled breathing—but calm in a peaceful, not caring way. I have become an observer, and I had not, until now, realized this kind of peace was the nature of death. At least, not my own. I do not know if I expected harps and angles or caldrons and pitchforks, but it just do not seem to matter either way now that I am here, with *here* being a state of indifference for the most part. I just remain calm.

I had often said I was not afraid of death, but more

the method of my demise. There is pain in methodology. A slow tortured death is the one I feared the most. Finger and toes tampered with or burning were the least desired, but they do not seem to matter now. Well, here I do not know the method, but I am calm in the condition, nevertheless. I am calm because I am lacking any energy or reason to be excited or otherwise. The energy is here, but it is somehow changed, or at least, it is changing.

I guess suspension in the act of falling is where my immediate and conscious brain functions ceased. My physical eyes have also ceased to function, but my mind's eye is still here, wherever *here* is. I do not know at this moment why I died or even if I should care. The method is no longer important. Oddly, I realize I have no care about my death one way or the other. I merely exist, or not, in this place of non-feeling, non-caring, nothingness as an inexplicable form of energy. In this form, the contractions in life and language are gone and I do not know why. Control is gone. Language is unspoken but still conventional and structured. I record in an unspoken, ordinary language I knew, knowing the experiences I describe will never be played back. Yet, I am compelled to give account, anyway.

That thing suspended there in front of me—me—is only the last glimpse of the last moment before I died. I find myself wanting to complete my fall, reach out and catch myself as any human being might. But really, I do not care if I catch myself or not. Completing the fall would make my death all so final. I sense that the desire to catch myself is a residual reflex from a world I no longer have contact with. Yet it is right there. No sensations exist here—no taste or smell or sight or sound. There is no cold or heat, to complain about, or love or any feeling akin to it, at least not yet.

I had always heard the deeper functions of the brain go on for fractions of seconds when someone dies, and those few fractions can seem like whole lifetimes flashing before the dying person's eyes. Is this it for me? Is this that time in my death experience? So many questions permeate my existence now that I am dead.

This state I find myself is all too confusing. What if my body, or my head, were obliterated at the moment of my death? Would I still have this moment of "lifetimes," this moment I am apparently starting now?

"I think therefore I am," seems somehow right for this situation. But not really, for I do not think I am anything at all. I do not think. I am just here, wherever here is, yet I am not here, and I exist, yet I do not exist all at the same moment. It is obvious something has changed. Something is new or different. It is like when the TV goes off, and for a split second the last image is burned into the screen. I am falling, yet I am frozen on the screen. But life goes on outside the screen. Everything from suffering to joy and love to selfishness continues. But inside the device, the circuits cool down slowly. My image slowly degrades from residue pixels to nothingness. Or maybe the residue is nothingness. I perceive, I wish I could explain better.

In any case, the visual only happens in the mind's eye. No not the mind's eye, but a third eye that can see everything. Maybe me falling, the room, and the people in it were always illusions of nothingness that can be seen only with the third eye. Complicated? Yes.

Now I see the answer so clearly. The history of our lives is residue to the living because the living are the witnesses. Witnesses? Witnesses? What are those? Why does that word feel so familiar?

I lay here on my side for what seems like hours, peaceful hours, perfect hours… My human eyes are fixed on a twisted piece of paper, just a shred, but I can make out the color red and the shape of a twisted heart imprinted on it.

"Awake!"

This is not a command to rise from death but more a summons to rise in death and see. But by who? What? In the hotel room, I see the remains of the end of life preserved before my eyes, but this time I am truly out-of-body.

Outside the room, I was in another room, I see my mother holding me as a baby. Her sisters were there, too. This corny scene was from a remembered life, but it rang so real. I see Aunt Kay and Aunt Josephine and finally Aunt Rosie, my favorite. They were looking down on me and smiling. Their breaths smelled of alcohol and decay. No, I perceived their breaths smelled like alcohol and rot. I perceived decay as a process and rot as a result. This perception is part of my new understanding of their lives now, but not back then.

They were secret alcoholics, and I always wondered if they knew each other's secret. Now, that I can see in this detached way, I understand that they not only knew about each other, but they also enabled each other by hiding pint bottles of rum from each other, and for each other, around their homes. I started finding those bottles when I was five years old. I had good naps in those days. Now, I do not care, and neither do they because they are all dead, too.

Someone said, "Goochie-goochie-goo," and they all laughed, and I would have laughed too, but it is—was—not funny anymore because I am dead.

Another said, "He's a big one."

Aunt Josephine said, "That means big poops," and she held her nose at me. Someone was changing my diaper.

My mama went out of the room, and Aunt Kay said, "Big ears and a big nose, too, like his daddy."

This viewing goes on for what seems an eternity to me because there is no sense of time in this new place. At one point, a man came in, looked down at me, and said, "That's my boy! Look at that big Johnson on that kid, just like his daddy!" He looked satisfied at me. He looked at my aunts and asked, "What are you three witches looking at?" and walked out.

I start to deliberate about my current circumstance, but I am not sure with whom or what. What would I see about my life? Would I see what kind of person I had been, or is understanding my life beyond my perception in this new place? Maybe I would just see, and there would be no judgment for what I see. That is what I prefer, but preferences do not register here. I see only the images I need to see with my third eye, and those echoes would be only reference points, much like in the world I left. These are questions and answers I have, but only bits and pieces seem to linger in some dimension where I am parked. I only partially exist, or maybe I only reside here temporarily. Yes, reside is the better sensation, but more in a homeless sense of a transitory observer of others' ongoing lives. This existence is a lone remnant of what I had been. Maybe my existence will only go on as someone's memory in the physical world where touch, sight, sound, smell, gravity, and physics continues to make sense. Yes! What will the living remember about me from the world I left? Will my life make sense to them?

A flash came from behind me, and I was in front of what used to be me. But how is that possible? And how did I know there was a flash? It is frustrating when you are the decedent. Now, how did I know that word, *decedent*? It's like witness, how did I know that circumstance? Yes! Circumstance is a better understanding of witness and decedent. To know things but not to know why I know things is frustrating. This place, or state, is frustrating because I am not myself, but I am not anyone else either. I am not quite sure of the images I see and if they apply to me. What I am conveying is not spiritual but practical. I saw a flash of light, but it was from my murder or from someone else's life? Maybe it is both. Maybe my murder was part of someone else's life?

Oh yeah! Also, in front of me now is the image of the flash of light, but it is still so strange. It is a mirror! I see the flash in the mirror, and I see a woman and a man also in the reflection, but they are behind me and reflected in the mirror, like an old piece of film that is burned in the middle, is in front of me. The woman's face…I can just make it out, hard and unfeeling. She is blond and partially dressed in a white blouse open to expose, well, her everything. She yells something at me. But I do not understand. She too is frozen in her own reflection. She is on a bed but standing on her knees and yelling something to me—at me.

I want to understand, but I keep wanting to telling myself, I do not care. That world is no longer my concern. Still, I cannot take my…my eyes? …off the scene playing out in front of me.

Looking closer, I see a box in the hotel room and, next to it, a hat on the dresser. Why are they there? Why is the hat, a brown fedora, so familiar to me? But now I can see the man behind me. The reflection is so clear now. I am wearing a fedora, but it is black. Why is the flash behind my head? The box is wrapped in paper that is covered in little red hearts, but some of the paper is torn away.

I will myself to care, but only by some instinct. I really do not care. Yet, I yearn for an answer to something I do not care about. Oddly, I deduce the fedora on the dresser must belong to the other man because the man in the reflection behind me is not wearing one. Do rules and logic exist in this new place? They must, but how? Why?

Someone or something else is here too, but I can see only a shadow. No. It is not there in that world but here in this new place. It hovers above me. It looks down on me, and no matter how hard I try to distinguish the shape, it is just a shadow in the shadows. I think therefore I am, or I don't think, but I am? Somehow, I know I'm here but where is here? I know the shadow is there, but there is here. This place is so bewildering. This condition is perplexing.

My first memories are in front of me again: I was sitting on the floor and playing Pat-a-cake with my mother. She was a handsome woman with a loving face.

"Pat-a-cake, pat-a-cake, baker's man... Who's at the door, hum? Hum?" Mama sang, "Who's that at the door? Is that Daddy at the door?" She pointed towards the door. The room was small and sparse but there was a little bed, a lamp, and a big picture of a big yellow duck, wearing pants, painted on the wall.

Oh! A big blue bird came in. He handed me his gun belt, with the gun in its holster, as he walked in the door. "Put that away for me," he said. He put his blue cap onto my head. My half-brother, Foster, was there—for some unknown reason I know I have a half-brother and his name is Foster—and Foster reached for the gun belt and then the cap, but his hands went unanswered. I do not know why I know my daddy was a policeman, because he looked like a big blue bird.

He could see the gun belt was too heavy for me, so

he took it back and put it over my shoulder. I ran and stumbled towards Mama. I wanted to show her, but the load was still too heavy, and I fell. Everyone seemed so happy except Foster. Mama was smiling down on me but, for no reason, she looked angrily at Daddy. Yes, that is my daddy. I understand that now. He was so tall and so big, like a big bird.

My murder scene is back now. My reflection and the mirror…Yes, the flash in the mirror and a box and the hat, all fade. At least, I think—no I do not think—I perceive it is a mirror and then it is all gone. No, do not go! I want to say, no! But I cannot understand why I want to say no. I have no reason to say no. I just need a little more time. This is a confusing place. Yes, time is the right thing. I need time to see the room. I am a detective—was a detective. I need to see rooms and spaces and cars and things and people and… No! I was a detective, so I do not need to sense these impressions anymore. This state of being is so frustrating, confusing… I think I sense now… Yes! I needed to talk to witnesses and suspects. But now I am a dead detective. Still, I need to see the guy, the one with the hat on, in the hotel room where I was murdered. My murder room, the other detectives would call it. I need to know what is in the box. No. The box is gone. Where did the box go?

I need to see who is in the shadows with me here and now. The scene is dissolving to blackness, so black, so serene, so calming but the shadow is still in this place. The shadow stands out against the darkness. I cannot quite make the shadow out, but it is there. Yes. It is here with me.

My father was hitting Mama, and I was in the corner of the room, crying. Foster grabbed me by the hand and pulled me outside. He started to beat on me for no reason. He asked, "Why you make Daddy so mad?" I opened my mouth but...

I am floating now. I am above my murder. Yes, this is better. I cannot imagine why I would know this was the place where I was murdered, but there is a sheet covering something lying on the floor. But I can still see everything. I can even see myself looking down on myself. I cannot even imagine how I could imagine to know what murder is. There is that word again, *murder*. I do not care, but I know I was murdered, "the unlawful, premeditated killing, of a human being by another human being." It seems so strange to know that. Maybe, I know that because one of the detectives in the room used that word, murder, gave that definition, then whistled.

"He never saw it coming. Poor guy was murdered where he stood. Shot in the back of the head," a female detective said. She was wearing a fedora, too. Do all detectives wear fedora hats? Was that me she was talking about? I really could not tell. I really do not care, but there I am, hanging around in the corner of the room nonetheless, so I will listen in.

"Wait! Wait! Do not lift that sheet!" needs to be said, but I cannot say it. So, I just look, and there I am with a chunk of my forehead missing and a stupid look on my face. The reason I know about the look on my face is because one of the detectives in the room says, "What's he got that stupid look on his face for?"

The female detective raises the other end of the sheet, and the dead guy, presumably me, has his pants down to his knees and has defecated upon himself—myself. They all snicker.

Hey! Why are my pants down?

One hat guy says, "Pew! I wondered what that was," and holds his nose. "Couldn't have happened to a nicer guy." He was being sarcastic, of course, because I have never been nice to anyone.

Another guy in uniform says, "I guess this is what can happen when you crawl in the wrong window and get caught with your pants down, so to speak." Everyone in the room laughs.

The lady detective says, "Yeah, and we get overtime to find out who's window our beloved co-worker crawled into. But there is another possibility." She takes the laughter out of her voice and asks in a questioning tone, "What if our co-worker, and victim, crawled through a window in this hotel—metaphorically speaking because we know he kicked the room-door open—and caught someone else with, say, his wife or girlfriend? And whoever she was with gets the jump on him?"

There I am with two extra holes in my head—one

entry and one exit—my pants down, a stupid look on my face, and I cannot do anything about it; just lie here and experience the crude jokes at my expense by my co-workers—my former co-workers.

"Break this up!" a voice booms from nowhere, and then another man, also wearing a fedora, comes into the room. "This is the murder investigation of a fellow detective, not a comedy club."

I know this new detective, but I cannot quite make out from where.

"Aw Sarge, you know how he was. He would be the first to…"

The room has no smell or sound or sight that eyes can see, yet there I am looking at myself and everything that is going on with the investigation. Maybe it is that I know bloody death has a metallic smell when the deed is fresh. So, I am sure the smell is there because it is always there. And so are the gore of violent death: the splatter, the distortions, and the crude jokes about the decedent to mask the splatter, distortions, and gore.

My half-brother ran over me with his bike. "I hate you," he said, and I cried out, but I could not get up. This new scene is different from being in the murder room, my murder room. I am actually living this event all over again, I believe. But the place and time also seemed remote, distant, in the past. I could feel the pain. I do not know what to make of pain in death.

Now, the shadow is hanging over me, again. Go away!

Mama asked Foster, "Why you treat your brother so bad?" But he just shrugged, cried, and walked into the house. Soon, Daddy walked out with a belt and started to beat on me to make me get up, but I could not because my leg was broken. He was lashing back and forth with the belt. Daddy had it folded in the middle so sometimes I got the leather, and other times I got the metal buckle, but most times I got both. I wanted Daddy to stop, but he did not know my leg was broken, or maybe he did. He just wanted me to "act like a man," he said, but...

This darkness is so sweet that if I could, I would taste it. There is no sense of time or distance or night or day or anything. I could stay here forever, and maybe I will. But there is this nagging of old voices and places. The places are sacred, and the voices are about God. Old voices talking about reverence, glory, and peace, fill this space I inhabit. I grope in the sweet darkness just to catch a word or two, but they pass my existence, leaving only a sense of regret.

Not so fast, the next scene is not what I suppose it is, is it? Who I used to be is lying on a stainless-steel table. I am seeing this from the corner of the room above myself, again. That lady detective is at my side writing something down on a clipboard. What is left of my brain is in a metal bowl next to my head. That man, the loud one who told everyone to "break it up" is there again. I know him, but I cannot recall him. He is there, and now I can clearly see him. I know him, and he feels so familiar.

A man dressed from head to toe in light blue scrubs says to the lady detective, "He was clearly shot from the rear just once. He probably didn't even know what hit him. You guys know who did this yet?"

"We have a couple working theories. The murder room was cleaned of prints and DNA, but we did find a scrap of paper on the floor that may have a partial on it. We'll see what we can do with that. We think the scene was staged. I believe his pants may have been pulled down to throw us off the track or maybe even to humiliate him." Her voice was thoroughly professional.

"You may be right on that Detective. There was no sign of him having had sexual relations or even an arousal," the light blue doctor said. "You said his pants were down?"

I know what hit me! And I want to tell the guy in the scrubs and the lady detective, but I do not care. A radio is playing a country song in the background, and the sound is filling this space I find myself. The song is something about a blond and a horse from Tennessee, whatever they are.

I know who shot me all right. I knew because it just hit me as hard as that bullet hit the back of my head. That guy wearing the hat, the one with the half-naked woman from my murder room, did it and now he is standing there with the lady detective, looking down at me. He shot me in the back of the head. He is wearing the same hat at my autopsy he was in my murder room. How do I know that word, *autopsy*? He is acting like he does not know who killed me. And for some reason, I still do not care. Yet, I exist in a state of pure frustration. I want to yell to the lady detective: ask that guy who did it! He was there, he knows! He is standing right next to you! But I cannot because I really do not care. I am dead.

It is interesting to see one's insides after one is dead. The man in light blue scrubs carefully examines me from head to toe, inside and out. He takes all my internals out, examines them piece by piece, puts them into a plastic bag, shakes his head at my liver, and puts the whole mess back into my shell. He keeps bits and pieces of my innards in little jars and small flat containers as though he plans to play with them later. He is weighing the remains of my brain now. He knows how I died, but he seems to be doing stuff only because he likes doing stuff to the dead. He says, "This is the damaged brain of an otherwise health Caucasian male. The weight is 1,280 grans with major distortions to the Occipital, Parietal, and Frontal lobes. The path of the bullet entered the skull at the lower, right Occipital lobe, traveled through the Parietal lobe, and exited through the Frontal lobe at approximately a fifteen-degree, upward angle. The entry wound indicates the barrel of the assailant's gun was no more than six inches from the back of the decedent's head when the shot was fired due to the gunpower stippling around the entry point."

How does he know that? How would I know what that means, but I do.

They slide me in a drawer, and the darkness is constant, yet I can see human beings coming and going from the autopsy room outside and the outer office as though I am out there, too. The lady detective says, "This looks like a crime of passion. Our victim kicked the door to the hotel room and came in unannounced."

"Shots fired! Shots fired!" My radio was at my ear. It was night and uniformed police officers were everywhere in this new scene.

My sergeant yelled, "You and Bill check out that warehouse over there!"

Bill and I headed out. We were both in blue uniforms.

But wait a minute, Bill is the same guy standing behind me in my murder room, the one reflected in the mirror. He is the guy who shot me in the back of my head. He is in a uniform, but it is the same guy.

We were both younger though in this new place. We went into the warehouse ready for action. It was full of shelves stacked with furniture all in the shadows. My heart was beating so fast. Bill was behind me when everything was slowing down. I could see down this long isle, but it was dark on the far end. Someone was running down there, on the far end, but I could not tell if he was...

I can taste the darkness again, but the shadow above me is still there. It will not speak. I want it to say something. Anything. If I could just stay here, then I would be simply fine. If the shadow would speak and tell me I could stay here, I would. If the voices would come back—the voices about God, and mercy, and peace, and love, and salvation—maybe I could grab one and I would be fine, but... Maybe, I could go with them.

This table is porcelain, long, and pure white, this time. I am stretched out, buck-naked, and someone is using crazy glue and parts from a box to put my head back together. Did my head come in a box? Shifting from place to place like this is all so confusing. The light in the new room is cold, blue, and harsh. I can see from the corner of the room as though I am standing over there. But I am lying over here on the table looking up. How is that possible? But it is happening. Oh yeah, that third eye.

They run a needle attached to a hose in at my neck and leave me to harden as fluids run out at slits cut at my ankles. People come and go in the room where they prepare me, but I just lie here. They do not seem to mind. Then, in a flurry, several people dress me. I want to slap her hand away as a lady puts makeup on my face and hands, but I cannot move. I do not care anymore.

I am in uniform again, but this one is dressier. At least, that is what one of the men says. "He looks peaceful in there in his dress uniform." *There* is my coffin. *There* is where they put me after I am hard, cold and dressed in my dress uniform. *There* is where the lady from the room where I was murdered, the one who was half dressed, comes to see me. Oh yeah, the half-dressed lady from the murder room is here looking down on me in my coffin. Now, she is smartly dressed in black and crying, but there are no tears. Her dress is short, and I should be angry.

Someone says, "Misty, I'm so sorry for your loss."

Oh yeah, I now realize Misty is my wife—was my wife.

The guy in the warehouse was running away from me, but I knew I had to shoot or he would get away. He was twenty-five yards away in the darkness. I was sweating but calm. I felt as if I were in a tunnel. I took dead aim and started the slow trigger squeeze—just like I was taught—while I concentrated on my front sights. Everything was still in slow motion.

I was surprised by my own shot. Bang! But I could not seem to understand why the guy running did not fall. Confusing. My gun did not move. It should have recoiled. I looked at my gun. Even in slow motion, I should have felt the gun recoil. What is recoil? I looked to my side and another guy, ten feet away, was falling backward. He had a gun in his hand, and he was falling. Did he shoot? It was confusing. I looked back at Bill and he had his gun in his hand, and the barrel and breach were smoking. Two more shots rang out from Bill's gun as the guy continued his fall. I realized Bill had just saved my life. He saved me twice, once from shooting an unarmed man—this I find out later—and once by killing a guy, I did not see, who was going to kill me.

Daddy said, "You guys can spend every other weekend and even summers with me, but for now, you have to stay with your mother." We were at home, but Daddy was packed and leaving.

Later, when Foster thought Daddy was not watching, he asked me, "Why did you drive Daddy away? Why did you even come into this world?" Foster was holding Daddy's pistol when he said those words. But, Daddy came up from behind, and he and Foster wrestled over the gun. There was a shot. Bang!

Why did I come in this world? That was Foster's question. My sense is I have—had—a purpose, but I do not know what it is—was. I should know when I came into the world and why, but I do not. Now, I am just dead, and I do not care anymore.

This is crazy! I see everyone coming and going from my wake, both from my vantage points of looking down from the corner of the chapel and from looking up from my coffin. Foster is looking down on me now. He is older than me by two years, but his face appears more strained from sadness than age. He is an older adult now, but we have not spoken since we were kids because he was taken away and I was so angry. He is crying.

My father is at my wake, too. He is in a wheelchair. He seems very thin, and his hair is whiter than it seemed before my death. He is also crying, but he always told me, "Men don't cry."

Bill is also there. He looks down on me and smiles, but I do not know what his smile means. He is comforting Misty, with his arm tightly around her as they both look at me. His smile is not a loving, but more a cunning smirk, like he is getting away with… Murder! He winks at me.

Firetrucks, with ladders extended, and huge American flags hanging in the wind, line the roadway as they drive me to a hole in the ground at the far end of a road, at the far end of town. I know this place because the guy that Bill killed in the warehouse is out there, too. I fly over this scene as though I am a kite being pulled by my coffin against the air currents. Up and down, side to side, I go, all the time looking down on my processional. I do not care that this is where I am. I do not care that the person who tried to kill me in the warehouse is buried out here, too. I only know that this day will come for everyone, and now it is here for me. I really do not want to be in a box in the ground.

It is a mostly sunny day. One of the men in uniform, folding the flag that drapes my coffin, whispers, "It's a good day for a funeral." Another honor guard flag folder nods slightly, awkwardly, but says nothing in return.

The ground is wet, so I perceive it has rained. I remain above it all—the puddles, the rising vapors drawn by the sunlight, the small talk, the crying, the noises fidgeting children make. There are accolades, both public and private, about a dead detective. Some are true, most are not. They talk about how kind I was and how I always want to be a public servant so I could help people. All lies. As I lay here with the sounds of familiar words filling the spaces around me, I realize I was kind to my dog Stretch, but never to Misty. I wonder if that is why Bill killed me. Yes!

Bill killed me! First, he saved my life back when he was my partner in uniform patrol and then he killed me in a hotel room when I caught him screwing my Misty.

An army of police officers are here. They all wear their best uniforms with chests sticking out like rare birds holding up traditions built on time itself. I have been to too many police funerals, and I know tomorrow will be normal again. If not tomorrow, then the next day. Tomorrow all the nice words will be gone. The further everyone gets from the event horizon—in this case my funeral is the point of no return—the more reality seeps back in in sad and sometimes shocking ways. Some will curse me for the last time tomorrow. Others may wait a year, but they will still curse me. Tomorrow, Bill will have free reign with Misty. But today, the birds all stand firm, fly in formation, and follow the protocols of traditions that have lasted hundreds of years.

They are finished talking over me now. The folded flag is given to Misty. She holds it close to her heart. They promise she will never be forgotten by her police family.

"On behalf of a grateful ..."

The woman detective is there, too. She is standing back with other detectives, all in dress blue uniforms. They look more like blue cats than birds. They are looking at Bill and Misty. Like cats hunting, they lick their lips.

I look down, but even the sky seems far below me now. The tether to my coffin—to my body—is gone. Now the darkness consumes me, and it feels final. The shadow is there above me and behind me, and I sense the shadow is me looking down on me. This darkness is so sweet, I could just stay here forever.

COP HOUSE STORIES

The First Week

"Have mercy!" boomed the voice of a bald-headed young black man. He was tall and perfect and stood next to a young, brown-haired Anglo man, also perfect. Perfect professional women outnumbered the men. Many of the women had let their hair down and managed to release an extra button or two at the top of their work fashion, a sign that the workday was over. They all stood close to each other, men and women, so close they could easily smell each other's breath. They had cascaded out onto the cobble stone sidewalk and into the street. The young black man was in the doorway.

There was lots of breath-smelling going on that afternoon all over the area but especially among the crowd gathered there at the Cop House Bar on Copper Street. This was a yuppy place just steps away from the triple-A ballpark and the business district in Edington, New Jersey. Apparently, the "have mercy" was in response to a joke that ended with the words, "and Jelly Roll made my mama fat!" Or it may have been an exclamation point to the final score flashing on all five flat screens, signifying a winning bet by the Anglo guy. The TVs were strategically positioned throughout the bar, to include one outside over the sidewalk.

It was hard for Pat Stanton to tell. In any case, the crowd pushed together so tightly that everyone had to yell in order to be heard over the noise of everyone else yelling something to somebody else.

In most bars on the street, Stanton noted, the crowd was not so thick. Those places, mostly located in new buildings made to look old, the crowds were more subdued, with the patrons' eyes stuck on cellphones and thumbs banging away. But this place, the Cop House Bar, was different. It reeked of history, grime, and rowdiness, dating back to the fifties and sixties, though the building was much older. That ambiance couldn't be washed away by all the Ax Bodywash and Vera Wang Perfume in the state of New Jersey. From the five sixties-era phone booths next to the front door to the bare brick walls, the place had a working-class character that most bars in this part of town would have died for. The Gen Zers, many of whom had never done an honest day of manual labor in their lives, loved that flavor.

When Pat pushed to the door, the crowd was even thicker inside. There were people on cellphones outside, some surfing and talking, and some taking selfies. Even the old pay phones next to the door were full of men and women who were, no doubt, lying to significant others about where they were, or were going to be. Some were setting up drug deals, and maybe a few were even trying to get through to an escort service. But inside was even more packed with young urban professionals not looking so professional. They were in various stages of undress. There was no room for selfies, but they somehow happened anyway. There were hoots and hollers, like at a rodeo, and twisted shirts spinning in the air. That's the kind of place this was, and the rowdiness showed most on days like this. The owner's only rule was no drug sales or use on the premises.

Captain Stanton, as he was called, was a retired-age man with stubble instead of a beard. He was pale with washed-out blue eyes and hair that had not decided to be blond or gray. He wore a canvas work jacket that screamed no nonsense. He had a bearing about him that made people leave him along. In short, he easily could have been a proper English gentleman out for a quiet walk on his estate. But this was no English anything and by the time he got to the middle of the room the crowd was already getting on his nerves. Though he remembered it was Saint Patrick's Day, he hadn't considered what that meant until then—

crowds, testosterone and green beer.

With a grunt, he pushed his way past an informal line, six deep and six wide, waiting at the bar. He moved towards the back room, but before he could get there, Whit, an older hippie looking waiter wearing a long white apron, cut him off. "Nubs is in the side room," he said, "and you better do something before Norris throws him out." Norris allegedly owned the bar.

Stanton immediately turned from Whit towards the side room where his friend Nubs was situated. The room had been strictly a pool parlor back in the days before the place was remodeled for the third of forth time. It had once comfortably held six pool tables, but that was before the banking and business crowd took over. Since Norris had removed a wall, the space was more and area. Now the former poolroom was more an extension of the bar, and the one remaining pool table, in a far corner, was covered during happy hour to make more space. There were a couple beat-up bar tables with two matching chairs at each, but the rest was standing room only. Stanton expected to see Nubs looking out onto the sidewalk from a table near the plate-glass window, with a row of shot glasses and beer bottles lined up across the sill. That's where Nubs sat when he was feeling melancholy. Stanton's quick look told him a different story.

Nubs was seated, with his back to Stanton, in the center of the room with his head flopped over on a bar table. Stanton couldn't see the worst of him, but he saw enough. He ruefully shook his head and rubbed his chin.

As he moved closer, he noticed shot glasses stacked in a pyramid in front of his friend. Saliva oozed from his buddy's gaping mouth in a slow-moving river, like lava, headed to its ocean. Stanton knew this was Nubs' way of claiming his space—of staking out his territory. It was rather like a dog peeing on a fire hydrant.

The crowd of after-workers in this part of the bar had been there longer than those out front. They were dressed, or nearly dressed, for the St. Patrick's Day celebration in everything from creased shirts with no neckties to fine neckties with no shirts. Even though they were a festive bunch—most of them fully in the bag—they still had the sensibility to give this old-time drunkard his space. They had created the shores of his ocean with their bodies, having formed an eight-foot circle around Nubs and the table. While it was clear that some saw him as the show, or just a topic of conversation, others saw him as an object of contempt and ridicule.

"Anybody in my office?" Stanton yelled over the noise.

"Commander's back there!" said Whit, while doing a doubletake over his shoulder. "And, looks like Moose and another guy just walked in."

"Moose, huh? I wonder what he wants? Get 'im!"

Stanton made his way across the no-man's-land to Nubs and started lightly slapping him on the cheeks. "Wake up m' friend!"

Nubs started to come to and Moose—given that name when he was a young police officer and for good reason, but not the obvious one—had parted the crowd and was standing there awaiting instructions.

Stanton gave Moose a second look, as though he had forgotten how big Moose was. "Well, get 'im over to my office."

Moose was big, Caucasian, and pale—some would say sloppy-big, at over 6' 6" and weighing in at nearly 400 pounds—but the reason he was called Moose was that he was the only police officer in the history of the Edington Police Department to hit a moose while on patrol. The big animal walked away with a slight limp. On the other hand, Sloppy Joe Baker, as he was known back then, walked away with a new and better nickname. The moose, it seemed, was an escapee from a little roadside carnival traveling through the city. The new patrol officer was glad he didn't have to go through the rest of his career as "Sloppy Joe."

The big detective had brown hair, graying around the edges, and wore a nice blue corporate suit and white shirt with a button-down collar, but no tie. The suit was so well cut, it was hard to tell Moose's service weapon was hiding under his coat. He pulled Nubs up by the forearm singlehandedly, and then a smaller, younger man, a detective that Stanton didn't know took the other arm. The younger officer was about six feet with a sandy low-cut afro. He wore a black suit, light-blue shirt, and was also tieless. Everyone knew he was packing.

The crowd parted the way they would if Moose were actually a moose, and the two detectives walked Nubs back into the main bar, took a right towards the men's room, continued through a short, narrow hallway that separated the men's and ladies' toilets, and went through a door at the end.

The place Stanton called his office was actually a private event room. At least, that's what Norris had called it before the old cops took it over as their private space. Remarkably, it was quiet back there—no sounds of the crowd or the TVs. There was no need for shouting and no standing-room only. They had walked in at the center of the front wall of a square room of larger than average size, all painted pale green. There were dirty, opaque, grated windows along the left wall. A door in the back-left corner led directly outside, but an iron bar laid across the door jamb blocked it. Along the length of back wall, also red bricks painted the same sick green, sat a built-in chestnut-stained oak bench without cushions. The wooden bench contrasted sharply to the walls. The floor was wide, oak planks and they, with the bench, showed decades of wear and tear. The original entrance to the space was on the right wall near the front corner, but it too was blocked—this one with boxes of inexpensive liquor. The blocked doors were probably fire code violations, but it never seemed to get reported.

There were two old bar tables in this space, too. Stanton used the smaller one as his desk. It was on the left side next to the back door. It was offset from the back wall and the bench in such a way that Stanton could look straight along the left wall—his right from his seat— through a small pantry, and on down the working side of the bar. Bartenders came and went through Stanton's office to get liquor stock under his casual gaze. Norris had had problems with disappearing bottles of his most expensive stock before he set up an arrangement with Stanton so that Stanton got an office and Norris got no more liquor thefts. It was rumored that Stanton had part interest in the place anyway and that's why he took such a keen interest, but Stanton had never confirmed that rumor. Norris, himself a disabled former cop, had been one of Stanton's partners on the job, and for his part, he would never even admit that he owned the joint. Why? Taxes.

Moose and the younger detective dumped Nubs in a seated position onto the bench next to Stanton's desk. To no one's surprise, Nubs immediately fell over on his side. The new detective grimaced, but no one else reacted.

Stanton, while taking a seat at his desk, shook hands with Moose and said, "Long time."

"Yeah, it has been. Wasn't even sure you guys were still holding court over here."

"Who's your friend?" Stanton jerked his chin at the younger detective who had helped move Nubs but didn't offer to shake hands. "I kinda like to know who's coming back here, you know."

"He's all right. My great-nephew—new to Homicide—Chops's grandson."

This brought raised eyebrows from everyone in the room except Nubs, who was then sitting up but still appeared completely out of it. Or perhaps he already knew Chops's grandson was black. It was clear no one else did.

Stanton stuck his hand out to shake. "So, you a newbie detective, huh?

"The kid asked, just this morning, when were we going to stop calling him 'Newbie,' and I told 'im when he fuckin' solves a case."

"I'm Lynsey Grant, and I have a case," the fresh detective said, sounding like a first grader on the first day of school, "but it's a throwaway."

The other detective in the room, Commander Bell, was female and wearing a navy-blue pantsuit with a white blouse, open in a vee at the neck. She had a cigarette between the usual fingers of her right hand. Smoke whirled to a point of stagnation above her head. The smoke obscured a stained "No Smoking" sign that hung on the wall, also above her head. She was taller than average and older than she looked. She sported a medium afro with greyish tips and had skin the color of orange pekoe tea. She sat at the larger table and had been casually looking at her cellphone while smoking when the group walked in. She looked up during the introductions but only waved and said, "Hi, Ann Bell," to the new detective.

Bell's greeting, though she was smiling, sounded like a threat to Grant because even though he had never met her, during his six years on the job, every detective had heard of Commander J. Ann Bell and knew she was not to be trifled with.

Moose said, "Yeah, meet the queen, Commander Ann Bell. She over Intelligence."

"Drama queen, you mean," Nubs said, and everyone

laughed. Dried spittle had caked on his cheeks, and the group laughed more at his appearance than at what he had said. He looked around like he was surprised to be in a new location. He reached for Bell's cigarettes and she didn't mind.

Commander Bell, showing some made up drama and lots of attitude, said, "Show 'em why they call you Nubs—Nubs."

Grant, while attempting to hide a look of surprise at these comments from this group of seasoned cops said, "I heard of you, Commander Bell."

She said dryly, "I know, and I've heard about you."

Nubs picked up the cigarette pack and held up his right hand to show that the little and ring fingers were missing their first joints. He then slowly curled all but the middle finger to reveal an obscene gesture, a bird, while all the time looking at Commander Bell with a featureless expression. Again, the room erupted in laughter.

Commander Bell looked at the newbie and said, "You'll have to forgive my former colleagues, but this is where I come to get a dose of reality every now and again."

Nubs called for Whit. It took two tries, but Whit finally stuck his head around the corner. "Speaking of reality, there's a little too much of it in here right now," Nubs said. "Bring me a bottle of my brown whisky and some shot glasses."

Stanton asked Whit, "You make any corn' beef today?"

Without having to say it, everyone knew Stanton was

talking about corned beef and cabbage. After all, it was St. Patrick's Day. But Norris sometimes had soup, clam chowder, or ham sandwiches for the crowd in the back room.

"Yeah,' said Whit, "And Norris wanted me to remind you all this ain't no restaurant and he could get in trouble serving real food outta here." Clearly, he said this for benefit of the new detective.

"Yeah, yeah, you ain't charging for it so this is just amongst friends as far as the new guy is concerned. Nothing for the health department t' stir about," said Stanton. He looked over at the rest of the group. "Anybody else?"

"Small bowl," said Bell. Everyone else waved Whit off.

Stanton rubbed his chin and looked at Moose. "Chops's grandson, huh? Man, don't that make me feel old."

Without realizing it, the whole room gave a moment of silence because Chops was dead, and he had been one of them. He died of a massive heart attack within six months of retirement from the department.

"If there was a fight, you wanted Chops on your side," said Stanton.

Bell said, "He had more complaints than any other cop in the department, and that was quite an accomplishment since his time was in the seventies and eighties when all the talk was civil rights and most of the cops were not feeling mutual on that topic. I was working the streets in Intelligence back then, and I should know."

In their world, complaints meant the public complaining about the police, not the other way around.

Nubs said, mainly to the new guy, "My favorite Chops story is the one where he goes into the evidence locker and gets out the Zorro costume. You guys remember this one, right! It was seized from this guy trying to sell it on the street after he stole it in a burglary at that costume shop off Fry. Anyway, your grandfather gets the cape and the head mask—now you got to picture this because your grandfather, as you know, was the size of your uncle here—the head mask is a scarf-looking thingy that covers the top of his head down to his nose with cut-outs for the eyes. The tights don't fit, so Chops gets his own, but they just black pantyhose. They got the guy in the interview room who was committing these serial street robberies, and he is half outta his head, you know, tuned up on drugs, and hallucinatin', and they gettin' nowhere. Well, Chops is wearing the scarf, cape, and pantyhose, but no shirt. Now remember, this perp had done like twenty, thirty strong-arm robberies. The guys in the robbery squad, including me, had been hammering on him for like four hours, and nothing. So, we leave him in the room alone for a while. Then, in walks Chops in his Zorro costume, but instead of a sword, he's carrying a three-foot piece of stiff rubber hose."

Just then, Whit walked in with the bottle of whisky and some shot glasses. He was holding the glasses by placing his fingers down into them and squeezing.

Nubs poured himself a shot and said, "To us and those more miserable than us," downed it, and goes back to his story. "So as big as Chops was, he walks in—in that stupid costume. He doesn't say a word—just stands there. But as soon as the guy opens his mouth, to say something—smart no doubt—Chops just starts to beatin' on him with the rubber hose. Then he leaves the room. This goes on four or five more times—Chops comes in, the guy opens his mouth to speak, and before he can get a word out, Chops starts beatin' on him. Finally, Chops walks in again, and before he can close the door, the guy says, 'I did it.'

"Two robbery detectives walk in, and one says, 'You did what?' The guy confesses to all the robberies they know about and some they didn't.

"You know they say rubber hoses don't leave marks, right? But this guy was all bruised up. When he gets to arraignment that same day, the judge is curious as to what happened to him—all the bruises I mean—but the guy is his own best witness. He says with a straight face, 'Your honor, this is the mark of Zorro!' The judge looks at him and his public defender and gives a look like what's going on here? The guy says again, 'It was Zorro. He came in the room and left his marks on me, and now I must tell the truth! I did it!'"

By the time Nubs finished the story, the whole room was in stitches, except for Moose. Chops was Moose's older brother by twelve years, and he had helped raise Moose both at home and in the department. But Moose wanted no part of Chops's brutal reputation, and it showed in his quiet demeanor at the mention of the violence associated with his brother. He never wanted to live up to his brother's reputation—not that reputation.

Whit was back with a large plate of corned beef for Stanton and a soup-bowl size of the same for Commander Bell. The spoons, forks, and knives were wrapped in napkins just like at a restaurant. Stanton tied the napkin around his neck, took a knife in one hand and a fork in the other, licked his lips, crossed himself in a religious ritual, and started to eat. With his mouth half full, and held open because the fixings were hot, Stanton looked at Bell and Nubs and asked, "Can you put those cancer sticks out while I eat? Then he looked at Moose, "So what's this throw-away case you talking about?" He was referring to the Detective Grant's earlier comment.

Detective Grant said, "The mayor wants me to find her missing daughter. She probably just a runaway, except she thirty years old."

"First things first, did the mayor herself ask you to do this or was it somebody in the chief's office?" asked Stanton as he carefully eyed others in the room.

So, they suspect she dead?" asked Nubs—before Grant could answer Stanton—his detective's instincts coming alive.

"I don't know. I'm the newbie," replied Grant, "so that's the shit they put me on. It was deputy chief Stow that told my sergeant to assign me, if that's what you're asking."

After a moment of reflection, Stanton swallowed

and said, "I'm thinking it's not just that, they're trying to bury whatever is going on. Why else would they put a new homicide detective on something like that? What'd you work before Homicide?"

Moose interrupted, "How can you jump to that conclusion? What could be the mayor's motive for wanting to bury the disappearance of her own daughter by using a new detective, especially a homicide detective? Her family may just want her found, and everyone knows Homicide always has the best detectives."

Stanton said, "Maybe the mayor don't know who is working on the case. Maybe that bunch of clowns manipulated her into it. You know them as well as I do."

It went without saying to everyone but Grant that when Stanton and his friends used terms like "bunch" and "clowns," that was code for anyone in power at the Edington City Hall or in the upper levels of the police department. Afterall, most of what Stanton and his crew did all day was sit around and talk about the "good old days" and what this or that "bunch of clowns" did, or was doing, no matter what administration was in power. Stanton and his followers did that even when they were active on the force.

Grant just raised an eyebrow as this group went on and on like that with their theories for some time. Then he Remembered his grandfather had often used the same terms and much worst when he talked about the higher ups at work.

"I worked the drug taskforce. You know, drug

distribution, stuff like that, all over the city and the county," answered Grant, giving a probable reason for his selection and hoping to end the endless speculations.

Moose said, "That's why I brought 'im to see you guys. Remember, the mayor was a Halifax. She goes by Gloria Blumenthal now but before she married, she was Gloria Halifax-Copal. Her mother's sister, Susie, was married to Jay Carter, but—I'm a little foggy on this—I think the missing woman, Skyler Halifax, is the granddaughter of Gloria's mother, Mary Halifax-Copal, and *she* is actually that councilwoman. You know, the one that was murdered back in the seventies. That case Jackie worked. Jackie would have been the one to know the ins and outs of that case."

There was another reflective moment of silence. The Jackie Moose was referring to was Detective Jackie Delmonico and she was also dead.

Commander Bell gave a low whistle and said, "Jackie took on one hell of a case when she caught and cleaned that one. Busted this town wide open. Them clowns running the PD back then shouldn't have made her mad— Caught the case, first day as Homicide commander."

"Acting Homicide commander," said Stanton, "Yeah, but she had unfair advantage, if you know what I mean." Then he winked.

Bell was not amused and showed it by glaring at Stanton. "Why don't you guys get off it? Jackie worked hard for everything she got. Every time a female cop gets rank, then she's automatically a slut, right? Jackie had some affairs around the office, but so did we all. I was brand new and got hit on by ten married men the first day outta training. Hell, two instructors in training hit on me. So, if you want to see sluts, just look around. See the man in the mirror. You'd think God made policewomen for the amusement of policemen. Well, I got news for you, God made policewomen so women in general would get some respect from men."

Nubs said, "But she ended up doing mayor Sullivan, right? And that black on white thing didn't go over well either. How else did she get from sergeant in Internal Affairs to Homicide commander in one promotion?"

Bell said, "You of all people, Nubs, shouldn't have anything to say about the black on white thing, as you call it, right! Besides, all that was just rumor, and you know it. I believe it had more to do with her helping 'Sergeant Sullivan' out of Shoe-gate than anything else, and that happened long before he was elected mayor. And as to the black and white thing, that never stopped you white guys from hitting on me. So what if she was white and maybe had a taste for black coffee." They all laughed but then Bell said, "In all seriousness, Jackie had her demons, but screwing power was not one of them, not like that anyway."

"Shoe-gate, what was that?" asked Grant.

"Before Sullivan was mayor," Moose answered, "once upon a time, he was *Sergeant Sullivan* and he worked uniform in the 12th Precinct. There is this story about him ending up first on the scene of a burglary call at a sporting goods store, and a *patrol officer* named Jackie Delmonico caught 'im coming out the back door with a whole bunch of basketball shoes and throwing them in the trunk of his patrol car."

"Yeah, yeah, yeah," Bell said sarcastically. "We all heard that stupid story. New shoes started showing up all over the Southside an' Johnson Homes—probably what got 'im elected mayor—like what—ten years later? Man, you guys really diggin' up the dead today."

Grant said, "You guys talking about the first black mayor of Edington? The one that's got the schools and park named after 'im? His picture is the biggest one up on the wall at the academy—that guy—that Sullivan?"

Bell said, "Hell yeah! That guy. There's lots of reasons for the true history of this city, especially during those days, to disappear. You only see the good stuff on the walls. All that questionable stuff that happened along the way seems not to exist anymore accept to us. You know the winners write the history, right? So, don't believe everything you hear. Besides, all Jackie had to do was get in her car and drive away from that burglary scene that night—which is probably what she did—and Sullivan would have been in her debt for the rest of his life."

"Those were the days, Newbie," Stanton said. "The Cracker Administration was in power."

Grant raised an eyebrow.

Stanton continued, "That's what they proudly called themselves, the 'Cracker Administration.' Mayor Jefferson Lee Carter and his bunch came up here from the South—mainly Georgia and Alabama—took power and started to administrate some southern politics."

"The northern political justice wasn't much different when it came to my people," said Bell.

"Oh, get off it," said Nubs.

"Why don't you give me some of that brown liquor, and maybe I'll 'get off it,'" said Commander Bell.

"Well, maybe you should get off some of that brown sugar for old-time sake," Nubs responded.

The whole room erupted with, "Oooooooooooo!"

Bell calmly responded, "What? You must have old-timer's disease, 'cause you know you don't remember the day you touched this!" She stood up and presented her body like a model in a beauty pageant, moving her hand smoothly up and down her side. Then she sat back down. There was loud laughter again and more "Ooooooooooooo!"

Moose said, "Newbie wants to get some deep background info about the family of his victim, and it's not like he gonna get any straight answers outta that bunch. I mean they are the same ones from the Cracker Administration, just a different generation. Matter of fact, them uncles—Jay Lee Carter's brothers and cousins—are still around with their hands in all the same ol' crimes. I was trying to recall that kid reporter, the one that got famous for that newspaper series he did back in the day. That family was all mixed up in that, the story I mean."

Grant spoke up, "Well, I did talk to some of the missing woman's uncles and some cousins, but all I got was bad feelings and crooked answers from them. There was nothing in the files, either. It was like somebody wanted to erase that part of the city's history. Even the newspaper wouldn't let me in their morgue unless I told 'em why."

"Trust me. That bunch had good reason to want that history gone. She into drugs?" asked Stanton. "Maybe that's why they put him on it."

He watched Nubs knock back another shot of liquor and slam the glass on the table, and Bell did the same right behind him. Nubs and Bell eyed each other as they did it as though it was some kind of drinking game only those two played.

Moose scratched his nose, squinted, looked at Stanton and said, "They never been that organized, or smart for that matter—to think to use a former narcotics detective to find a person that may have disappeared into drug culture. Naw, that's just happenstance. Or, more likely, just like you said, that bunch wanted the case to disappear in the hands of an inexperienced detective and have somebody to blame when it did. And then they could just let the whole damn thing die on the vine."

"Shots for everybody," Nubs said, and he poured them out. Moose and Grant chose not to partake. "We got to get back to work," said Grant.

"Maybe one more before I go back to the funhouse," said Bell.

Nubs asked Grant, "So you homicide police, and they got you looking for a lost family member, huh?"

"That's about it. And we ain't homicide police no more. We just death investigators now."

"Back in the late sixties," Nubs said, "I worked

Missing Persons, and I can tell you there's no sense in looking for a thirty-year-old woman if she don't want to be found. That's like looking for a tomcat to neuter on an island of cats—seen everywhere and found nowhere.

"Where was she living, anyway?" Nubs quickly added.

"Lives in a loft on the south end of River Street. The newer places down there."

Nubs, Stanton, and Bell chortled and looked at each other suspiciously.

Bell said, "That's where they found her grandmother—"

Stanton interrupted, "Except all that was old, dilapidated warehouses back then. Warehouses stretched all along that end of River Street." He used the knife from his cutlery like a wand, pointing over his right shoulder in the general direction of River Street. He swallowed a chunk of corned beef before continuing. "They found her grandmother back in there. Matter o' fact, by the time they finally cleaned all that out, around five years later, they'd found 'bout thirty more bodies in all that junk. Some had been there over twenty years. It was a real dumping ground. Jackie was in the middle of all that investigation, too."

"Yeah," Nubs added, that used to be canneries and tanneries, full of old vats and machinery and shipping warehouses. For a while, there was even a high-class shipbuilding company making expensive yachts on the upper end. Then the seventies came, and people just started throwing they junk there. The eighties came and everybody went broke. No more expensive Yachts. It was a mess. Funny she was living down there. I know it's all yuppified now, but it's still funny in an odd way—all them bankers and doctors and Indian chiefs got no idea the ghosts they livin' on down there."

Stanton said to Moose, "The guy you thinkin' about is Jackson James B—" He searched his memory for the last name.

"Boodro, or something like that," Nubs said. "We always called him J.J."

"Yeah! Boodro." Stanton continued talking to Moose, "Creole name. He's got, or had, a column you'd see in the *Edington News* from time to time called the *Jackson James Crime Journal.* You know 'im. He was always talking about Edington being in the shadow of Manhattan and Jersey City—saying we get crime, crooks, and corruption on a smaller scale, but we get it just the same. I haven't seen him in a long time. I believe I got his number in the Rolodex. He was right, too! We had—got—the crime here just like in the bigger cities."

"Yeah." Nubs agreed, "You get Boodro on your side, and maybe the chief's office a lay off it this case becomes a hot potato. Boodro was good friends' wit' Jackie, and he helped us out a lot. Come to think of it, he did a series of articles called "Shadow of the City." I was in the hospital then, so I had nothing but time to read. He was pretty good. He covered all that stuff, including that serial killer and all them bodies they found down there."

"Was that really a serial killer case? I mean all of 'em

was prostitutes. Nothing ever really came of the case." said Stanton.

Everyone looked at each other sheepishly, as though they had some secret knowledge—everyone, that is, except Detective Grant, who wasn't in on their secret.

"You really pushing it today!" Bell said, showing her displeasure with Stanton's use of the title *prostitutes* when referring to the victims. "Pat, you workin' that last nerve of mine again!"

"Some say they were better than just friends," Stanton responded, speaking of the relationship between Jackie and Boodro.

Bell rolled her eyes. "Don't you start, Pat! You know all that's just rumor, too!"

"Yeah, but the way she took care of that kid…"

"So what? Some folks said she was like a mother to 'im, too. You don't hear anybody spreading that. I do believe Jackie and Boodro had a history of some kind. That kid would probably be what, late fifties, early sixties now? He wasn't much younger than us. He was a teenager when we were young on the job."

Stanton looked at Grant and Moose, "Come by next week and I'll see if I can find J.J. Call first, though."

"Not me," Moose said. "The newbie is yours now. I just told him I would introduce him to you guys. I got enough going on. Besides, I got enough stink on me from my own cases."

"Stanton, you got a call. It's Mavis!" The voice belonged to Whit. He was in the pantry opening.

"Tell her I'll be home in a while. And you bring me another helping of that beef an' cabbage and a round of beers."

The Second Week

It was Thursday of the next week and raining when Detective Lynsey "Newbie" Grant next arrived at the Cop House Bar. He shook his raincoat at the door, folded it over his arm, and went directly towards the toilet hallway under the watchful eye of Whit, who was wiping bar glasses with a rag that was not exactly sanitary. The bartender wore a white apron that showed the same stains as his rag. The place was almost empty, but it was early, 1:00 p.m., to be exact. There were a couple of rummies, regulars at the bar, and a couple guys in the side room shooting pool in silence. Only the occasional sounds of colliding resin balls came from back there.

When Grant went into the back room, Nubs was alone at the large table with his usual pyramid of shot glasses, but Stanton wasn't there. Nubs wore the exact same clothes as the previous week. They were just more wrinkled.

"Detective!" Nubs greeted Grant. "Take a seat. Have a shot. Stanton's on his way, probably."

The two men sat at the table in an awkward silence for what seemed like a long time then Grant said, "I never knew about this place. Over in Drugs we hang out at this biker kinda place off Pearl Extension, where all the strip joints are—the 'Raw Hide Rama.' Out there you never know who's a cop and who's not, 'cause a lot of the plainclothes county guys hang out there, too. We all look like bikers and drug dealers to each other. Even some narc guys from the city come over. Everybody likes it like that. It keeps everybody honest, if you know what I mean."

The place fell silent again and Nubs just eyed his guest while enjoying the last of whatever was in his shot glass and the awkward silence that seemed to make his tablemate nervous.

"Whit! Whit!" Nubs finally shouted, and Whit soon came through the pantry with a bottle of white liquor—vodka. He put the bottle on the table along with four shot glasses, carried in his usual manner.

"You got ham today?" asked Nubs.

"Yeah! It's Thursday, ain't it?" Whit responded.

"We'll have a couple—if you got time."

"When has that ever made a difference?" Whit said over his shoulder as he walked back towards the pantry opening.

Nubs stared at Grant. "Newbie, you know this is our place. The cops and robbers both come in here, but we can tell 'em apart. It's a neutral spot, though. At least that's how it used to be. Now all these yuppies and generation shitters, or whatever they call themselves... well it's changed. Except back here, and it's the closest to what we had back here. Sometimes Norris and Captain Stanton even let the old bad guys come back here. It's still neutral ground."

Nubs poured out two shots and slid one to Grant.

Picking up his own, he added, "Raise your glasses, you sorry sacks of blue. Here's how!" He forced the full shot into his mouth, swallowed hard, and winced.

Grant didn't know how to take that toast. He was no Commander Bell and didn't know the drinking game. He wondered if it was a threat of some kind or even a warning to get out. But then, he didn't know how to take Nubs or Stanton or any of this crew. They seemed stuck in some world that was long gone. They had created, or recreated, a world made of nostalgia that only existed for them. He was about to excuse himself and get back to his current life, where time was more like a river and he moved with the current. He liked being in the present and had no time for eddies that stalled his forward motion—no time to circle back for long past days or lost friends. Also, his right leg was getting jumpy. His impatient youth was showing.

Nubs pointed to one of several pictures behind the door where Grant had entered. The younger man had not noticed the photos before because they were just part of the room—part of the wall décor that had turned invisible with time.

"Those pictures are this building back in the fifties, sixties, even the seventies. See the one with all the cops in uniforms out front?" Nubs pointed at the largest of the framed images. "Those faded-out cops are us. This was our precinct house. This very room was Lieutenant Stanton's office when he ran patrol out of here in the late seventies. I was upstairs where there's a insurance office now. I was in Detectives at the time. Of course, that was before they centralized Detectives downtown.

Whit walked back in with a plate of ham sandwiches in one hand and a cleaning towel in the other. He wiped the tables down and threw the towel over his shoulder. Without invitation, he slumped down in the chair across from Grant and started to talk as though he were already in the conversation. "Just like it says on the sign, this is the 'Cop House Bar.' Most of them yuppies think it's 'cause back in the 1800s this used to be the offices of the old copper forge on the next block. They used to smelt copper, and horses pulling sleds hauled it down to the river on this very street. They put it in the holes of ships. The same horses pulled copper ore from the ships back up the hill to be smelted.

"This place has been a lot of establishments since then, but from the forties to the early nineties, it was a police, precinct house. There was a schoolhouse right across the street where I went to school. I still remember marching from the school to Main Street for the schoolboys' parade in the early sixties. I was in high school. We had to wear school uniforms back then. The precinct closed the street and gave us a escort to High Cotton Street every year. That was the heyday for this area. We was the only city except Boston that had the boy's parade like that. I didn't appreciate it back then."

Whit pointed in the general direction of the river. "On the corner towards the copper forge was a firehouse, and sometimes they'd close the street just so the cops could play the firemen at softball."

Nubs interjected, "You mean so the cops could murder the firemen at softball. I was new back then, and we beat them lazy S-O-Bs every time!"

"The Atlas Coffeehouse was on the other end of the block," Whit continued, without missing a beat. "They had a big copper sign of this guy holding the world on his shoulders. I wonder where that sign is now—bet it's worth a felony conviction now? Anyway, across from that, where the hippies hung out—I was one of them, too, as soon as I graduated." He smiled and used his hands to smooth his greying blond hair to the back, where a rubber band narrowed the ends into a ponytail. "Where the funeral home is now, there was a garage, and one of the bays was rented out to Kim's House of Wings. Good wings!"

Nubs picked up the memory at that point, "So naturally, this building being the Nineteenth Precinct House, everybody called it the Cop House. You could say to anybody in in the city that you was going over to the Cop House or you worked out of the Cop House, and they would know where you meant."

Whit smiled. "Now we got our own micro-brew and if you say Cop House brew everyone knows what you mean.

Grant held up a hand for Whit to stop. "You keep talking like you was a cop, too."

"Far from it. I was more a cop-hater, or maybe just a hater. Everything was counterculture back then. I loved everybody but... The war was going on. Civil Rights was all the talk—you know it was all 'fight-the-power' back then. I mean, you could go to any party, and they put pills, horse—you name it—in your hand, and you slipped to the clouds. Yeah, I loved everybody but really I was a hater, and that included myself. That was me, anyway. I was pretty messed up. I been clean and sober for over thirty years now." He stopped to enjoy a moment of pride at his time in recovery, or maybe for a round of applause in his head, then he continued, "I used to clean this place back in the day when it was a precinct house. But before that I was living rough in those old warehouses they were talking about last week. That's where Norris, Stanton and Bell found me. I was snitching for Bell to make enough to get a fix. Norris and Stanton took a likin' to me and put me to work off-the-books cleaning up the precinct house for snitch money until Norris got me approved to get paid, regular, working for the police. I used to cut they hair, too. Still do, sometimes—shined the cops' shoes, all that stuff." Whit smiled at the memory.

"When the city was gonna sell this building back in the eighties," Nubs added, "Norris bought it and put Whit to work here. At least that's the word. This place has seen some stuff."

Whit didn't refute Nub's statement but said, "It was pretty common for the cops to take suspects in the side alley back then, right out there..." He pointed to the wall with the windows and the barred door and continued, "and administer some street justice. Even the cops that didn't like it just kinda went along to get along. And not all that street 'justice' went to black people if that's what you think."

They both looked at Grant then, as though they knew what he should have been thinking, probably because he was black, and considering the years they were talking about, that's what they would have been thinking. But Grant just gave them a blank look.

"It seems that long hair and tattoos, like mine, were also general offences back then so more than a few hippies got their share of street justice back there, too, including me. That was before I started to helping Bell and got to know Norris and Stanton." Whit added. "Now, every cop in the country 's got tattoos. How times have changed."

Nubs chuckled. "Half of them new ones' smoked dope before they got hired, too. The world has sure changed."

"All of 'em," Whit corrected. "All of them smoked dope." Then he looked down at his hands and clamped his lips as though he had overstated his thoughts.

Whit and the others seemed to have invisible lines in their room—lines only they knew existed—lines only they could really traverse. The lines protected some and exposed others. It was a strange room to navigate. At least, that's what Grant considered when he thought about how Whit had just retreated into himself for crossing one of those lines. This confirmed the uneasiness he felt at how oddly Stanton and the crew interacted with each other from time to time. He'd had the same feeling a week earlier about Bell when she was teasing Nubs about his fingers. Who does that?

Just as their conversation was winding down to blank stares and awkward silence, again, Stanton walked in with two black men. One was light-complexioned, the color of antique brass, and tallish, very much like Detective Grant, but with graying, black hair. The other man was dark copper and stout. Both men were older but not as old as Stanton. The lighter one, looked distinguished in a black sports coat and jeans. He carried an old, plain leather, satchel over his shoulder. The stout one sported a straw fedora with a small, yellowish-red feather at the band. He wore light brown wingtips, a deep brown pin-striped suit, tan shirt, and bright-yellow tie with small brown dots. Grant suspected he was bald because he didn't take off his hat, something men of his generation usually did—If they wore one—when they came indoors. This one carried himself like a fighter, not a boxer, a *fighter*.

Stanton sat down, grabbed a ham sandwich, and after the first bite, said, "Look who I found hanging out at the men's room door." Everyone but Grant laughed.

The taller man stuck his hand out to Grant with a smile and said, "I'm Jackson James Boodro, retired reporter and friend to all humanity. Captain Stanton tells me you wanted to see me."

Nubs also stuck his hand out to Jackson James and said, "J.J., how you been? How's it hangin'?"

"You would think after all these years, I would outgrow that kiddie name, right?" Jackson James sounded good-natured but not jovial.

"Yeah, well you would, wouldn't you? But if I'm

stuck with Nubs, then you got J.J. for life."

"Yeah, but it feels like I'm stuck as a seventies sitcom character."

They all laughed then, and the mood really lightened. Everyone seemed to loosen up.

Then Nubs looked at the shorter man and said, "Geech! Long time brother. You still doing that private thing?"

Geech stuck his hand out to Grant and introduced himself, "I'm Murphy, Charles Murphy. If you get to know me better, you can call me Geech." No one smiled at that introduction, and Grant wondered why.

Both the new men sat at the big table. Whit stood and asked, "What can I get you gents?"

Geech said, "Two fingers," and looked at Nubs, and then added, quietly, "No offense, brother."

Nubs held up his shot glass in an empty toast," None taken."

Geech used his left hand to touch the tip of his hat. Grant noticed Geech was also missing the first joint of his little finger on his right hand. Although curious, Grant was not bold enough to ask about that story. This group was free with each other, but he was definitely not a part of them. He was an outsider, on eggshells around them. The lines in the room were always shifting.

The new detective looked at Jackson James and responded to his earlier inquiry. "Yeah, I got this case, and I need some background on it. There was nothing in the files at HQ, and I was told you might be able to help." This was an awkward moment for Grant. He had been a detective long enough to know you don't question anybody in a group, especially a reporter—and especially a group of cops.

Nubs stepped in and saved Grant in his moment of ineptness. "If you want a be a murder detective," he said, "then you better start thinking more like a murder detective and less like a death investigator. Working Homicide 's an art, my friend, more than science. It's more like Sun Tzu than Sherlock."

Stanton slapped his knee and laughed aloud. "I never thought I'd see the day that retired Detective Sergeant David 'Nubs' Cooper would be caught waxing poetic. I think they call it, talkin' 'bout Sun who?"

"I actually watch PBS when I leave here, you know," Nubs said, with a straight face.

"Yeah, but Sun Tzu is a stretch for plain old po-lease like us," Stanton replied.

"Don't you believe there's a art to what we do—did? I mean, didn't we use strategy to solve crime, even if we didn't call it that?"

"Naw," Stanton replied, matter-of-factly. "We used brute force, a soundproof room, maybe that alley back there and a good slapjack—fear mostly."

Everyone except Jackson James thought his assessment was accurate. Even Grant nodded.

Stanton shook his head at Jackson James. "Loosen up, J.J. You know that's just cop talk."

Jackson James said, "Now I know why I stopped

coming around you guys." He was being sarcastic, but they didn't seem to catch that nuance.

"Who's your Sun Tzu?" Asked Stanton. "I don't recall any master strategist coming out of the Edington Police Department in my lifetime. Do you?" He was looking at Nubs.

"Well, our best version of a strategist was Jackie Delmonico," said Nubs, confidently. "She's an example of what I was talking about. She was one of the best detectives this town ever produced. Brought down that bunch running city hall back in the day." The group paused for a reflective moment of silence.

"I asked around after you spoke about her last week and everybody thought she was a good detective, but a strategist? From what I heard, Jackie had a few demons— like men and alcohol," Grant said, instantly regretting speaking his thoughts aloud, remembering the company he was keeping, and the lines he needed to respect.

Both Geech and Jackson James looked at Grant, almost as if they were in physical shock. Everyone else in the room looked at him as though he were about to die.

Jackson James seemed to let this moment pass, but Geech continued to look the new homicide detective squarely in the eyes. "Maybe you should get to know who Detective Delmonico was before you go passing judgment. Bless her soul!" His eyes were red and his anger was palpable.

Grant knew he had stepped over one of those lines and was wise enough to let it drop. He said to Jackson

James, "Can we speak in private?"

"Sure, but not today," said the retired reporter. He didn't offer an excuse, and none was asked.

Grant felt on the outs at that moment—not that he ever felt in—and he thought flattery might figuratively get him back on track, so he asked Jackson James, "So you had a column in the newspaper, huh?"

"Yeah!" said the journalist, sounding as though he'd just remembered his career. He played along but was smart enough to recognize a suck-up. "Yeah," he started again. "It was called 'Shadow of the City.' It was all crime—cops' and criminals' stuff—in an our-town series."

"Why did you call it that?" Asked Grant.

Stanton interrupted. "This here is the best detective you ever want with you in a fight," he said, referring to Geech. "He ain't just a fighter; he's a brawler, and he loved to brawl." Stanton was attempting, in his own way, to do the same thing Grant was doing with Jackson James—that is, get Geech's mind off what Grant had said about Jackie Delmonico.

Ignoring Stanton, Jackson James answered Grant's question. "Everything happens here is in the shadow of the same stuff happening in Manhattan or Jersey City. We get the bodies from Manhattan when they float across on the river tide; the tough guys from Jersey run here to hide out; and, the Twin Towers, when they stood, used to literally cast a shadow over us at the right time of day."

Geech finally smiled, letting Grant off the hook, and referring to Stanton's last comment, he said, "Not no mo'.

I'm a lover now—a lover of God—not a fighter." He had a gold tooth on the front.

The room got quiet for the time it takes a man running from the devil to take five deep breaths.

"There's still luck involved, but when you do a thing, you do it for a reason. You expect it to get a result." Nubs was back on the topic of strategy and investigations. "Sun Tzu said he could put his finger on a map and have his enemy go to that spot or from that spot."

"Yeah. Well if you want to find out who did this crime, whatever it is, you got to make 'im tell ya," Stanton countered.

"And just how am I supposed to do that?" Grant asked. "Bring 'em in one by one and beat it out of 'em? They all relatives of the mayor." He was being sarcastic, but the old cops seemed to consider his proposition as serious. They all nodded.

Finally, Nubs smiled. "That's more our speed. Captain Stanton, you remember when we went after Baby Doll's crew? They were killing more rival gang members than Carter had liver pills. That was when drugs first hit us big time. It was like a rite of passage for these guys—a way to get noticed by the mobs around Jersey and the City."

Everyone understood Nub's meant Manhattan when he said *the City*.

"And that was okay," Nubs continued, "until they killed that night watchman at St. Jude's. Then the situation went off the rails, and the gang ended up killing five innocents, trying to cover their tracks." Everyone also understood innocents to mean innocent bystanders, people that just happen to be in the church at the time.

"I remember," Stanton said, "but we broke that case with some hard interrogations. That's what we called it, not strategy."

"But that was the strategy," Nubs insisted. "Go hard and make the right person break. That motivates the rest to scatter like roaches and start doing stupid stuff. Then you watch where they go and what they do. You remember."

Grant asked, "So what was that case about? I've never heard anything about it."

"It's like with Mayor Sullivan, there's a lot of cases you won't hear about in this town because of who all was involved," Stanton said. "That crowd you messing with now is all related to that same bunch from back then. They just older and better criminals, and when it comes to corruption, they still in the middle of it. It's all women, money, power, and drugs, and that all amounts to the same when it comes to them—control of women, money, power, and drugs! Back then the mayor's brothers and cousin all worked for the city, but their kids were mixed up with this street hood named Robert 'Baby' Doll. Everybody called him Baby Doll. He was using young girls as prostitutes and to distribute heroin and cocaine. He was kicking back all the way back to the mayor's office through the mayor's family."

The regular group nodded because they understood *kicking back* meant part of the drug sales proceeds was being paid to the Mayor and his cronies in exchange for their protection.

"What about that big pedophile case Jackie had?" Geech asked, just throwing out another of the cases that was covered up in Edington's history.

"Which one?" Stanton asked, not that he couldn't recall, but more acknowledging there had been so many.

'That was some strange case, too." Nubs added. "Jackie drew it after being on a five-day bender. They found a bunch of kids in a rooming house over on the south side. They were from outta state—some from outta the country. The youngest one was eleven. You remember her partner at the time was Clyde the Clown—you know, Clyde Drew. He had been on the force a hundred years, and all he could talk was: 'They all just runaways. They all better off than they was if they was at home.'

"That bunch at city hall didn't want the kind'a national attention that case would bring so, while Jackie was out doing real police work, Clyde went to his only strategy—the tried and true, sweat-somebody-in-the-box, or an alley, until-they-confessed and case-closed strategy."

"Yeah, I remember," said Stanton. "Clyde the Clown got some dope fiend off the street, took him over to the rooms where the kids were found so his fingerprints was around, then sweated 'im in interrogation till he begged for a fix. The doper went down for the crime with a confession then hung himself in the holding cell the same day. Clyde wrote it up: case closed. That's how he called it. That's how they did it back then, never mind the real asshole was still out there. That was Clyde's *strategy*."

"Clyde was always an idiot," Geech said. "And who says the guy hung himself? It wasn't no surprise he left Jackie to do all the legwork while he sat around drinkin' with that fool of a sergeant they had back then..." He snapped his fingers as though the sergeant would appear before him, but he didn't.

"Rat Man... no... Rathman," said Stanton. "I haven't thought of the Rat Man in years. I wonder if he still around, even." There was no moment of silence for Rathman because they obviously didn't care if he was dead or alive.

Stanton looked at Grant and Jackson James then, and said, "There's no proof that anything nefarious happened on that but the department always had guys like Drew around—guys that could make things happen any way they wanted.

Nubs raised his shot glass. "Here's how, and I forget when!" He knocked back a shot with a swallow of beer chaser. "But now with all that DNA and stuff, you actually got to do some detective work."

Stanton said, "You remember that rape case that Bell and Jackie worked on together—all them girls raped in broad daylight?"

Geech said, "I do," and chuckled. "That poor guy never knew what hit him."

"What happened with that case?" Grant asked.

Stanton said, "Well they didn't cover it up, if that's what you mean. Clyde was up to his old strategy. He was shouting 'they was all prostitutes' to anyone that would listen. He even had his next suspect picked out. In the meantime, Jackie had started doin' some real police work. She ran backgrounds on all the girls, and it turned out they all frequented a little street market just off Pearl Avenue. One got her hair done over there; another one walked through on her way home from work, and so forth.

"Anyhow, a guy was following them home from the market. He would put a stocking cap over his face and attack 'em in broad daylight—pull 'em into an alley or something. Bell played the decoy for over a month with Jackie backing her up, and finally the perp took the bait and followed Bell. He jumped her and tried to pull her in a alley off Baxter. The guy was a real nutjob, only nineteen. His mother owned a sandwich shop in the market."

Everyone laughed then, except Grant, but he didn't know the punchline.

"Bell beat that fool a good fifteen minutes before we pulled her off," Nubs added. Jackie stood there and kept the bystander away.

"Yeah, that was good strategy," Stanton scoffed. "How did we get on this stupid topic anyway?"

"I was going somewhere with this, but now I can't remember," Nubs answered.

Whit yelled from the other room, "You guys want some soup? There's plenty!"

Without asking anyone, Stanton yelled, "Yeah, soup all around!"

"Oh, yeah," Nubs said, remembering where he was going with the strategy topic and looking at Grant. "If you want to stir that bunch up, you got to use some strategy on 'em."

Stanton threw his hands up in disgust.

Nubs continued, "Now hear me out! If you want to find out what's goin' on with that bunch, just put the word out that you want to pull them in for questioning, then watch what they do. Maybe put the word out that you going to start searching for your victim 'cause you think she dead."

"What do you mean by that?" asked Grant. "The chief is never going to let me pull them in, and he certainly won't authorize surveillance on them or to do a search."

"You got friends in narcotics, right?" Nubs asked.

Stanton jumped in solemnly, "Ask for forgiveness— never for permission—if you get caught."

"Just watch what your main suspects do for a couple days," Nubs continued, "and you'll know if you onto somethin'."

Jackson James handed Grant a business card and said, "I got to go. I don't want to be part of no conspiracy. It's been fun seeing you guys again and, as always, it's been real. But it hasn't been real fun." They all laughed, recognizing the old but good refrain.

Whit came in with bowls of soup on a tray, carried high on one shoulder. "Got soup for you, too, J.J."

"Thanks, but I don't have time today. I do appreciate the effort, but I have a doctor's appointment. Had the best bowel movement I had in days, yesterday, so I better find out why so I can do it again." Then Jackson

James smiled, looked at the new detective, and said, "Give me a call."

"Yeah, I know what you mean," Stanton said. "Something I been eating 's been givin' me heartburn. Makes no sense, 'cause I eat the same things on the same days almost every week."

Whit looked at Grant. "Don't get old Detective," he warned, "'cause every conversation you have eventually goes to aches, pains, and shits. You got to go all natural, man." Grant smiled and shook his head at the group.

The phone rang in the pantry, and one of Whit's bartenders appeared in the doorway. He was a young kid, by their standards, in a long, white apron. He had thick, red hair and too many big, white teeth for his mouth. "Captain, your wife is on the phone." He held the phone receiver in his right hand, and it was obvious Stanton's wife, Mavis, would be able to hear every word anyone said. This obviously disturbed Whit who saw it as part of his job to run interference for the guys in the backroom.

"Tell her I'll be home when I can. It's still early, and I'm busy!"

Whit took the phone from the young man, went back out of sight, behind the bar, and could be heard relaying a series of sounds that were probably close to what Stanton had said.

Whit came back and warned Stanton. "She said you need to come home now, or she's coming down here."

The Third Week

The place was quiet because it was early—9:30 a.m. on Sunday morning. Detective Grant got only a nod when he passed Whit, who was doing what bartenders do, only this time the rag on his shoulder was clean. Whit was also licking his thumb and using it to rub out spots on the beer mugs and shot glasses before wiping them down and putting them away.

Grant was in a pair of khaki cargo pants and a white polo shirt. He had a portable police radio in-hand. Before he could cross to the restrooms towards Stanton's office, Jackson James hailed him: "Detective Grant, over here!"

Grant looked in the side room area, and Boodro was sitting at the table nearest the window with his hand up to call attention to himself. This seemed odd to Grant because there was no one else back there.

Jackson James appeared to have been looking out the window, waiting for Grant to arrive. There were two, unbroken eggs in front of him; they could have been either raw or hardboiled. It was impossible to tell by looking. An empty beer mug and a cup of steaming-hot coffee also sat at his place setting.

"Join me for breakfast? I doubt Stanton's office is open, and Whit won't let you in unless he or Nubs or one of the others are back there," said Jackson James. "Or maybe you one of the boys by now?"

This comment drew a smile from Detective Grant because he knew it was all sarcasm.

A manila folder, with newspaper clippings exposed

around the edges, lay on the table in front of another chair and place setting. Grant sat down at the other setting, placed the radio on the table, and addressed the reporter. "How you doing, brother?"

And this familiar greeting among black men surprised Jackson James because Grant was Chops's grandson, and considering his history with Chops, the greeting just seemed out of place.

Whit brought a fresh mug of beer to the table for Jackson James.

"Your breakfast?" Grant repeated, with a quizzical look at the reporter.

"Want some?"

"It's a little too early for *breakfast* for me."

"Suit yourself."

"Whit, that coffee looks good," Grant said. "Can I get some?"

"Sure. But Norris forgot to order cream, so black 's all we got, unless you want to sweeten it with a little rye."

"Black is just fine. I'm working."

When Whit left the table, Grant asked, "So why did you want to see me so early? I suspect everyone 's gonna know we talked, especially since we're in here—"

Jackson James interrupted. "By the way, do you mind if I call you Detective Grant? I never really understood that ritual of police nicknames, especially 'Newbie.'"

Grant nodded and smiled.

"So, is that radio on? I have to ask because I don't

want our conversation transmitted all over the city," said the reporter.

"It's on but not transmitting. It's on a tactical channel and nobody knows we're up irregardless."

"What are you *up* on? You got a tactical operation going today?" Jackson James's reporter juices were flowing but he got dead eyes from Grant.

The reporter looked at the device suspiciously but spoke openly anyway. "Well, Detective Grant, at heart I'm an investigative reporter, and I don't want to share my files with the group. I don't expect you to break my confidence, and I'll never break yours. I don't mind if they know I told you stuff, just not what I told you, and the same goes in reverse. I don't care if they know you tell me stuff, just not what you tell me. It's an old habit, but it works best for me and protects you."

Grant slowly nodded again. "I can live wit' that, but I'm not your police snitch. Just to be clear on that."

This comment took the reporter by surprise, "First of all, in real detective work—not just chasing Dairy Queen dope—the best detectives all work with the press. It's part of the package. I tell you what I can, and you tell me what you can, and nobody's snitchin'. You just pretend to hate the press to keep your buddies off your back."

Grant slowly looked the reporter in the eyes, ignoring the "Dairy Queen dope" crack, but considering how to take his source.

Jackson James continued. "That file is just copies of a few clippings and some personal notes I brought you for background—about the police and politics here in Edington—to help you with your missing persons case. That'll give you a little history on Mary Halifax and her murder case. Mary Halifax was a city councilwoman killed back in the eighties. She was the sister of Mayor Jay Carter's wife, Susie Halifax. The big secret at the time was that Mary and Mayor Carter had a son together and they named him Jefferson lee Halifax-Carter, and everyone actually called him Junior. Susie and the mayor never had kids. Yeah, I know it's confusing but so were those times. I believer Junior married Gloria Blumenthal but she kept her last name. Their child, Skyler, is the young woman you're looking for. Right?

"After you read my notes, I believe you'll understand why the current mayor chose not to take the Halifax name. The Carter's have ruined that name forever. That's the connection you're looking for, though. I hope that helps. I was in the military back then, so it's not all first-hand information, but it is good for background. Jackie—Jackie Delmonico—worked the case of Mary Halifax's death. It was her first case when she was acting-homicide lieutenant. Unrelated to all that. I know your victim's father was killed about ten years ago, the target of a robbery over in Manhattan. I know you said there was nothing in the files at the department and I'm not surprised. Read my notes and I believe you'll be surprised to learn who Jackie got on the murder of Mary Halifax but that's not important as to what you are working on now."

Grant started to thumb through and scan the

dossier. He casually asked, "Just out of interest, can you also give me some background on Captain Stanton and this group? I mean, did I detect more than a little tension among them last week, even though they seem to be so tight. Didn't I?"

"So, you are a real cop, huh? That was smooth the way you went right to pumping me for info right after my little recruitment speech." Boodro shook his head, smiled and rubbed his chin. "Yeah, there is tension, but they close—closer than you or I will ever get to them. I think the tension may have had to do with the history some of them have with each other. It doesn't go away. You being black and Chops Baker's grandkid didn't help, either. You self-identify as black, right brother?"

"Yeah, I do, but I never thought that was important, especially as a police officer."

"You would if you knew your grandfather's history with black people in this town. Well, enough said about that. I didn't mean to make you uncomfortable."

Jackson James then cracked an egg in his beer—it had been raw—and drank until it was gone, with part of the concoction running down his chin. "This is the only bad habit I picked up from my active days of hanging around cops and robbers," he said, laughing. "So, you want me to talk about Stanton and crew behind their backs, huh?"

Then the laugh went to chuckle, "They have been on the ins and outs with each other so many years, it's hard to tell if they are either in or out now. Before the other day, I hadn't been here in years, but it was just like I never left. They are still just like family to each other, sniping and cutting each other for laughs, but it's really passive-aggressive, if you ask me."

"So, you were part of their group at one time?"

"Naw, not really. My only connection to them is through Jackie. They are right, she was one hell-of-a detective, but she had a brother, Bruno, they don't mention, and he was one hell-of-a criminal. They were the perfect storm for me getting into stuff. She treated me like a son; but he's the one got me to join the army by treating me like a criminal."

"Was she corrupt?" Grant asked, not getting distracted by the comment about Bruno.

The conversation was getting too rapid-fire for Jackson James, and he slowed it down by deflecting. "You know, I really don't want to talk about Jackie right now," he said. "You should go read my series, Shadow of the City, at the *Edington News* morgue if you want to know about her. As for the rest of that group, I'll give you a little of their history—why they're so close—if you believe it will help you understand them."

"I tried to get in your morgue the other day, but they wouldn't let me in."

"Show them my card. Tell them you want to see my series, and they'll let you in. I'll make sure of it.

"Now as to the group of cops, a lot starts right here in this building."

"Yeah, I know about some of them working out of

this building when it was a precinct house, if that's what you're talking about."

The reporter reflected a moment, checked his watch, and said, "That's a start, but it goes much deeper. Nubs—Detective Cooper—was part of what they called the Cracker Administration when he was a young detective."

"Yeah," Grant said, "I heard about that, too—some of the same folks I'm dealing with now, right?"

"Well, let me start again then. You know how one relative moves from someplace, and another one follows until the whole damn family relocates? Well, that's what happened with Mayor Jefferson 'Jay' Carter. He moved up here from Georgia in the early sixties—sold used cars or something down there—from Jewel, Georgia. And the next thing you know, he had married Susie Halifax. With help and money from her wealthy family, he was elected mayor. When Jay got here, he didn't have money for chewing tobacco or a place to spit. Within five years, he was literally spitting all over city hall. The first to follow was his first cousin, Howard 'Howie' Reece, who moved up here from some little town in Alabama. Jay appointed him chief of police; he'd been a sheriff back where he came from. He was tall and lean and had the reputation of being the trifecta—lowdown, dirty and mean. Before anybody was paying attention, one of Jay's brothers, Braxton, was up here too, running the sanitation department. Another brother, Nathan, took charge of street maintenance. These were the three biggest pots of money in the city, so this was power they wouldn't give up easily. And as for Cooper,

Detective David Cooper—that's Nubs's real name—he just kind of got caught up in all that at the time. He was the mayor's eyes and ears, and a little bit more which I'll explain later.

"Geech comes in the story in a slightly different way, but he's connected just the same. He came up here from Georgia about the same time as Jay Carter, from a little place down near Savannah. He was still a teenager, like seventeen, but his mother was already a maid at Jay Carter's home at that time. After Geech arrived, he got his GED and two years of night-school college.

His mother got him hired on as one of the first black police officers in Edington. Correction, he was the first one to last through training. There was pressure from the federal government to hire black cops, but none ever seemed to make it through training here. You can imagine what those days were like, and frankly, Cooper was one of the worst bigots I'm told. All this was long before I even thought about being a reporter, but I did the research later. I don't think there was a lot of love lost between those two, Geech and Cooper, I mean.

"'Coop' as he was called back then, before he earned the Nubs nickname, made detective and was assigned right here at the nineteenth precinct house. Geech Murphy, on the other hand, went to plainclothes and was assigned to Vice and Street Crimes. He was the only African American to work out of uniform, and that was a privilege that many Anglo officers resented even though the police force, at that time, didn't want to put a black man in a police uniform. A uniform would require respect they did not want them to have. But he made it through. He worked undercover or surveillance all the time.

"Another name, Ann Bell, first black woman in Intelligence, was hired about that same time; but I doubt anybody outside Vice knew she was on the force, including the mayor. But he profited from her being there nonetheless."

"I met her last week for the first time, considering I been on the department for over six years—only heard of her before then," Grant interrupted.

"They assigned her to Vice, and I don't even think she had gone through training yet. They had plans for her." Jackson James continued, as if he hadn't heard the detective. "You see, she worked plainclothes—tall, brown and fine—and mainly walked the streets up on the north end of Pearl Avenue trying to attract black pimps for the Vice detectives to shake down, and Anglo johns that the mayor and police chief could blackmail for political favors. It was a nice little racket. Bell played it cool. She knew she was being used. But she also knew how to use them back. She ended up keeping book on all of them, all her bosses I mean. But long before she made her play on all that stuff, civil rights protests were going on. Vietnam war protests were ongoing. The FBI's COINTELPRO operation was running around spying on people all over the place and it was all a big mess. And she was in the middle of it. Bell even did some work for the FBI until she balked at going in undercover on some civil rights leaders over in

Manhattan. That was a line she wouldn't cross. She told the FBI they should hire some black women of their own, instead of using her, if they wanted to work investigations on their so-called public enemies. You can imagine how that all went over. She told that story many times and laughed about it.

"Anyway, the Klan was out in force over here, probably attracted by Jay Carter's mayoral administration. You know how one racist attracts another. Those were the days!"

Jackson James looked as though he was enjoying a good movie playing out in his head, and he knew the ending, as he continued: "But events were spiraling out of control when it can to the local police rackets, Cooper had risen to detective sergeant in a short year due to his faithfulness to Jay Carter's administration. He was the chief's main bagman with a connection to a serious young criminal out of South Africa named Osmond Weights. This guy, Weights, was a psychopath with attitude. He had vertical and horizontal scars across his face from where some guys tried to skin him alive in Joburg, South Africa. At least that's the reputation he perpetuated—looked like something out of a horror movie.

"Notwithstanding, Weights's crew got busted—but not Weights—on a city-county drug sting, and the county cops confiscated a bunch of dope and credit cards the Weight's crew had stolen from some Manhattan wise guys. Cooper never admitted he was a bagman for the chief— you know a go-between for Weights and the chief—but that's probably what he was. The next thing you know, Weights had kidnapped Cooper and was sending him back to the chief in pieces—as in a finger at a time—until the chief gave up the seized drugs and money. Weights never asked for his crew's release, but he wanted the money and drugs."

"That took some nerve," said the detective.

"You have to think, Weights didn't see the police as authority, but more as a rival gang. That's the kind of relationship he had with the police. People lose all respect for authority when that type of connection exist.

"Well, the county had control of the evidence, so Chief Reece knew the release of cards and money to Weights was not going to happen. Don't get me wrong, the county was corrupt too, but they were into other rackets.

"Geech, Bell, and Jackie's brother, Bruno got all tied up in this case. The chief didn't want the public to know about Weights kidnapping a detective because…well, because they were both criminals, the chief and Weights. To Chief Reece, this was just a dispute amongst criminals, but he was chief of police—no other way to put it. He was paralyzed. I believe the chief would have been willing to give up the drugs and plastic cards if that would have gotten Cooper free, but they were not his to give; or, sacrifice Cooper if it would have made the whole thing go away, but he knew that was not possible ,either. So, he did neither."

"And all the while, pieces of Nubs was arriving every day—two fingers so far, huh?" Grant contemplated what

Jackson James was telling him and shook his head.

"Well, Stanton was patrol lieutenant at the time, and he was good friends with Cooper even back then. They were working right here in this precinct house. I know what you might be thinking and as far as I know, when it comes to dirty-cop corruption, Stanton is a straight arrow. In fact, it was Stanton who unofficially solicited Bell and Geech to go on the streets and see if they could find Cooper. They were the only two plainclothes officers with the kinds of connections to find him. I later found out that Geech reached out to Bruno, Jackie's brother, to start looking, because Bruno personally knew Weights. Geech asked Bruno to find out where Weights was hold-up and where they had Cooper stashed.

Jackson James looked at his watch again and then swept a glance around the bar.

"You expecting somebody, or what?" asked Grant. "You got someplace to be?"

"No, but I expect Stanton will be here soon. I want to get this out and talk to you about something else—the reason I wanted to meet you so early.

"Anyway, in the process of Bruno and Geech's 'unofficial' investigation, Bruno found out that Cooper was here in Edington in an old dry-cleaning factory just off River Street. He passed that info to Geech but Bruno wanted to stay out of it beyond that. The place is a bike shop now. Geech went in alone to try and bring the kidnapping to a quick resolution. But as soon as he got through a window and was close enough to hear Cooper struggling, Geech got cold-cocked from behind.

"This is where the situation got really strange. It turns out Weights had a thing about taking the fingers off people when they crossed him or whatever. When Geech woke up, he was missing the first joint of his little finger. But get this, Geech wrapped his finger up and kept searching. But Weights and Cooper were nowhere to be found.

"Finally, Jackie came through with another tip from Bruno that Cooper had been moved to a boat drydocked in a little yard on the edge of Jersey City. He had a couple of street guys guarding him. This time at Jackie's urging, Bruno and Geech went in together. They've never told what happened, but Cooper turned up the next day in the hospital, and Weights has not been seen since. He was gone just like Hoffa. By the way, Bruno was interviewed in that case, too—the Hoffa case, I mean. You can't make this stuff up! Rumor is that Weights in still around but who knows?

"When the police caught up with where Weights had been living, they found a necklace of finger bones. Seems he collected fingers. All that was just so bizarre."

Grant was trying to digest everything he'd heard. It wasn't that he'd heard enough, but more like he had heard too much. "So, what else did you want to talk to me about?" he asked while still contemplating the story he had just heard.

Boodro looked at his watch, glanced around the room again, lowered his voice, and said, "I'm about to start a series of articles about police corruption. More accurately, a different type of police corruption—a type that Stanton and this whole group is less familiar with but engage in all the time—at least used to. I need some background on it from you."

Grant thought, puzzled. He mouthed the word "corruption." He was actually looking at dead flies on the windowsill and noticing how they had been joined by two live ones—the new flies were constantly bumping their heads against the windowpane as though they could miraculously break through the glass. That wasn't working for them, but they kept trying just the same. Grant secretly felt sorry for the flies.

The reporter resumed speaking carefully and deliberately. "Detective Grant, as bad as some folks thought cops were in the old days, when it came to abuse of authority, it's gotten even worse. Some cops nowadays have no capacity for self-reflection or criticism about your profession. You all have become an insular society. And that, in and of itself, is a form of corruption. I think that's what I want to write about—what I call this new form of police corruption."

Grant looked blankly at Jackson James.

"Insular," said the reporter slowly, as though the young detective didn't know the meaning of the word. "As in not willing to acknowledge problems exist or look for solutions to anything about policing outside your own culture. Not acknowledging you have problems from within your own ranks—problems with the excessive use of force and authority."

Grant continued his blank stare.

"You know—police shooting unarmed black men and all that stuff—to make it plain. I need to know what cops really think on these topics. As close as I am with many police officers, they are very reticent to speak to me on these issues. I monitor a lot of police groups online, and I see only the worst of our society when it comes to policing and shootings in those groups. The comments these cops make are cold, unfeeling and some downright racist; though, I doubt if they would think so. I think—no believe—there has to be another, internal, narrative to all this. There has to be a silent majority of police officers that recognize what has happened to their profession and doesn't see everything as binary or us against them."

Grant yawned, batted his eyes as though coming out of a daydream, and said, "I don't feel I'm your man for this. I'm Newbie, remember? I mean, you put me in an awkward position if you expect me to give you quotes on what you just said. I mean, I've only been on six years, and that would be a career killer for me."

"And therein lies the problem," insisted Jackson James. "Nobody wants to risk a frank discussion because of— because of—well, because of I don't know what."

"You're asking a lot of an officer who's just trying to make his way," Grant insisted.

"That's true, and I realize that, but I need some real insight. I need to know all sides of the story if my series is to, you know, balance."

"Balance what?" Grant shot back, forgetting he didn't want to get into it. "I mean, what are you gettin' at?"

"Change," replied Jackson James. "That's what I'm getting at. I want to contribute to changing a system, or at least spur thinking about this current place we find ourselves. It's like we're at a place where if we go any further, we might not be able to go back. The police can kill unarmed people. In defense, they claim fear for their own safety. The union says, 'the officer had no choice,' the chief says, 'the officer followed his training,' and the jury says, 'not guilty!' That makes the killing nice and legal, and all is right with the world."

"Well, I don't know about all that. I come from a place where we speak of being police officers with pride. I mean, we keep the peace, my grandfather told me, and that's what his father told him. If that's what you're talkin' about, then he was enormously proud of that, and so am I."

"I understand that. I get it, but I just want insight into police culture for my article, that's all. I won't quote you," Jackson James pleaded. "All these cops talk about the old days and refer to them as the good old days—I mean the violent police conduct, the overt racism, the sexism, and all that stuff. What was good about that? They call it police misconduct now. I call it corruption."

"Well, it's still the same now," responded Grant. "Most of the guys—black, white, or whatever—I work with don't believe a female can do the job. They know they can't say that to them—to the women, I mean—but they can damn well say it to each other. Many of the white guys also think black officers are too sensitive if we speak out about race, and they say so. All the white officers talk like they have a grievance when they get caught out of line or don't get what they want, like a promotion or whatever—like it's always someone else's fault. In fact, the only difference between then and now is the technology. Cops get caught on video now doing stuff they used to lie their way out of. What am I going to do about that? White cops tell me I'm different, as a black man, because can I talk like them and they think I think like them, but the fact of the matter is, I'm only different when I'm in uniform or they know I'm a cop. Other than that—and sometimes even that's not enough—I still might get my ass all jacked up!"

"Really?" said Jackson James, encouraging the young detective. He sensed a change in his new confidant's wellspring.

"Really!" confirmed Grant. "One time I was doing a buy-bust at the garage and—" He stopped because the reporter had seemed to light up with a little too much interest.

"The garage?" Jackson James asked. "You talkin' about that gravel lot behind the old Edington school building? I thought that place was long gone. They should've torn it down years ago and made it a Kmart."

"Too much asbestos to tear it down, I heard. It's a perfect place for drug deals, though. We used to use it a lot when out-of-towners came in to sell us dope." Grant stopped and rubbed his chin, considering what he had just said. "Are we off the record here, 'cause what I just said is kind of like a trade secret."

"Yeah. This is just all on background, and I'm not interested in drugs unless it involves traditional police corruption. You were saying something about the garage?" Jackson James paused, took a cleansing breath, pursed his lips, then started again, "I think, in all fairness, I should tell you I had my own experience with your grandfather, Chops, at the 'garage' one Halloween night when I was a teenager. Did you know they call that place the garage because that's where they took people to 'tune them up' back in the day? I haven't been back there since that night."

"Yeah—well, yeah!" Grant continued, awkwardly because he didn't quite know how to take what the reporter had just said. "I was undercover doin' a buy-bust one night. That's where we buy the drugs and arrest the guy at the same time. All us cops met in the alley behind the old Feldman Department Store building, and we were planning how to do the takedown once the guy showed up with the dope. We had some county guys with us, 'cause they brought us the case. My sergeant put his flashlight on me and said, 'This is Detective Grant. You see how he's dressed, right? He's wired, and when he gives me the takedown signal, I'll give the go.'

"Well, when we get to the garage, this black guy I was dealing with gets in my car, and that was fine with me because that was the plan, the closer the better. I show him my money, about a thousand bucks, but it looks like a lot more. But then, he sticks his hand out the window and waves in another crew with the dope. I admit, I should have expected this, but this wasn't part of the deal me and the guy had discussed. They drive up in a SUV. As soon as they pull up, one of the guys from the SUV also gets in my car, without my permission. Things are happening fast, too fast. I get nervous 'cause I think it might be a rip, so I give the hard code."

"Hard code, meaning you believe it's going to be a rip-off, right?" asked Jackson James, as much to keep the detective talking as to learn anything. He knew very well that a rip or rip-off meant a robbery.

"You don't know how it is to be UC with two strangers sitting in your car—one behind you in the back seat." Grant reflected, then continued, "You don't know if he's gonna try and blow your head off before or after you do the deal. You have to remember; he believes you one of them—a drug dealer I mean—and fair game to be robbed and murdered. And to make it even worse, the first big deal with a new guy is always the worst 'cause nobody trusts nobody. This was my second meet with this guy but our first deal. I knew he didn't usually carry a gun, but this second guy getting in my car was a wild card. He had a package with him, but that could have been his laundry or a submachine gun for all I knew. They want you to know it if they got a gun though. But I wasn't expecting a crew to pull up, especially when this second guy gets in my car without an invitation.

"The hard code means for my backup to come in hard like gang-busters and get the drop on the dealers and not to worry about me. The soft code would be for my backup to come in easy 'cause maybe it's only one guy and everything is under control—I already got the drop on the guy or you don't want to spook anybody into doing something crazy.

"Well, when backup came in, it was hard—automatic weapons drawn, shouting and everything—draggin' people from cars. One of the deputies got carried away and dragged me from my car. I knew the guy from around and he knew me. He knocked me to the ground and got on top of me with his knee in my back and whispered while he handcuffed me. 'This is how we cover a snitch's ass in the county,' he said. 'We make it look good.' Then he proceeded to kick my ass while I was in cuffs. My sergeant pulled him off but actually stuck up for the guy later, saying something about he couldn't tell who I was in the dark. Well I knew better! So, I know both sides of the black-man-white-cop game, inside out."

For Jackson James, the old reporter magic was working. He had sat back and let Detective Grant go on and on, even after he'd said he didn't want to talk about it.

"My grandfather Chops told me about making black officers fight random black men on the streets back in his day," Grant continued. "He said if his training officer had a black officer assigned to him, like on the first day outta the academy, he'd take 'im to Johnson Homes, you know the projects, put 'im outta the car, point at a big black guy and say, 'Go jack that guy up.' He did it just so he could see if the black officer would fight other blacks. He said if the officer lost the fight, they would lock the other guy up for assault and resisting. He also told me he did the same sometimes when he was a training officer."

"See, that's what I mean! Why would your grandfather tell you something like that, to pass it down? By the way, I grew up in Johnson Homes." Jackson James said in disgust. "That's just wrong on so many levels. Was he proud of that? What if that had been my father, a good hardworking man, forced to fight a black officer in Johnson Homes? He was going to lose if he won or not— his job or his life. And where would I be now if I had grown up without my father?"

"So, you tell me then," Grant added, to make a point, "What's a new black officer in that situation supposed to do? If he tells, his career is done before it even starts. Do you remember that black guy in California, back in the nineties who was filmed being beaten with seven or eight cops all around him? What do you think happened to those officers who testified against the ones who beat him? They have to watch their backs even today. Men like my grandfather didn't even consider the beating wrong. The important thing to guys like him was to be able to trust the guy next to you if you got in a pinch, whether it was a fight or a lie to cover up something that went bad. That was— is—the system. It gets passed down from generation to generation. That's why he told me that story about having to beat up black civilians. He wanted to emphasize that I'd better know who I could trust in a pinch. Besides, no better way to know if you can trust someone than to make them complicit in the same acts."

Jackson James said, "That's just what I mean. A wise old preacher once said, 'It's the system. The system is evil!' I didn't know what he meant at the time but as I talk to cops who tell me stuff like that, I now know exactly what the old guy was saying. Only the churched listen when you talk about evil. Cops listen when you talk about corruption. That's why I use that word to describe what's going on now. But even within that 'evil system,' something has changed. Most police don't like dishonest cops who steal money or drugs, stuff like that. They called them 'dirty cops,' even if they wouldn't tell on them. Now that type of corruption has gone way down, but a different type has taken its place, and it's supported mostly by that old system but has its own means and ends. Do you understand what I'm saying?"

"But what if I tell you I understand it just fine?" Grant replied. "We police officers have to survive in that system your preacher calls "evil" the same way we black men have to survive in that same system. That doesn't change, no matter what race we identify as. I can call myself mixed race but cops, black and white, see me as black. Unlike with Caucasians, when people see me, they see black and all the baggage they choose to put with that. Do you accept it's right for young black men to need training on how to act when they're stopped by the police just so they can survive? But that's the system."

"But at what cost?" This time the reporter was careful to measure his tone, to avoid sounding partial or preachy. "My question is, why is change so difficult in that system? And do you recognize that the system needs changing? Can there be a system change? Can the police at least agree on that?"

Grant rubbed his lower lip and said, "Well, if we don't stick up for our brother officers, black or whatever, then who will? Who will back me up when I need help out there? The public? Shouldn't cops enjoy the same rights as anyone else? We deserve to be able to protect ourselves just like everybody else, right? Even though our job comes with built-in dangers we can't become lambs to the slaughter." Grant paused to consider the debate going on in his own head before continuing. "But at the same time, if we as civilian black men think we're being targeted, then we have a right to stick up for ourselves, too. The problem is that, as police officers, we carry deadly force on our hips and have the authority to use it—the right to use it. On the other hand, we ordinary black men carry our skin color on our faces, wear it as a badge of honor, and that's not always respected by the police, the courts, or juries—unless it's dressed in a blue uniform. In other words, they'll always take the word of a cop, black or white, over that of a civilian black man; at the same time, they'll take my word as a police officer over someone I may shoot." He paused again to consider his conclusion. "Strangely enough, that works for me. It's complex I know but that's the system I understand, and have to work in.

"But all this corruption stuff you're talking about, I don't know. It's just how the world works."

It was clear that this conversation made the new detective uncomfortable, and Jackson James backed off to ease the tension.

"To make a point, I'll tell you about one case that Jackie Delmonico took me on." Jackson James appeared to want to prove his earlier assertions about the evil system. But more, he wanted to keep the detective engaged.

"One night, on the night she made me a reporter," he started. "She called and said she wanted me to ride with her. This was the second time she was in Homicide—she was there twice—and she hadn't been there long. I had just come back from Vietnam and I was literally emptying trash cans in the newsroom that evening because the night custodian was out sick. That's how far I was from being a reporter. She picked me up at the newsroom and took me over to a small, shabby house off Ward Avenue where a little child had been scalded to death."

Jackson James's eyes went down to the table, took in the dead flies on the windowsill, and finally looked at his faint reflection in the window. It was as though the scene was there in front of him and he was trying not to see it again. But like any good reporter, he recalled everything and described in detail what he'd seen and heard.

"I'll never forget it," he continued. "The young dad was in handcuffs, sitting on the couch, and his girlfriend, the child's mother, was in the bedroom with the detective. She was moaning and crying like I never heard a human sound before. I never saw her because I never went in there. I mean, I could have because Jackie let me go wherever I wanted, but the woman was in an anguish so deep, I could feel it when I walked in the door. I didn't want to see her or take away from her private moment of grief. The boyfriend was a skinny kid with thick, long black hair. He didn't have a shirt on. His skin was still red with rage. His nose was broken and stuffed with bloody tissues. He had tattoos of stacked skulls going up his forearm like he was keeping count of unspeakable acts. He held his head back to staunch the flow of blood, opening his mouth so he could breath. His jaws were bruised and smeared with blood.

"The baby? Well, the baby was perfect and bright and pink, having just come out of a bathtub of scalding, hot water. He was lying dead on the bathroom floor. He wasn't even a toddler, yet. This was clearly not Jackie's case but Chops, your grandfather, was there, too. He and a couple other officers let her take me through the crime scene, and I took some pictures. The ambulance crew had gone, and the cops were waiting for the coroner to arrive.

"While I was walking through, I heard your grandfather say to one of the other officers: 'He won't be putting his hands on another baby. Wait till we get him back to the station. A broke nose will be the least of his problems.'

"Chops didn't recognize me from our run-in when I was a teenager, and I knew what he was capable of. I'd had my turn under his fat hand. He clearly trusted that Jackie wouldn't bring in anyone that would cause them trouble. That meant me.

"Nevertheless, Jackie let me take all the pictures I wanted." She said, 'This should get you in at the paper. Don't squander it, but don't blame me if you get just what you want.' I didn't understand what she meant at the time, but later I got it. She knew that I, just like her, would soon be living on other people's agony to fill my own wants and needs. I was going to use this family's troubles to make my proper entry into the news business—making my living off the misery of others. That's the sin of my profession. I knew what Chops and those officers meant about dealing with the suspect back at the station, but I wasn't brave. I knew that if I quoted the officer's comments, when I wrote the story to go with my pictures, I would probably get Jackie in trouble and ruin my own chances of ever getting into another crime scene." Jackson James paused for a moment to compose himself. "Besides, I wanted to kick the guy's ass, too. The next day, when I picked up the police incident report, I read that the guy had resisted arrest in the booking room, resulting in a concussion, several broken fingers, and cracked ribs. So, you see just how quickly the system can suck you in and make you complicit—and I'm not even a cop."

This comment led to further self-reflection by the semiretired reporter. His mind raced with thoughts of his dead friend Jackie Delmonico. He wanted to keep talking about her: "Months later, I learned that after Jackie dropped me off that night, she went to another crime scene on the lower end of River Street, not that far from here. Somebody had found what they described as the body of a young woman left buried in a trash pile. The woman was half naked and had been strangled. It was Jackie's case. The victim spent two or three weeks in the morgue before she was identified.

"It was lucky that Jackie got the case, because the poor woman may never have been identified if it wasn't for her. It was like the male cops thought a woman, hooker or not, should be under the protection of some man or other—husband or pimp, a male relative—like that. If she was out alone at night, she deserved whatever she got.

"It turned out that the identification took so long because the victim was so out of place in Edington. She didn't live or work here, so she just lay there unidentified. The best and worst that happened on that investigation was that the victim's father was a prominent minister in Jersey City, where she lived. She worked for Peter Arlington, a bigtime criminal lawyer in Manhattan who also happened to live over here in Edington. The victim was finally identified when Jackie started calling around to other departments. Jersey City reached back with a missing person that matched her description.

"When it hit the news that the young woman—and I'm sorry to say I can't recall her name—worked for this attorney, the shit hit the fan. The attorney demanded complete access to police information and insisted on the assignment of his hand-picked detective to the case. That detective was none other than—Clyde Drew. You heard of him, right?"

Grant nodded.

"Chief Reece, being no fool, however, kept Jackie on the case so she could do the work under the supervision of Drew. Even after the victim was identified, Clyde refused to stop calling her a prostitute. I can remember rumors of a quote from him, saying, 'Preacher's daughter or not, what was she doing out alone with money stuffed in her bra?'

"It was true, the victim was found in one of the warehouses on River Street that some prostitutes did frequent. Jackie said Detective Drew classified the woman as a prostitute because, other than him being a 'chauvinist asshole,' there was five hundred dollars stuffed in her bra. You see, it shouldn't have mattered, but it did to this department—maybe in a lot of departments. That was part of the system back then.

"Notwithstanding, this was before DNA and all that. The best you could do scientifically was a blood group, and that was pretty worthless in court unless the judge wanted it to count and that meant the victim had to count. You had to have an eyewitness or fingerprints, or both, to get a conviction with most juries, especially if a suspect was influential and had money for a good lawyer. The cops were famous for taking suspects deep into the precinct house—or in this precinct, it was that alley back there— and beat the hell out of them till they confessed, especially if they were poor or minority.

"So, Jackie was working hard on this woman's murder case, trying to find suspects and witnesses, but nothing was going good for her, especially with Clyde Drew constantly cutting in. Lawyer Arlington demanded constant briefings and second-guessed her every move. The victim's father was in the newspapers every day asking why the police couldn't make an arrest. Jackie couldn't do anything right in their eyes, and Arlington rode her ass every way he could. It was tough for her.

"Everything started changing, though, when Jackie went back to the crime scene and searched the warehouse again. She found evidence that other victims might be there; and, in a strange way, that gave her leverage.

"Meanwhile, the victim's father started calling for Jackie to get fired because she had dared to request an interview with him. Apparently, he thought to even make a routine inquiry about him was a firing offense for her because of his stature in the community.

"They were both in the papers—the lawyer and the preacher—demanding Jackie's head. And the press was no better when it came to that case. The senior writers at the News were more than happy to help bury Jackie Delmonico, one of the early women detectives in your department, if it sold papers.

"Jackie once said to me, 'I've never been under that kind of pressure before or since, and I had nowhere to go. There were no leads, just pressure.'"

"Well," Grant said thoughtfully, "she must have had somewhere to go. She stayed on in the department, didn't she? I mean, what did she do?"

"She got smart and stepped out of the system. She did a deep search of all the warehouses in the area looking for clues, and she did it without Drew's or the chief's permission. She convinced the warden at the county work camp to send some inmates to move stuff in the warehouse so she could look."

"Yeah! She find anything?"

"Yeah!" Jackson James said smugly. "You gonna find this hard to believe, but she found about twenty-five more dead women in there! Some had been there for over twenty years. Two were recent enough to tell they'd been strangled. The ligatures were still around their necks."

Grant interrupted, "So that's the case they mentioned a couple weeks ago."

"Did they tell you about when the word of the search got back to the chief and Jackie told the chief and Arlington, at the same meeting, what she'd found, Arlington accused her of trying to cover up the death of his secretary by diluting her death with a 'bunch of whores,' as he called them?

"Chief Reece immediately took Jackie completely off the case and gave it over to Detective Drew. And, Drew promptly eased all those bodies out of there without alerting anybody. It was not clear at the time if this was a political decision, corruption, or police incompetence. Either way, that's what happened, and they got away with letting a probably serial killer case go uninvestigated.

"Drew immediately went to his old standby. He found a patsy, a kid sleeping around the warehouses. They sweated him, got a confession, and that got the preacher off their case. They rushed the case through the court system. The patsy was just a kid too. A hippy that looked a lot like Whit at that age. Anyway, he was convicted of the murders and died of AIDS in prison seven years later."

"So, what would be the motivation for them doing that?" asked Grant. "I mean, why wouldn't they want the real perp caught?"

"That's the question—why?" answered Jackson James. "Jackie was pretty sure they had a serial killer at work, but her superiors never told that to anybody. They buried the whole investigation and it was not until a year later that Jackie learned why."

"Let me guess—the killer was related to someone in the department, right?"

"Not in the way that you know it. It had more to do with the suspect that Jackie developed in the case who was related to the whole system of justice."

"Well, who was it?" Grant asked, somewhat impatiently.

Jackson James would not be rushed, though he looked at his watch again. "Detective Drew slowly buried the case and the bodies. But on her own initiative, Jackie went to her friend, Detective Geech Murphy, in Robbery and got copies of all the incident reports on the victims she'd found. She could do this because in those days Robbery automatically got a C-C on all homicide reports, and Geech was her best friend.

"Jackie found out they had identified twelve of the women through clothing and jewelry, and a couple on picture IDs they found on the bodies. She went through all the records and noticed that Drew had identified them all as prostitutes in the reports. She originally thought the prostitute label was just a reason for Clyde to sweep the cases away as unimportant to the Department.

"But she went to the actual courthouse records and found a totally different reason for Drew's cover-up. She checked the records just to see how many of the women actually had sheets for prostitution, and that's how she cracked the case. Only one had prior arrests for solicitation. She started looking for any other connections, or interactions with each other, or with the court system, and that put her on the trail. Being the curious person she was, Jackie went to the clerk of courts office and learned that some of the victims were going through divorces and others had restraining orders against the men in their lives. But that didn't explain how or why all of them got killed and ended up in approximately the same location, the warehouses.

"Because she did this all under the table, the whole thing took another year. In the end, Chief Reece found out about it, though. To make a long story short, Jackie found that the women had one circumstance in common—they all had the same lawyer of record. You got it! They were all clients of Peter Arlington. He was the only connection. He was the divorce attorney for six of them. She also found out that Clyde Drew was Arlington's paid investigator, off the books, which is why Drew was so anxious to make this whole thing go away in favor of Arlington.

"They still didn't clean out the warehouses. The fact that they found those girls was never reported on by the press, and Arlington was never arrested. In fact, he filed to have a seal put on the investigation in the interest of his clients' privacy, and the case died on the vine. Clyde got promoted to detective sergeant, and Jackie was also promoted to sergeant to keep her quiet. She was sent off to Internal Affairs, where unwanted detectives went to die or be forced out of the Department. But she came back, and I covered that comeback in my 'Shadow of the City' series. You should read it. What she did was—."

"Gentlemen!" A voice boomed from nowhere to interrupt Jackson James. Stanton, dressed in blue uniform trousers and a white uniform shirt with no insignia, appeared from the same place as his voice.

"What're you two scheming about this fine Sunday morning?" Stanton asked heartily.

"Oh! We planning the takeover of America when the revolution comes." Jackson James smiled.

Grant looked uncomfortable at that comment and said, "I got to get to work," before grabbing his folder to leave. Then he asked the reporter, "Do you believe anybody will want to read about that stuff?" He was talking about the police corruption angle.

Jackson James said softly, "I honestly don't know. But I know they will never search for answers if they never hear the questions."

Grant slowly nodded, absorbing what he had just heard. The radio broke squelch but nothing was said. The detective said, "I got to go."

"Got a break in your case, Newbie?" asked Stanton.

"Can't say, Sir," were the young detective's last words as he turned the corner towards the front door, while putting the radio to his lips. He was last seen jogging down the street towards the river.

"Have a seat, captain?" the reporter invited.

Before Stanton could scoot his chair up and get comfortable, Whit was there with thin cuts of cured sausage, cheese, tomatoes, and two sliced, boiled eggs on a tray.

"What was it?" Stanton asked about Grant's abrupt departure. "Do I have bad breath?"

"I was just talking to Detective Grant about police culture for a piece I'm working on, but he wasn't very helpful."

"Police culture? What the hell is that!? You mean like getting up to go to work every day and dealing with the scum of the earth?"

"Something like that," Jackson James smiled, recognizing his companion's sarcasm. "But I was talking about how corruption in the police department has shifted."

"Corruption! What are you talking about, J.J.?" Stanton made a sausage-and-cheese hors d'oeuvre, shoved it in his mouth, chewed, started to make another, then finished his thought. "Are you making out that we all crooks? You saying I spent my life as a crook—that Mavis is married to a crook? The good old days are gone?" It was all sarcasm.

"I'm not saying it's not a noble profession," Jackson

James was quick to add. "But I am saying it's just like a lot of things, it's changing, and it was never what we imagined it was in the first place. Besides, you and I probably had different visions of the good old days, though."

"Don't start that," Stanton moaned. "It's Sunday, man. You ruinin' my breakfast. Now I know why Newbie left. Nobody wants to talk about that stuff."

"Yeah, Captain, I get it. It's hard to talk about it, but while we've not been talking about it, the noble profession has been taking a beating. I want to understand that shift, and I want to write about it. Maybe all I'm saying is dysfunctional relationships don't ever get better if people don't talk about them!"

The captain sipped his coffee. His mouth was full and crumbs filled the corners of his lips, but he was clearly listening. The flies on the windowsill were all dead, as the room was heating up.

"It's like everybody thinks the right change is going to turn up at our doorsteps and say, 'I'm here!' But right now, change doesn't even know where it is. It's just dead when it comes to policing. At least that's what I accept," said Jackson James.

"Who says we need change? Especially the 'right change,'" the old captain shot back, looking the reporter in the eyes. "Looks to me like we're finally ahead because the cops are winning now."

"Finally winning what? A major movement of unrest, a—?" The reporter stopped to compose his thoughts. "Don't you realize the house is on fire, Stanton?"

"The police are finally getting the respect we deserve. Juries and judges finally get it! The Supreme Court finally gets it! The public finally gets it!"

"I'm not so sure. From where I sit—as a reporter, I mean—the police see it as black and white. You either with them or against them, and there is no in between. It's a binary choice." He added ironically, "And that's a fine position for public servants to take."

"Public servants? Nice to say, hard to be," said Stanton.

"Well, think about this: Police used to accept praise as humble servants of the public for doing heroic stuff— taking down really bad guys, running towards the gun battle, saving kids from drowning, running into burning houses, and stuff like that—now they demand praise just for putting on the uniform in the morning. All the heroic praise is more than fair when they do it, but the police have taken it too far. They seem to hold it against us mere mortals if we don't put them on a pedestal for something we pay them to do.

"You cops have started to create symbols and flags—an American flags with a blue stripe—for yourselves like cults and religious orders. Since when did it become unacceptable to just do police work under the American Flag? You have to create your own flag?" Jackson James was getting more personal than he had planned but he was caught up in the moment and the frustration came through in his voice. He was frustrated and speaking the grievances of a million black men and women who had grown up in an Anglo-male dominated society. "Now officers go on crusades and refuse to work if they don't get to police like they want. It just not—." He ended his thought abruptly out of frustration.

"I don't agree," Stanton said. "I'll give you one thing, though. This new breed of police officer—white ones, I mean—are afraid of blacks. Not blacks in general, but the consequences of something going wrong with a black perp. They don't put hands on them like I did when I was active. And they really believe that old adage that being judged by twelve or carried by six is a good reason to take the quick solution to ending a confrontation. The other part of and adage goes: 'the dead tell no tales.' That held true until the age of police videos and cellphone cameras, you know. But even now, good juries find ways to acquit good officers. This all has to be simple for the cop on the street, J.J. They start thinking about all this stuff too much, and meet the wrong guy in the wrong ally, and the officer is dead."

"Stanton, you really believe that tripe? It's a matter of opinion as to what's a 'good jury.' You telling me Anglo officers aren't trained to be afraid of black people just because they're black? They believe black people are more dangerous, so they have to be more cautious. Do me a favor and find a stat on how many Anglo officers are killed by black men each year, on average. No such stat exists—not published anyway. They keep statistics on everything else, like how many black people kill other blacks, or how many whites are killed by blacks. —why not on that? Why are there so many unarmed black men killed by white cops in America? Tell me that! And tell me why the first inclination is to cover for the officer, no matter how egregious his action! There is one big difference between your workplace and many others. You have a distributed workforce, which means you have very little direct supervision over what are sometimes split-second decisions made by the officers under your command. Is it their training?"

A blank stare from Stanton told the reporter he had lost the retired police captain, but he continued, nonetheless. "You were a supervisor, so you should understand what I'm saying, right? Your workforce, Captain, was distributed all over your precinct, and supervision for your officers' actions—your sergeants and lieutenants—were blocks, minutes, and sometimes days away. That supervision was almost always after the fact. In addition, your officers all carried deadly force on their hips and had discretion on whether and when to use it. They even got to decide for themselves how to enforce the laws they were sworn to uphold. In many instances, their decisions weren't supervised until after some terrible action or mistake. Because judgment and discretion are always factors, the officers can't usually ignore things like racial prejudice." He looked Stanton in his gray-blue eyes. "Yeah, prejudice—and other personal attitudes that creep in."

"So here we go, where you were headed all along. Now you telling me all white cops are prejudiced. Right? Because, I don't believe that for a minute. I'm not!"

212

"Everybody's prejudiced man! We all have preconceived ideas about other people. From the foods they eat, to their mental abilities or anger quotient, we all make subconscious judgments all the time and with that comes our own preferences. From the type of ice cream we enjoy to the people we prefer to associate with, we all have prejudices. We spend a lot of time trying to avoid that word these days, but words like bias don't carry the same cachet. Preferring your own race and believing the other race doesn't deserve the same rights and privileges you have are different mindsets, though both are illogical because there is only one race—the human race. Whereas, having a bias simply means having a preference. This is bigger than that."

"J.J., you've changed. It sounds to me like you don't like cops very much anymore—like you've developed some kind of grievance—and that's surprising, considering all the favors this department did for you," said Stanton, his eyes narrowing. "And considering how close you were with Jackie, that surprises me."

"Jackie has nothing to do with this, and your conclusion is just the opposite of how I feel. It's just that I'm an old man now. Just like older Anglo guys have their conjured grievances about jobs or promotions they didn't get because of minorities or women, old black men have the market cornered on grievances about things we didn't get, because of old white men. In fact, the grievances of men from my generation started before this country was even born. No. I have tremendous respect for the police. Most black people do. When I call one, I want one. I want drunk drivers off the roads. I want criminals put away and not breaking into my house. When they do something heroic, I want them treated like heroes. But whether I call the police or not, I don't want to risk my life because a scared or racist cop—or one that's just having a bad day— shows up and I become his victim. And I'm not just talking about the victim of one officer, I'm talking about becoming the victim of a system. In my article I want call out that system as a shifting kind of corruption. It is easy to pluck off unarmed men or women, one at a time, and blame the actions of individual officers or the victims themselves, but we know it's all fed by a corrupt system.

"It was a police officer that made me a reporter. Strangely, I used to resent her for it, but now I understand what she did, just not why. She did warn me. And yes, I'm talking about Jackie Delmonico. Before she came along, I was just a clean-up boy in the newsroom who they occasionally allowed to take some pictures for the paper. She took me out on a homicide run, and the next thing I knew, I was in the news business, for real. But I soon realized I knew too much about how the system worked to happily live off that same system that is supported by misery of others. That's what she warned me about. That's why I eventually became an investigative reporter."

Stanton put his hand on Jackson James's arm, patted it, and said, "When I was a kid, the cops came down on me just like every other kid, even though I was white and my daddy was a cop, too. And guys who acted like Chops came down and got me out of trouble a couple of times, and beat the hell outta me a couple times, too."

Jackson James removed the napkin from his lap and placed it on his plate, a sign he was finished. "I hope you're not trying to equate your experiences with the police with mine. I was under the hand of the real Chops once, not 'guys like Chops,' so don't even try that.

"You have to remember, back in the day, there were always cops and robbers. Corrupt cops were considered bad guys and they knew they were bad. They made a conscious decision to be bad. Even good cops hated those corrupt officers, although they didn't always turn them in. Now-a-days some officers see it as a rite of passage to push a situation to the point where they get to use excessive or deadly force.

"Remember the Knapp Commission, all those officers in Harlem chasing those bags of money they called the 'Nut?' Those guys knew they were bad cops. But nowadays cops don't even know they're corrupt. They just see it as a political choice."

"The Nut, yeah! That should be ethics 101 for every police officer." Stanton responded, ignoring the political choice comment. "That's where the NYPD collected money from the numbers and prostitution rackets they let thrive. They systematically passed portions of the proceeds up the chain of command. Yeah, those were different officers and different times."

"Well, I could argue we have our own version of the Nut right here in Edington," Jackson James said evenly. He was starting to calm down. "In our city, the money is derived from excessive fines in the black and Hispanic neighborhoods. It makes its' way throughout city government in the form of pay raises and bonuses. The' Nut!' That's the system."

"I know what you're talking about, and I don't disagree. While it isn't right, the officers are enforcing the laws on the books here in Edington. What happened in Harlem, that was just plain illegal. If you don't want those laws on the books, change them. What are our cops supposed to do?"

"And that's the real shame, because the City of Edington made it legal. And what political power do black people in this city have to change anything?" said the reporter. "The officers don't even know what they are doing is wrong. They have discretion, or perhaps they are under orders, but either way it's wrong.

"You know—and I'm being frank—so just follow me on this. I believe it took a while, but black people, in general, have figured out that no matter how they adapted in the world they are never going be truly accepted and treated the same as Anglo folks. That epiphany has to happen to each generation. So, we learned to create our own societies where we would be accepted and be heroes in our own narratives. That's why we have black colleges and black churches, institutions like that. And there's the rub."

"What do you mean, 'a rub?'" Stanton asked, seeming to give Jackson James's proposition serious consideration.

"The rub is the belief that some officers can't be comfortable letting black people control their own narratives as being regular, law abiding, people in our society because black people have to play a role in the officers' narratives."

"That sounds crazy to me J.J. I don't see what you are talking about."

"I'm talking about those officers who consider themselves some sort of class heroes. For them to be heroes, there must be a steady supply of villains—a class of people the officers protect everyone from. Don't you see it? That's the rub I'm talking about, and that's what I want to figure out. For example, if something goes wrong out there on the streets, then those hero cops feel obligated to cover for each other and ostracize other cops who don't tow the blue line with them. The unions are caught in the middle, because they have to maintain hero-status for all their members, including the worst of the worst. That means they sometimes have to defend cops' most outrageously bad behavior."

Stanton rubbed his chin and looked at the remains of his food. "I still don't really know what you mean. We do take on a certain amount of risk on behalf of the public every time we put on the uniform and so the union is what protects us from unfair persecution. That should be worth something. But what does that have to do with this hero and villain stuff? It sounds like something from the comic books, if you ask me."

"In logic, Stanton, in comic books and the real

world, if you have a hero class then there has to be an enemy of the hero, or a villain class. That's why I chose that ancient word to describe what I think is going on. Villains are important to all plots. That's not just in the ancient plays, or comic books; that's real life, too. One could not exist without the other. If police can make black people the villain class, then it's okay for the heroes to kill them. The really destructive concept is when people are forced to make that binary choice and there is no middle. The officer is either guilty or 'not guilty.' Juries are forced to choose between those two alternatives, no matter how heinous the actions of the police are. The pressure is always on to find the heroes not guilty. That's how a police officer, deemed unstable and unfit by one department, can move on to another, commit other outrageous acts, and have his union, fellow officers, and most importantly, prosecutors all find ways to let him off the hook. None of these people can say they are not in favor of the hero, because then they themselves would lose their hero class status and become villains. That's where we've arrived, and that's what I'm talking about. I'm not saying the officers are all bad. In fact, I'm saying most are good people but that's all, just people. They are just human, and we should acknowledge that. I'm saying once you accept that hero status then you accept a system that keeps you from confronting this corrupting behavior in a real way. I dare say, Captain Stanton, some people, no matter their ethnic leaning, would see this discussion and question my motives just like you did. But that's the point. We need to have the discussion; and that's what my article is going to be about—the need for the discussion. It seems to me the most heroic thing an officer can do these days is speak out about changing the system."

Stanton rubbed his chin and thought for a few seconds. "Each situation is different," he said, finally. "Each police officer is different, but—"

The reporter cut him off, "—But the results are the same, at least in the cases we hear about. Everybody on the police force either sticks up for the accused fellow officer or gets very, very quiet. That's the kind of corruption I'm describing. I'd like to know why those officers are standing behind the police flag rather than the American Flag. Is it because they no longer control the narrative behind the American Flag and the Constitution—you know all that 'All men are created equal' and 'justice is blind' stuff? Could that be it? If not, tell me your side of the story, and let me write it in quotes. Tell me what the police—the honest police—really feel."

Stanton took a deep breath. "I think it's you liberals, J.J., that make the heroes and villains, as you call it. Even if an officer admits he's wrong and the black victim's death was an accident or an overreaction, the liberals still want the officer's head on a pike. They want to make him represent every other officer on the force. Consider it this way: The public pays the police to keep the peace, right? If we don't do that, you want us fired. If we do it and the wrong person gets arrested, we get fired. If we do it too aggressively you want us fired. We're not Goldilocks: we can't try these beds out before we lay in them. There's not time for that on the streets. We often have to make a decision before we know if it's too hard, too soft, or just right."

"But wouldn't you agree," Jackson James asked, "that there has to be accountability both before and after the fact? I mean, if an officer demonstrates he has a prejudice against certain people or is a racist, does his fellow officers have a duty, for the sake of the overall profession, to call him out on that before his Goldilocks moment? Can the system get to that point?"

Before Stanton could answer, Whit's voice boomed from the bar side of the building, "Mavis want to talk to you, and she already knows you here!"

Stanton stood and said with a snarl, "J.J., I can see a bit of your point of view and why you see it as corruption but I'm not sure anyone else will. I've got to go, but we can continue this later.

"I especially want to know where all this Anglo stuff comes from. What are you talking about? Is that some new idea, because I heard all about that in the sixties and seventies."

The Last Week

"Hey, Turk!" Whit shouted from behind the bar, over the regular happy hour bar noises. It was Friday of the next week at 4:05 p.m. The bartender held up a newspaper with the headline visible to the detective formerly known as Newbie. The large block print read: "Killer of Mayor's

Daughter, Uncle." The subtopic read: "New Turk in Police Homicide Captures Killer Red-Handed!"

Norris was trying something new in the bar. He was having a winetasting, though he wasn't there. When Stanton heard about the idea and saw the crates of wine stacked in his office, he went ballistic and threatened to leave his daily haunt. Norris thought Stanton's reaction was hilarious and laughed in his face. Norris knew the only way his silent partner was leaving the Cop House Bar for good was after a wake where Stanton was laid out between the bar and poolroom—something they did from time to time for the old guys that served in the nineteenth precinct.

"If you don't shut your fuckin' mouth, I'll knock you outta that fuckin' chair!" Stanton had shouted, speaking of Norris's wheelchair.

Norris, a big man with shriveled legs because of his handicap—what Stanton called "cripple," was always the calmer of the two men even when they'd shared a patrol beat and were partners in Robbery. Norris said to Stanton, in a matter-a-fact voice, "You put your hands on me, and you'll draw back a lead keepsake."

Stanton, and everybody who knew Norris, suspected he kept his old backup—a Smith and Wesson, thirty-eight, Airweight, five-shot revolver—secreted somewhere on his person or in the wheelchair. As a result, Stanton didn't feel inclined to test that assumption and the wine flowed out as ordered that afternoon. This was not the first time Stanton and Norris had clashed, and undoubtedly it would not be the last.

It seemed having wine cases in his space was an intrusion for Stanton and serving it in the bar was a major change in the character of the place. Those were his major objections. But here they were, and Stanton seemed to be the only person upset about it.

All the regulars had arrived in Stanton's office that afternoon, save Nubs, when Detective Grant showed up. Commander Ann Bell held a wine glass half filled with Chardonnay—probably a first for the bar—in one hand and a cigarette in the other. She seemed to be in her natural afterhours habitat. Whether due to the wine or not, she appeared quite merry.

Holding a bottle of beer, Stanton stood as Grant entered. This was also a first. Stanton never stood for anybody.

Geech held a glass of Coke in his hand. "You can call me Geech now, Turk, now that you a real murder detective and earned your new name." Everybody laughed at this comment, but it seemed out of place to Grant.

Moose had entered behind Grant, and to the young detective's surprise he placed both hands on Grant's shoulders. Whit brought in beers for Moose and Grant and a Merlot for himself. There were others there, too—strangers to Grant—but they all clearly belonged. They all raised their drinks and toasted the newest successful murder detective.

"To Detective Turk Grant!" someone said, and they all drank.

Someone else proposed a toast: "May all his cases go

down so easy, and you always better that bunch at city hall," and they all drank. It went like that for a while… And they all drank.

Grant was shy about this attention, and to deflect it, he asked, "Where is Nubs?"

Then a voice from the pantry shouted, "Captain! Mavis is on the phone!"

"He's at St. Mary's drying out," said Stanton, answering Grant. "He'll be there a few days, but he'll be okay. I'm sure he'll catch up with the adventures of Detective Turk Grant." Then he looked at Whit and said, "Tell Mavis I'll be home in a little while."

Bell's eyes appeared brighter than usual, even passionate. She said to Grant, "You got to tell us how you got 'im."

"Not this stuff in the paper," added Moose.

"You know the story as well as I do, Moose," replied Grant.

Moose slapped Grant on the back and said, "You caught it, Turk. You cleaned it. You tell it."

For the first time in his four weeks of coming to the Cop House Bar, the cops gathered there seemed to wait for his words. It was as though a baby was about to cry for the first time and prove his lungs. There were no defects in the baby. Turk's voice was confident and strong. For the first time he felt he belonged to their little private clique, and he guessed this was the reason Moose had brought him there in the first place. He was part of their group now, and he felt somehow under their protection. And in a strange way, he wasn't sure that was a good thing. Still, he was sure he liked the feeling and he was ready to talk.

"Well, credit for the article goes to Jackson James," Grant said, raising his bottle.

"But credit for the work goes to you," said an anonymous voice, one of many still congratulating him while continuing to drink.

"I got lucky," said Grant. "Here's to Jackson James!" And they all drank.

"I took your advice," Grant added, "and got my suspects to do the work—to lead me to her body. I stirred the pot. Here's to Detective Nubs Cooper!" They all drank, and he continued, "After I left here that first week, I put the word out in city hall that we suspected a member of the Carter family was responsible for my victim's disappearance. I also got some of my buddies from the drug squad to run an unofficial surveillance on my three key suspects, her great uncles. It took a few days, but all three of them finally met in the back of the sanitation department last Sunday morning, and the one that did it, Braxton, took a sanitization truck to a dumpster yard at the edge of town. This is the place where the city keeps the old, beat-up bins until they sell 'em for scrap. He had to use the truck to move more than twenty dumpsters to get to the one where he had put her. That showed prior planning." Everyone in the room nodded at the legalistic conclusion. "Then he moved that dumpster, with her still in it, back to the main recycling center. He was going to bale her up in plastic. It was plastic and paper bales, bound for the

Philippines."

It was not considered bad manners for someone to butt in on a good story to add insight and make the story better, and that's just what Bell did. "If that body had been baled in a bundle of plastic and put in a cargo ship," she said, "there's no telling when—or if—it would have been found, or if it could have been linked back to Edington."

Turk jumped back in. "She was just a tiny little woman, and her remains would probably have been mistaken for a big dog after a few months in that that hot container. My investigation was improvised, but we may never have caught him if you guys hadn't told me how to do it."

Stanton asked, "What was the motive?"

"Drugs," Grant said dryly. "I doubt it will ever really come out, but the uncles were running a drug distribution network, and she was one of their mules. Looks like she got greedy, or needy, and things got out of hand." Then, trying not to sound cocky, he added, "I guess they picked the right detective after all."

Whit appeared at the door and yelled, "Captain! Captain!"

Mavis Stanton stood in the doorway behind Whit. She appeared to be a thin frail woman, turning jaundiced around the edges, but her looks were deceiving. She'd probably stood there, just that way, when the room was Stanton's police office and their children were small. Stanton had always underestimated her.

She said calmly, "You got to come home, Pat. I need

your help. You can't sit up here like you still work here. Those days are long gone. You got to come home and help me clean Paddy up. He's not having a good day." She said this quietly, but then the timbre of her voice and the stature of her body changed. The softness was gone, and she became noticeably louder and taller. "He needs you. We need you. As thin as he is, I still can't lift him."

Her hair was white and brittle, but she had hastily arranged it in a bun. "You sit up here all day, every day. Why don't you tell your friends why you won't come home, why you can't even look at your own son? Tell them how you ran our daughter out the house and into the streets because of the race of the boy she brought home. Go ahead and tell them how you tried to run our home like you ran this prescient house. Why don't you really tell them what's wrong with your son?"

Captain Stanton's wife stood barely five feet tall, but she commanded any space she inhabited. She had been a schoolteacher by profession, and that's what she became again that day standing in the doorway, as though she might be lecturing a class.

Clearly frustrated, she continued. "Times have changed. It's no longer anybody's concern if a cop's son has AIDS. You need to come home. You can't keep sitting up here being the honorable cop but avoiding the honorable things at home. I need your help! You're up here living in a world where you still run the show—where it's all about doing the right thing and watching your partner's back. But your family has fallen apart. What about our backs?"

She steeled herself, taking two deep breaths, reset her tone, her mood, her everything, and took a step forward before starting again. "I mean, do they know about your drinking at home and all that? Do they know about the terrible things you've swept under the rug to keep your cop groupies out of trouble? You think I don't know what you glorify when you come home and argue with me? Do you forget what your kids heard you brag about? Did you believe your children weren't listening? Can you imagine how many families you—and those like you—completely destroyed, either directly or indirectly by arresting fathers, mothers, sons, and daughters when you or your officers could have made better decisions—better choices. That includes your own family. You all laugh about your actions within your group. I know you have all become callous about what you do, seeing so much of it. I guess you have to laugh and pretend you don't care to keep from crying, but here you all are. You're retired, Pat. I need you at home now. Your son needs you at home now."

She turned towards the door, looked back, and said in a calm, quiet voice, "I won't be calling or coming again." Then she left.

Pat Stanton just sat there with his head down. He was stunned. His wife, this small-framed woman, had dressed him down the way he'd criticized rookie officers in his command. And he took every word in. It was clear to everyone that her mind had been simmering for years, and today was the day she had let it boil out and embarrass

Captain Stanton in front of his friends. As quickly as she had appeared and boiled over, she was gone, leaving an odor of poison thoughts and Tabu perfume to linger in the silence.

The Cop House Bar—and Stanton's office in particular—had become a place where the exploits of police officers and detectives became real over and over again. The good stories were told until they became part of the DNA of the place, like the pictures on the walls. But now the group was quiet for once, just looking at each other, until Detective Grant said, "The uncle shat himself when we caught him red-handed pulling her corpse from the dumpster!"

And they all laughed. And they all drank.

GOOD COP BETTER COP

Everyone always called Dan Ferryman a good cop—his neighbors, his friends, the people on his beat, and even stray dogs lick his hand. So, as he picks up the newspaper that morning from the dew-wet lawn and opens it briefly, more out of habit than urgency, he stops in his tracks after seeing the headline. He takes a second look at the face of the paper, then he looks at the American flag hanging next to his front door and finally he glances up and down his street at the assortment of other flags and banners. Some are American, some college banners, some celebrate the season, and many stand for absolutely nothing at all. One has an egg on it and still another a rainbow. He briefly shakes his head before walking back inside.

His son's folded American flag, displayed on the bookcase next to the front door, deserved a slight nudge to make it perfectly straight. It bugs Dan because he can never seem to make it balanced. The rectangular shape of its display case makes it seem slightly out of kilter to the picture of his son and the departmental patch placed on either side.

The picture is that of a square-jawed, handsome, dark-haired, fair young man. Dan always thought Danny's hair was too long in the photo but now he believes it's perfect and regrets he never got to tell him so. For Dan, the photo makes bad days seem better and good days seem sadder. *Funny how that works*, he thinks.

Dan is working second shift, so he has time to assemble the breakfast Margie, his wife, left the fixins for on the kitchen table. He pours the coffee she started before leaving for her job at the hospital. He pours the cereal in the bowl and adds milk from the fridge. He takes a deep breath hoping he can keep it together while reading the article about his son who died in the line of duty just one year earlier. The article, which Dan helped with, was supposed to have been out the next day which was actually the one-year anniversary of his son's death. Both Dan and Margie had planned to be off the next day and read the article about their son and his sacrifice, and mourn, but here he is alone with the article and his grief.

"Young Cop Remembered in the Places He Served," the headline reads. It is below the fold but still a headline as far as Dan is concerned. He thought the article would be more about his son doing the things that police officers do—things like running towards gunfire or into burning buildings to save lives—all things that Danny had done. But after reading the perfunctory lead: "Local police officer, Danny Ferryman III, killed while responding to domestic dispute is remembered one year later by family, friends and those he served," Dan is confused.

Horseshit, he thinks, then he whispers to himself, "'The people he served,' how ridiculous is that—sound like command-speak. I taught my boy how to police, but he didn't listen."

The newspaper reporter interviewed a teenager from the south side and the article shows his picture. The kid looked to be tall and lanky. He is holding a basketball with two hands. He said he knew Officer Ferryman as the cop who answered a call on his street and ended up organizing a game of soft ball. Officer Ferryman and his friends, other police officers, had blocked off the street one Saturday and just watched them play.

"It was one of the best afternoons I ever had. They brought balls, bats, gloves, everything!" the article quoted the boy as saying.

"I told Danny not to ever trust any of 'em. It's all a lie—this business about them being just kids like anybody else. A kid can kill you, too. They'll steal anything not nail down." Dan realized he was talking to himself but didn't care. He was home alone, and he often talked to himself, complained to himself, argued with himself, and became pissed with himself when he thought about Danny's death.

He thought about killing himself when he was home alone. But good cops don't do that. Do they?

Dan sighs and thinks about Danny and what a trusting kid he was. *Product of that damn public school. Liberals! My Daddy saved and sent me to a good private, Christian school. I should have insisted with Danny, but Margie…* His thoughts trail off.

There is a yellow wall phone next to a small desk and a white refrigerator next to that. A door that leads through the utility room, and on out into the garage, finishes that end of the kitchen. He refolds the paper and places it under his arm. He picks up his cup of coffee, and walks over to the desk, leaving his breakfast untouched. He picks up the receiver to the phone and rest it on his shoulder while at the same time scattering a stack of papers Margie had arranged on her desk. He picks up one note, starts to dial the number on it, stops, slams the phone down and walks through the utility room into the garage, balancing the coffee in the cup.

It's dark in the garage but instead of turning on the lights he hits a button next to the door jam and watches as the big garage door glides up. The sound of the motor on the garage door opener is somehow relaxing. Light floods the open bay. He looks around and notes everything is neat, just as he left it. He looks out onto the driveway at is patrol car and he can't think if it makes him happy or sad. He used to have a definite opinion about his squad car but now it's just there and he can't muster a feeling about it, one way or the other. There was a time, the authority that went with it, the feel of it, his pride in it, and the admiration of all his friends and family that culminated in his possession of it was his whole world. But now he doesn't know how to feel. *I just wish I had Danny back, but all the wishing in the world...*

He walks over to his high bench and sits on his high stool. He thinks about the model cars and other stuff he and Danny put together at that bench and smiles. *Remember that carrier ship Danny?* "We had so many parts left over," he whispers. "And that Corvette model car? Wow, you said you were going to get a real one someday and get me one too." *They're still in your room just like you left them.*

Thanks Dad! Dan's brain responds. But it was not the police officer Danny in his thoughts. It was the sensitive little boy that he imagines. The one that didn't like baths but loved to swim in the ocean. He decided to give in to a short cry before re-squaring his jaw.

The light radiating into the garage is broken by low thunder clouds that threaten rain. "How I could spend this day with you Danny, right here working on our stuff," he whispers and wishes. Then he opens a jar of nuts and bolts, he keeps on a shelf above his head, to remove a key. He uses the key to unlock the drawer to his work bench. He takes out something wrapped in an oily rag and places it before him on the bench. He carefully unwraps the object as though it were a fragile gift.

He hears the ringing of a phone and instinctively reaches for his cellphone that is usually in one pocket or another. He realizes he is still in his pajamas and it must be the house phone ringing.

"What're you doing?" Margie ask, and before he can answer. "You're not in the garage, are you?"

"No. I'm having breakfast and reading the paper."

"So, you've seen the paper then? You going to work today?"

I don't know why she would think I'm not going to work. "Yes, I plan to go in. I almost called that reporter and give 'im a piece of my mind. That article is not what I expected."

"Did you read the whole article? I mean it puts Danny in a very flattering light."

There is silence from Dan.

Margie continues, "And promise me you'll stay out the garage today, okay? I know what you keep in that bench, by the way? Danny told me a long time ago."

Dan scoffs, "What do you mean? I don't know what you think you know but—."

"Just do me a favor. I'll be home early, and we can spend a few minutes together before you leave."

There is silence again from Dan.

"Love you hon!"

"Yeah, me too."

Dan goes back out into the garage and stands over the bench, looking down at his prize. A Model Nineteen revolver is laying on the rag just as he left it. He picks it up and checks to see that it's uploaded, though he knows it has to be. He looks down the sights and pull the trigger twice just to hear the hammer fall. He places it back on the rag and picks up the newspaper.

He snaps it open and on page "A2" is a picture of Dan, Danny, and Margie. The picture has the caption: "Officer Daniel Ferryman III came from a law enforcement family. He is pictured here (L to R) Daniel Ferryman III, his mother Margie, and father Daniel Ferryman Jr. His grandfather, Daniel Ferryman, (not pictured) was also a Grand, County sheriff's deputy who served this community for over thirty years." The picture shows Danny and Dan in uniform. It is Danny's graduation day from the academy, and everyone is smiling.

"Why did they have to mention Daddy?" *I never mentioned him to the reporter.* "Oh well, I believe most people have forgotten him by now, though."

I don't know why I keep his old pistol anyway? Dan picks up the pistol, examines it again and neatly folds the cloth around it before placing it back in the drawer. He leaves the drawer unlocked.

Daddy why do you keep that thing around? This is the adult Danny speaking in Dan's brain.

"To remind me of who he was," Dan whispers.

But he killed himself with that thing. You never even talk about him. You should let it go.

No need to whisper anymore. Only Danny can hear himself now and he gives way to a full-on conversation but half of it is in his head.

"But he was my daddy. I was a better dad to you than he was to me, wasn't I?" Dan's brain wants an answer, but Danny never answered that question, not even when he was living.

Then Dan remembers an argument he and Danny had two years earlier like it was yesterday. He remembers it word for word. It had played out in his head over and over so many times. It starts with the question Danny keeps asking: Why did Granddaddy take his own life?

"Policing messed my daddy up Danny. He didn't trust anybody—gun, badge, liquor—that got all mixed up for him. When he retired and didn't have that anymore—accept the liquor—that was his end. It was too late for me and him."

Then the adult Danny said, *Well that's your problem Pop? You want me to hate the same people you and Granddaddy hated for the same reasons. You want me to have the same grievances you have. Well I can't live my life that way.*

"Is that a word your liberal college taught you—grievance—huh? Well you'll see! We built this country. There was nothing here worth having before our ancestors came here and built this country and all them you believe care about you; they just want what you got. They can't ever have what the white man 's got, and it's best you remember that and keep your distance.

But Dad, I don't think that. They just want the same things I got, not what I got. They want the same opportunities, that's all. This is the land of opportunity, right?

"Well you wait until you have a son and you have to make sure the government don't take from you to give to them because of their rights and not yours, then tell me what you think. Everything is our fault—everything right?

They get the schooling and jobs your son is supposed to get. Tell me what you believe then?

"God damnit Danny! Now you won't even have a son!"

Dad, you got a big break and a second chance, even if you had to move out here. That jury did you a big favor.

"Ain't no favor for a grand jury to no-bill a case on a police officer. I'm out there doing exactly what they pay me to do. It's that chicken-shit chief that ought t' be run out of town. The district attorney could indict a ham sandwich if he wanted to. You better wise up. They owe us for what we do. What do you think ol' Dick Morris 'll do if they try and break in his house and get to his family? What do you believe happens if we don't come, or we get there just in time to shoot one? Do you think he gonna care if he's black or not, or even if he's armed or not? No! You better wise up!"

Dan was referring to 'Dick Morris' the district attorney who prosecuted him for shooting a black teenager. The teenager was running away, with no gun on him when the fatal shot was fired. "It was fortune that the jury saw it right, just like I knew they would. The chief didn't have to fire me—"

Dad! Dad! I'm not saying you should have gone to jail. They found a gun but even if they hadn't, I wouldn't want you to go to jail. I'm just saying not all of them are out to get us, the police I mean. I don't for a second question your actions. You did what you thought was right for your safety, but what do you think would have happened if that had been me in that alley and another office killed me? What would you do then?

"You talkin' crazy now. There is no way in hell you would have ever been in a alley like that. I raised you better. Don't go to work talking that shit, they'll stop covering you? They'll stop backing you up. You just don't know what this world 'll do to you."

You and Granddaddy were the same way. "I don't know nothin' about nothin'" you both would say, but Daddy you got to loosen up! All the people we suppose t' serve ain't all bad.

"Well you just keep that attitude and see where it get-cha?

"It got you dead. I tried to tell you," moans Dan and he wipes tears away.

Dan decides to go back to the kitchen table to finish the article. He pours another cup of coffee, crosses his legs and holds the paper in the window's light, meaning to get comfortable.

The next bit in the paper is an interview with Mary Dorn McEllerbe. She was an eighty-six-year-old retired homemaker from a part of the city that went from Italian to Black and on to Latino in one generation or two. She is pictured as a small woman with an Irish twinkle still in her eyes. She is standing with her friend, Dora Sweets, a black woman of the same age, who's eyes have lost their color due to cataracts. The caption under the photo reads: "These neighbors never really met until Officer Danny Ferryman insisted they come out and sit on their front porches one Autumn afternoon. He said it was too hot to sit indoors."

Dora Sweets said, "Danny knocked on my door one afternoon to introduce himself and noticed that I had all the windows closed with no air conditioning. It was hot in there and he just started to open windows. I thought he was crazy. He told me he would be in the area all day and that I could enjoy the fresh air. I did."

Dan could not shake his dead son's next words. He could not let it go.

Any part of the city—I would police any part of the city the same way I policed any other part of the city because they are all just people. And if I died doing it that way, you would miss me, but I would be fine ... And, I don't even like the word "police" for what we do. It sounds like we picking up trash and I don't feel that way about it.

"You lettin' smart-ass and guilt—white guilt—talk now and you don't have nothing to be guilty about. We supreme beings in this world. It's our Manifest Destiny. We talk and they listen. You need to be proud to be a white male."

Are you listening to yourself, Daddy? Do you hear the words coming out of your mouth? I'm proud to be who I am. I proud to be your son and I'm proud to be an Irish, Anglo-American but not the kind of pride you are talking about.

"Well, what other kind is there?"

Pride in being part of America and in where my family came from, and that I can provide for my family. None of that has to do with me being a 'supreme being' or that I have to keep other people down to feel any accomplishment.

"Is that what you think I do? Because I don't care

about black pride and all that. Show me what they've done for this country? That's what I'm talking about."

Well you served with some black people in Vietnam, didn't you Dad? You never mention those times, but they were there too, right Pop? In school we learned that black people served in all the wars, even though they were kept as slaves in the south.

"Here we go, that whole slavery thing! I don't know that much about our family, but I don't believe we ever owned any slaves. That's what I mean by that 'liberal education.' Our family came here from Ireland in the late eighteen-hundreds is all I know. Your great grandfather spent his first days living on the street. He made his own shoeshine box and lived on that until he met your great grandmother and went to work at her father's tanning business. That's where he got his start." Dan feels satisfaction, even now, hearing those words come out of his mouth.

I know Dad, but I do think about the slaves. They couldn't marry their way out of their situation or buy their way out or even live there way out. Even their children were destined to be slaves. They just had to die or hope their master died and let 'em go.

"You talkin' crazy again. That's just the way it was. That was their part in building this country. Do you believe any white man would have stood for letting their wives and daughters being subjected to that? That's the difference between us and them!"

Us and them? —they had no choice about it. If you had come here like they did, you wouldn't have had any choice about it either. Great Granddaddy never would have married well, Granddaddy never would have become a sheriff's deputy, and you and I might never have become police officers. You remember? You got me on the force. That's what I'm trying to tell you.

"Yes, I remember. That was a proud day of me, for our family."

Dan let his thoughts trail off and read the rest of the article satisfied he had held his own against his better educated son. The article was a lot of the same—all stories about how Danny and his partner had gone out of their way to get to know, and help people, in their patrol areas.

"Horse Shit! It's just like the guy said in a book I once read. They're the sheep in this world and we, the police, are the sheepdogs. We protect them from the wolves. We don't play with the sheep and we damn sure don't play with the wolves."

Dan hears his name. It is coming from the garage again and he doesn't want to go but he has to because it's Danny the little boy calling.

Dad you need to put this away before mom gets home. This is the adult Danny talking, when he gets back to the garage, confusing Dan's brain. *You need to take this gun away from here.*

Dan walks back out into the garage, hitting the button to close the big garage door as he walks past. The door goes down and only the light from the door to the house pushes his shadow back to the workbench.

Dan stands there in the shadows looking down at the gun and remembering how he had been reminded once before by his adult son to put it away, or better yet, take it away. The echo of Danny's voice is as real as his mind could make it. *I miss you Daddy, but I'm fine.*

"I don't believe you." Dan says softly.

He hears a car pull in the driveway and knows Margie is home. He opens the bench drawer, removes the revolver and runs his hand under the top of the bench to a place where he has a box of cartridges hidden. He hears the front door open. He quickly takes a cartridge and chambered it in his father's revolver. He knows Margie will go back to their bedroom and freshen up before coming to find him. He snapped the revolver shut and indexed the round to rotate under the next hammer-fall. Margie is calling his name from the kitchen, heading in his direction. "Dan! Dan!"

He turned the gun on himself but hears the young Danny softly say, *Not today, Dad. Not today. I fine.*

KILLING MOONY JR.

OR

TWO MILES FROM HOME

"Lordy" was the somber word that brought me back into the austere kitchen at my parent's house—though *Lordy* was not really a word, but more a thought uttered or a reflexive grunt. Mama was shelling red-hull peas into a colander and dropping the hulls into a paper sack positioned at her bare feet. This was her daily routine. If it wasn't peas, it would have been butter beans, snap beans, or collards being washed. At the same time as her work passed, she was staring at one of dozens of envelopes, each with the end torn as her preferred way of opening the mail. She kept it—the mail I mean—in permanent stacks on the kitchen table. This surface, this piece of Americana in most southern homes, also served as her dining room table, her food prep counter, and finally her reading stand. This is also where she kept a medium-size black *Holy Bible*, copies of *Home Magazine* someone had given her, a few old newspapers, and … well, you get the picture.

Her bright but aged face showed deep lines of worry most of time, but the wrinkles almost disappeared when she was happy. And that day she was happy, probably because I was home.

I realized she also kept envelopes in small piles on the bottom of a flimsy TV stand. It that managed to support a broken, medium-size, Zenith brand that in turn supported a smaller RCA portable model, TVs I mean. The RCA worked just fine, more or less, and was always on in the background during the day with soap operas and game shows providing background noise.

On this particular midmorning's soap opera, a rich young woman was trying to entice a much older man to leave a cocktail party with her. Everyone in the viewing audience knew the older man was her father's half-brother, except the rich young woman and me. She was full of joy, Jack Daniels, and jewelry and giggled all over the screen to my secret delight.

I had assumed Mama was bemoaning one of several unpaid bills with her previous call on the Lord. Or perhaps another bill was coming due. Maybe the amount of peas she had left to finish shelling had caused her to sigh. Strangely, Mama and Daddy kept their finances secret from me—like I was a criminal of some kind—yet she always spread the evidence all around, in those piles of envelopes, for anyone to see. For a brief moment, I thought I could help her with the peas, but that notion evaporated before it fully formed. I soon reasoned there was nothing wrong with the papers in front of her or her daily food prep. The annunciation of her pronunciation of the religious icon—the Lord—was probably the result of the depraved uncle on the television screen. She reacted with the sounds of the TV. It was clear that Mama was listening but not looking in that direction, something she often did.

A radio came on in the back of the house, an announcer blasting out the Georgia hog and grain reports.

"Turn dat down!" Mama shouted before I really registered the radio. I guess I was used to Daddy having it on in the morning. And as quickly as she said it, the announcer's voice went away.

Mama said, "He been retired from all that for ten years. I don't want to hear dat fuss in the mornin', do you?"

Now Mama was just looking at the screen door and, I suppose, wondering the same thing I was: *what good is it doing?* The screen itself had been patched many times, and the doorframe sagged, leaving a good two-inch dip along the top right corner. You had to literally pick up the right side to open or close the thing.

"I can't help it that my son loved you first," wafted a voice from the TV, and I gave a glance in that direction. The older man was pulling the young woman into a kiss as she resisted, but not really. Mama didn't want to see it, but she heard it.

Mama said, "Dat gives me goosebumps. He just a ol' dog. You know that's his niece and his son's first cousin on his side of the family?" Without waiting for an answer because she was talking to herself, she grimaced as though absorbed in the real lives of real people.

No. I didn't know.

Mama then reached under a stack of envelopes to grab a strategically placed fly swatter. She used her left hand. She hid swatter like that. She had me thinking if the flies couldn't see it, she had a better chance of getting them when they landed. She was a hefty, right-handed woman with sandy hair gone to gray and light skin almost gone to Caucasian. She also had the usual freckles and liver spots of a woman her age. In fact, she had all the maladies of other women in their seventies, including varicose veins and small moles that cropped up around her eyes. She wore a drab housecoat printed with pale squares of varying sizes and pale colors. While holding her busywork in her lap and removing her reading glasses with her free hand, she came down hard on a fly. She mumbled something about the screen door, but I didn't understand her.

I just had to smile. *She still sharp*, I thought. A handful of hulls dropped into the bag.

"Lordy," she said again. This time, it came as whisper. All in one motion, she let drop her glasses tethered to a cord looped around her neck, swiped a tissue from a box on the table, removed the evidence of her swatting accuracy, and replaced her glasses exactly as they had been. The tissue and smeared dead fly rested crumpled on the table. I couldn't help but beam with pride. No way did she just do that.

Then she stood up from her mail stacks, leaving her colander on the table, and turned a gas fire on under a black iron skillet. "I guess I better get your daddy's breakfast ready," she whispered again, this time to me.

She took a carton of eggs from what they still called the "icebox" and went to the sink, filled a dark pan full of water, and washed her hands under the same flow.

I heard Daddy rumbling about somewhere in the back of the house, probably near that radio. Just that quickly, my mind drifted to my parents' bedroom and how sacred a place it had been when I was growing up. It was always clean but dark and full of Mama's hats on the dresser and Daddy's shotguns and rifle placed barrel-up in the corner near his side of the bed. He was the protector of his home. I was forbidden to go in there when I was little, probably because of the guns. Now that I was a full-grown Federal agent, I still respected that threshold because that is just how much I respected my strict parents. My mind was wandering into that mysterious place of their bedroom when I heard my mother exclaim, "Lord! Don't be messin' wit' dat doe."

Suddenly, I was mentally back in the kitchen again. I guess she thought I was staring at the door the same as her. That door had been a frequent topic around our house since my semi-annual visits started five years earlier. Before then, I only came home on special occasions like Thanksgiving or Christmas. This time the visit was nothing special to them and in the middle of the week.

"I'll get somebody to replace it, Mama," I said.

Daddy was coming up the hallway carrying his brogans in one hand and a pair of grey tube-socks in the other. He was almost eighty but looked only fifty-five or so. He was slim built and sun roasted to an even brown. He had once been as tall as me, but the years had taken him down an inch or two and the sun had taken him a shade darker. A very slight stoop reduced him just a little more, to just under six feet.

Mama was cutting fatback into thick strips with a butcher knife. The fat was thick, hard, and all white. She strained to cut a last chunk to put in the pot of water, but she paid no attention to the effort because it was her routine, something she did almost every day.

"Can I help you wit' dat?" I asked, and Mama raised an eyebrow. I understood that look was most likely about the easy way I fell back into that old southern way of speaking that I grew up with. Mama never thought for one minuet to improve her dialect, but since I had gone to college, she expected better of me. But strangely, she let my lapses pass without a correction. I guessed she understood that the familiar food and familiar surroundings would inevitably bring about familiar language.

She almost grunted with her efforts on the fatback as she spoke. "No, I got it. Do you plan to see Mrs. Cora while you home?"

Mrs. Cora was the neighbor whose house was the mirror image of Mama and Daddy's. Her house sat slightly up a hill about a hundred yards up the dirt street, across a weedy field. We could see Mrs. Cora's kitchen door and side porch just like she could see ours. Both houses were built of cinder blocks. Hers was light beige, and ours light green.

Seeing breakfast wasn't ready, Daddy went back down the hallway again. I heard water running in the bathroom sink and I guessed he'd decided to shave. Soon a radio came back on to a country station, and the bathroom door closed, muffling a bluegrass tune. Mama shook her head but stayed quiet.

"We can't do this!" exclaimed the young woman on the TV, as she climbed out of the old man's bed, his hand holding her by the waist. His hair was thick, graying, and artificially perfect, and hers also maintained a flawless shape. But the off-color screen made her hair seem purplish blond with black roots.

I looked back towards the screen door again, this time thinking about Mrs. Cora. My mind had wondered up there to our neighbor's house again. I had thought on and off over the last day about something I had to do and how it involved Mrs. Cora, her son Mooney Jr. and Melissa her daughter. Mama's earlier question about visiting Mrs. Cora only made my thoughts more pressing.

When I was eleven, I had a crush on Mrs. Cora, and by the time I was twelve, I had a crush on Melissa, too. I was much too shy to follow up on my not-so-secret romances; however, on one summer evening when I was sixteen, Mrs. Cora trapped me in her bedroom, pulled me close against her, and kissed me on the lips. I still remember the feel of her tong sliding in my mouth.

"Now that's why you been looking at me all crazy lately, ain't it?' she asked.

"Ye-yes, ma'am," I stammered and immediately regretted using the "ma'am."

"I could use a young, strong man like you maybe when you get a little older." She kissed me again, this time deeper and longer. She whispered, "I been so lonely for a man since Clarence died."

She had me begging to get out of there before she let go, much like the young woman on the morning soap opera. I smiled considering I had missed my "Mrs. Robinson" moment. It's funny now, sitting in my Mama's kitchen, but not so much back then. She kissed me on the lips one last time, apologized, and made me promise never to tell. I was thinking, who would I tell? Who could I tell? My friends wouldn't believe me. She was lonely and told me so. She rubbed against me, and I cried to get out. Why would I tell that?

A pretty special and secret relationship grew out of that moment Mrs. Cora—not sexual or motherly—no, it was more like an older and wiser female friend giving womanly advice to a young boy in puberty. Yes, a bond was formed.

Melissa, on the other hand, let me chase her around the public swimming pool a couple of summers, but I never even got close. She was all legs back then, with a big Afro, perfect eggshell-skin and naturally, perfect teeth. She was much too fast for me, both figuratively and literally. She claimed girlfriend status with everybody but me at the time. But I got to hang around her because Mooney Jr.'s, or Juney as I called him, was her brother and my best friend.

"Mrs. Cora 's still up there," Mama said as though she was confirming a question in my mind. "She's just as crazy as ever. You keep looking and she's up there," Mama said again and smiled. Mama had lost some teeth on one side and was not wearing her bridge, but she was still a pretty woman to me.

"Melissa was home just yesterday or the day before. She's been home more regular, lately," Mama continued.

My mother and I could always talk, and with Daddy in the bathroom, with the music going and Mama on the topic of Mrs. Cora and Melissa, I had something I needed to say just to her.

"You know, Mama," I started. "I been havin' bad dreams about all that mess. I guess I been thinkin' about it too much."

My mother was not a diviner of dreams, but from the time I could talk, she had asked me about mine. She had always said that dreams were where our emotions came out into our thoughts. That's not how she said it but that's what she meant.

She asked, "Nightmares?"

"Yes and no. It feels like one, but I'm not frightened when I wake up, just cold and nervous."

Mama just looked at me, the yellow coming out in her brown eyes.

"I'm at Reidsville in the death chamber with Juney," I tell her. "And people are strapping him down in the electric chair. There's a sign over the chair that reads 'Old Sparky'. Juney is very black, almost as black as that skillet." I point at the stove. "You know the way some dark-skinned black people get when they die, after a few days? But he was very clean and shiny, like when you use to grease me up for church." Mama smiled, and so did I.

"Anyhow," I continued, "at first, Juney was all calm like he was waitin' to eat or somethin', and then all of a sudden, his head is shaved, and he is struggling to see who's behind him, strapping him down, but he can't turn around. No matter how he struggles, there are straps in place that keep him sitting there looking straight ahead. Then all of a sudden, he's looking back at me like eyes in the back of his head, but it's more like his face is on backwards. I see Mrs. Cora and Melissa over in the corner, but they are very small, almost like live Voodoo dolls. They look at me and start to beg, but I can't understand what they're saying, and I that's when I wake up."

Daddy emerged from the bathroom and rejoined the conversation but not the one Mama and I were having. He says, "Yo' mother won't even let me stop by Mrs. Cora's no mo'."

"You got no business stoppin' in to check on her or anybody else," Mama shot back, her eyes as sharp as her tongue. "We got cnough to keep you busy here."

"Well, I thought she might need a strong man around the house every now and then." It was obvious Daddy was just picking on Mama by then. He was smiling with his big tartar-stained teeth the whole time. Of course, I was thinking maybe Mrs. Cora had found her big, strong man after all, just not so young.

"She can get a man if she need one," said Mama. "She never had trouble doin' dat, even when Moony Sr. was alive. Bless his soul."

Clarence Moony was Mrs. Cora's late, common-law husband, and everybody called him "Moony Sr.," just as almost everyone called their son "Moony Jr.," almost everybody except me.

"She doesn't come out so much now that the date's been set." Daddy was done jousting with Mama. He was talking to me now, looking at the screen door from his seat at the table and sizing up the project with his eyes.

"What's the point in having a screen door if it doesn't keep the flies out, Daddy?" I said, half kidding. "Daddy, I'll be happy to have a new door put in."

"Don't you spend no money on no new doe'," he shot back. "And don't go gettin' smart."

I could tell he was serious.

The eggs were starting to fry, and Mama had cut off and grated a huge chunk of what everybody in that little town called "government cheese" to make cheese-eggs. She and her neighbors got the cheese from the local county Farm and Home office in Louisville, the county seat. Taking it didn't seem like welfare to them because everyone in town took it either firsthand or second, and I supposed some Wisconsin farmers were glad they did.

Mama said, "You been lookin' up there at Mrs. Cora's house all yesterday and now this morning. I thought maybe you wanted to go say hello to Melissa, but now I don't know." She wouldn't talk about my dream in front of Daddy. He would think it was silly and say so.

Daddy said, "That girl got a good job, you know. She workin' fer a big airline now. Still pretty, too, just like..."

Mama shot a look in his direction.

Melissa had gone off to Clark College in Atlanta, and I headed off to war in Vietnam after high school. She'd had one marriage and no kids, and I'd had two marriages and four kids. I had come home from Vietnam, joined the police force, and gone to school, all the time making my way through those bad marriages. My kids were teenagers now, and all of them stayed with my second ex-wife, Naomi. I had lost my first ex-wife to drug addiction and suicide. I usually brought at least one of my kids home to with me when I visited Mama and Daddy, but this was not the trip for that—besides school was in.

I shook my head at Daddy and laughed.

Mama said, "Like I said, you been looking up at that house. What's up?"

"I guess I have a letter to deliver."

Later that same morning, I sat in a straight-back chair in Mrs. Cora's kitchen looking down across the field at my dad examining the outside of his screen door as though it was his first time, and not his hundredth, seeing it. He looked up at the sagging corner and gently tested its steadiness. Watching the old man, I silently thought he was on a fool's errand, though I could never tell him that. It was his door, his house and, as I had been told many times growing up, his rules!

Mrs. Cora sat in a chair next to me, apparently looking out at some flowers next to her well-house. I could tell by her pointless conversation that she was probably considering the situation of her son Moony Jr. She had a pot cooking on the stove just like Mama, and her house smelled of boiling, fat meat, just like Mama's.

The beginning of summer was weeks away, but Georgia summers always started early, so a sticky humidity was already coming on. Mrs. Cora wore a pink, flowery duster with a light pink print apron holding it in at her waist. I still imagined her younger bosomed form, though it had long ago sagged to the reality of a sixty-something year-old woman with a fifty-something looking body. She had skin that black men called "yella" and big hips and a small waistline that men in this little South Georgia town still lusted after. And she sometimes encouraged them.

I said, "I bet there's more than a few rabbits in that field."

She said, "I bet there's more than a few rattlesnakes, too."

"Now that this is all city, I 'magine the snakes have move on a long time ago.

"If they rabbits, they snakes."

"If they rabbits, they screwing."

We both laughed.

"There's a neighborhood dog going to come by here and piss on my flowers in a few minutes. Would you do me a favor and kill it for me?" she calmly asked, as though talking about changing a light bulb. Her facial expression was frank but matter-of-fact.

I chose not to answer.

"Good of you to come by," she added. "This is a hard time, but I reckon you know that."

"Whose neighborhood dog?" I snapped the question showing some frustration before catching myself, and then comely added, "Yeah, Daddy told me they set the date for Juney."

As I said earlier, Juney and me grew up together and were best friends. His nickname was a mixture of Moony and Junior and is what I had called him since we were seven or eight years old. He hated it, but it stuck. Now most people who knew him well called him that, too. Mrs. Cora called him Juney, too, but only when she was expressing love or joy for him, and especially when she was pleased with him.

"There it is." She said, looking at an ungainly brown puppy with white spots sniffing her flowers. One front paw was white.

"You got your gun, don't you?" she asked, looking at me as I sat there in short pants, flipflops and a printed tee-shirt that read, "IT'S NOT URANUS; IT'S DJIBOUTI."

"Mrs. Cora, does it look like I have a gun on me?" I answered with some sarcasm. My use of her title was no longer a sign of a child's respect for a married woman; it was just what everybody in town called her.

"Moony Jr. said you was one of them undercover cops, so I figured you had your gun on all the time."

"That was a long time ago. And if I was undercover now, where do you think I would have it—the gun, I mean?"

"You don't want me to answer that," she said, laughing. "Well, I still got that shotgun Moony Sr. left back there. Bless his soul. You can just use dat or maybe I can use it. You can just show me how."

"Whose dog is that, anyway?" I asked again.

"Oh, he just hangs around here, eats there. Thinks it belongs here and there, just like Moony use to." I assumed she was talking about Moony Sr., but she could have also been referring to Juney.

"Well, I'm not killing it, and neither are you. What if you shoot down towards my house and hit my daddy or somebody?"

"Oh, they just like everybody else. They believe I'm crazy, so they would understand. Well, he's doing it," she said, this time exasperated, and running to the back door, which was actually on the side of the house.

"You git!" She yelled at the dog while flapping her apron up and down with both hands. The startled puppy ran away. She spat into the dirt yard and came back and took her seat.

"You want me to fix you some cheese-eggs?" she asked and then quickly added, "I guess your mama already did that?"

"Yeah. We had some and fatback. It's been a while since I ate like that."

"When did you get in, anyhow?" she asked. This was the country version of small talk and was expected even among old friends, but we were closer than old friends and I believe both she and I expected better than small talk.

"Yesterday morning."

"Gonna be a hot one. S'pose to rain, too," she said. Then she nervously moved directly from small talk to big talk, taking me by surprise. "You know, Juney's new lawyers told me the date set for about three weeks from now. He says no mo' appeals and he didn't want to get our hopes up wit' some kin' a pardon. I heard me an' Meliss can visit an' bring in a home-cooked meal or cook one there. I don't know which, but the sheriff s'pose t' be workin' dat out. But I don't think I'll be goin' over there." She said this with such conviction and such certainty that it made me confused as what she was trying to tell me. I wondered what she expected from me—saying that to me.

Juney and me had gone into the marines together and on to Vietnam together, but in separate units. Like I said, when I came back, I went into law enforcement and on to college, but Juney came home shot up in mind, body and spirit. He was a different person. I wasn't there to see it, but Mrs. Cora told Mama how Juney had changed.

On one of my trips home, Mama said, "You know, I

COP HOUSE STORIES: Seven Allegories

don't let Juney come by here no mo' 'cause Cora told me that the boy steal everything ain't locked down."

"What's up wit' Juney, Mama?" I had asked back then. I had tried to find him during several of my visits, but wherever I went, he had just left. Wherever he was supposed to be, he never showed up. I got his intentions loud and clear and just quit looking.

Mama hadn't answered my question about Juney, and all I could do was shake my head again and look back in my mind at our distant past. I guess that was contagious, because Mama did the same.

"He wasn't the same boy you played wit', ran wit', fought wit', ate wit', left home wit'. Mama had said. That time he spent in the army and going to Vietnam changed him,"

"It was the Marines, Mama," I insisted.

"Yeah, I know, but all that stuff just the army to us old people."

I had to let the topic drop.

"I know Juney is a disappointment to you, Mrs. Cora," I spoke from the lack of knowing what else to say, thinking about what Mama had told me. "But I heard he reformed in prison. He's a born-again Christian now, leads Bible study and all that stuff. I know he would appreciate your visit."

"Never said he was a disappointment!" she shot back. "I never told nobody that, but everybody believes it. I never got over what he did, and I hope that family can find forgiveness and peace, if they deserve it, and I told 'em that in a letter. But he my son, me an' Moony Sr. had him, and when they take him, he'll still be my son. I did my best, without his daddy around most of the time, but he wasn't no disappointment. He was on that stuff back then; it was that stuff, that stuff and that war that took my boy. He went to war just like you—got a Purple Heart and all kinda other medals. They back there in his draw somewhere. I use 'ta have 'em out, but then I couldn't stand to look at 'em no mo'. All you boys went to war, and he come back here, and …. Lord, I thought he was going to kill me one night, it was so bad. At one time, I even blamed you. You come back working and going to college. Your mama was sho' nuff proud of you, showing off your medals and pictures."

Mrs. Cora was staring out across the low weeds and the unseen rabbits and snakes, the good and the bad. The hot air was rising between our houses. She was staring at nothing in particular and, I'm sure, looking into her own mind.

"That's not it," she said to herself, and then she said to me, "He still my son and he didn't turn out like you. I love him, and I would go see 'im if I could. I would switch places wit' 'im if I could."

I could hear the frustration in her voice and see the beginning of tears taking birth in the corners of her dark-brown eyes.

"What you mean, 'If you could?' It looks like the hard part is done," I said, meaning the arrangements were already made for her to visit. "Sounds like all you have to do is cook a good meal and show up, be brave, and hold it together for 'im."

"Well," she started again, her tears now fully formed. "You don't know how hard ..." And there came a tapping on the front screen door, ending her thoughts and stopping any further words on the subject.

"That would be Pastor Jame," she said, almost whispering. Glancing at a clock on the stove-top, she stood, wiped her eyes with the tail of her apron, straightened he frame, and willed her composure back.

I thought she was mispronouncing the preacher's name the way country people do until she said to me in a whisper: "Why his family couldn't leave the s on that name, I don't know. An' he got the nerve to clear his throat like he annoyed when you use the s. The man clear his throat entirely too much irregardless, even in the middle of a sermon."

She proceeded to go to the front door.

I stayed in the kitchen, looking down to my parents' house. Daddy was still working on the screen door with both hands, trying to take it down, but he was also kicking at the same puppy that was agitating Mrs. Cora earlier. The animal was trying to sniff Daddy's leg.

"You get 'im, Dad," I whispered.

"How you doin' today, Sister Cora?" The pastor spoke to her, his baritone voice booming through the screen door, but he apparently caught a sense of lingering emotion. She opened the screen door and he craned his neck and walked on into the house uninvited, sensing someone else inside. I'm sure he wanted to see whomever it was, whether he knew them or not, and what they had done to upset Mrs. Cora. I couldn't blame him for that. He was a short, stout man, and very neat; with skin the color of French toast and freckles like cinnamon. He wore black pants and a gray-plaid, short-sleeve, dress shirt with a black belt and expensive black loafers. I thought his shoes were much too expensive for those of a country preacher, but I was prepared to not hold that against him. His deep voice revealed a rich, southern milieu. I don't know why, but I expected to see a huge gold or silver cross around his neck, and I felt strangely disappointed when it wasn't there. My unsure opinion of him was firming up to be more positive.

Before Mrs. Cora could answer his greeting, he stuck his head in the kitchen, waved to get my attention and asked, "Do I know you, young man?" He was older than me by at least fifteen years.

"No, sir," I said out of respect for his vocation, and moving to Mrs. Cora's side, "but you probably know my parents up the road." I nodded towards home, where Dad was throwing a piece of scrap lumber at the puppy. Fortunately, he missed the poor animal, and it went scurrying away.

"Oh yeah!" he said, turning his attention back to me, "I'm Pastor Jame."

"Pleasure to meet you, Pastor James." I just had to test it out. Mrs. Cora cornered me with a look and a smirk in my direction.

He coughed, "That's Jame, young man. There's no s."

"Oh," I said, smiling at Mrs. Cora. "I didn't catch that."

"Well, whatever," he said and then cleared his throat again.

"I just stopped by to pray with you a few minutes," he continued, looking at Mrs. Cora.

She glanced at me. "Well, I appreciate it, but I'm a little tie up right now."

I said, "I can come back later. That's no problem. I kinda wanted to see Melissa, anyway."

"She won't be back until the day after tomorrow or Friday. Will you be around that long?" Mrs. Cora asked me. "She's working a flight to Mexico or somewhere and back. But you stay; I can see the good pastor another time."

"Well," the good pastor said thoughtfully, rubbing his chin. "You must be that FBI man that everybody around here talks about from time to time?"

"No," I answered. "Everybody says that, but I'm a postal inspector."

"Ain't that the same thing? You federal, and you arrest people, right?" He smiled.

"Not really, but whatever …" I coughed then.

He said, "Well, maybe I'll see you later today then, Sister Cora."

"If looks could kill, I would be six feet under in that graveyard over there," I said to Mrs. Cora after he left, pointing to the neighborhood church, Mrs. Cora's church, and its adjacent burial ground. The church and cemetery were a block away, but actually just across the street on the far side of the block from Mrs. Cora's house. The headstones looked disarranged and out of place like gray, crooked teeth, but in perfect symmetry with the small, slightly crooked, whitish-gray church.

She smiled, "I'm glad you were here." She opened the door again and went out on her front porch, holding the screen open for me. Not knowing what else to do, I walked out behind her. I was deciding whether to deliver my letter then or not. We sat in rusted, metal porch chairs that had seen too many days in the sun and rain; the remnants of pastel crème green and white were still fighting through. The chairs rocked easy with the bending of the metal.

Mrs. Cora spat into the front yard and sat back.

"That church is where I grew up. My mama and daddy's house set right there where the church is now, and I use to play all over that area. Everybody called this the quarters then—the black section with Daddy's little farm in the middle of it. That was before you was born. They donated the land for that church, and they left me this little plot. They buried right over there." She pointed towards several headstones against a backdrop of sparse pine trees, but I didn't know exactly where she was pointing or which graves she meant. I suspected Moony Sr. was near them but I had also forgotten where he was buried.

"My son's gonna be buried in the back corner over there next to Bobby's little gin joint." She pointed again to a different place I couldn't see but of course everybody knew about Bobby's joint was located. It was a bucket of blood that had served this community for over fifty years, and it seemed to stand against storms and progress.

"That's a shame." She shook her head while talking. "A mother knowing the exact day her son is going to die and where he's going to be buried—no parent should have to know all that," she said, more to the dirt ground in front of her than to me. "Anyhow, he should be put next to Moony Sr. He wasn't much of a husband, but he was a good daddy to Moony Jr." Then she hastily whispered with a bit of remorse in her face, "Maybe I wasn't much of the wife.

"My daddy told me that that church started meetin' in their house, and now my son is gonna be buried in the back corner next to a juke joint, they tell me. Yeah. I'm glad you was here when Pastor Jame come by. It's not him, though. Just a couple other people who don't want a killer buried over there. Said it might become a shrine or somethin', and I'm thinkin' a shrine to who, to what? It was fine when he was really killin' over in Vietnam. They give him medals for that killin'. Other killin' veterans buried over there, some wit' honors."

She unconsciously waved a fly from her face. A cooling breeze, that felt so good, came across the porch just then and I wanted to believe it was the slight movement of her hand that made it so. Her hand had somehow brought a wave of coolness on the sticky air. I was considering how a breath of air that started somewhere near the Arctic Circle could work its way through thousands of cities and small towns and finally blow cool, just for seconds, across Mrs. Cora's front porch at that precise moment, with a wave of her hand.

"We never went there." I said, looking over at the little church and speaking my thoughts, but it was something Mrs. Cora already knew. "At least not regular. You remember Juney and me showed up a time or two on those special days when we knew the girls would be out there. And me and Mama and Daddy went there one other time when Moony Sr. was buried, and I think Mama and Daddy went when your big mama was funeralized."

"Yeah, I remember."

"Other than that, I don't remember Mama or Daddy ever going," I added, awkwardly. "Unless it was after I left. You know we always went to Flat Rock."

I paused and then asked, "Why did you say you were glad I was here when your pastor come by? Did you think you would unload on him?"

She was crying agin. "I know what he wants, and I can't do what he wants right now. That bunch of busybodies!"

"What you talking about? What did he want, if you don't mind my asking?" Which, I believe was the point of her starting this conversation with me.

She repeated, "I was born in a house that sat where the church is now. I went to school at the old colored school that use to be at the end of Johnson Street, and I go to the Bobby's IGA grocery store at the other end of

Johnson Street. My doctor, Dr. Willis, is downtown, just two blocks from the post office. I clean four houses to make a livin', an' all them houses is within two miles of here. I walk just 'bout everywhere I go. Before that, I was a teacher's aide at the elementary school, just four blocks from here, but I had to quit that 'cause I… I couldn't do field trips. Beyond that, I don't have a reason to go nowhere else."

"Just curious, why couldn't you go on field trips?" I asked, but she sighed and ignore my question.

"Yeah. So what? Lot people stay right here," I said after waiting a silent moment.

"Pastor Jame wants to see me about going to see Juney, maybe cooking for him"

"Is that a bad thing—to see your son? Juney would probably like to see you."

"They want me t' cook for him his last night, his last supper. Pastor and the sheriff fixed it with the prison and the State. I mean, it won't really be his last night, but it would be the last night he can have a family visit. I could cook it at the prison kitchen or maybe bring it in. But I just can't do that."

"What do you mean, you can't do that? You keep saying that like it's a fact. You can't do what? You just said you loved your son. Why can't you cook him a good meal? This is a rare opportunity. Have you talked to Juney about this?"

"Yeah, we talk once a month on the first Tuesday for thirty minutes. That's how I know Pastor and the

Sheriff set up this meal for 'im. He wants me to do it, but I can't, and I can't tell 'im why."

"You know Juney didn't really kill nobody," I said. "I mean, not before he got to prison. He was just with the two boys that did the killing. He was with Cricket and Stanley, and Stanley did the killing. You do know that's right? Juney waited in the car, but the other two killed that man, and Juney went to prison just the same because that's the law. And then, well, Juney did what he had to do in prison to survive. So, there's no reason for you to feel that way."

"You have no idea how I feel or what you talkin' about!" she raised her voice for the first time, then caught herself. "I ain't standing up for Juney, and I ain't excusing Juney. He knew when he did grown man's robbin' and killin', in the car or not, he was gonna have to pay a grown man's price if he got caught. He knew better. I know everything that happened. The sheriff stopped by and told me when it happened. The old sheriff, not that thang da' got now!"

"Who? Holly?"

Mrs. Cora got quiet then. She took the tail of her apron, waded it up, and wiped her tears again. It was strange because I could see the lines of hard work on her hands I hadn't noticed before. My view of her was changing from the woman of my crush to the woman of her reality.

"I got a problem!" Mrs. Cora continued. She blurted this out like I would instantly know what she was talking about, or that what she was talking about should be obvious to me.

"And what's that?" I asked, calmly. "What's the big problem that you can't go see Juney?"

"I went to the library and looked it up 'cause I know it ain't natural. But there it is."

"What do you mean? What is it you have that means you can't go see Juney? Is what you have contagious or something? That don't seem reasonable to me." I said this before thinking. Naturally I was just being a smartass.

"I can't leave here. I have to stay right here in this little red dirt town. If I leave, I'll die. I know it. And then what good can I do fo' Juney? They gonna call off his execution so he can attend my funeral?" Now she was being the smartass.

I had to regroup. "So, you have this phobia or whatever, and because of that, you can't go see Juney? That just doesn't make sense to me but... Does he know this?"

"Yeah, that's the word, phobia. No, and it won't make him a bit of difference. Just like this town—if I tell anybody in this town about it—I really will be called the crazy mother of that crazy killer. But if I don't go, they'll just call me that crazy mother, you know, that didn't want to see her son."

"You rationalizing. Is this phobia stuff or what?"

"Yeah, that's what people do to get by this kind 'a stuff," she said. "It's within my right to rat-iona-lize. If they just think I'm mean, or don't care, or crazy, then they leave me alone. But if they know I'm crazy, they gonna try and run me out 'a here. But I can't leave, so I'll just take the first option, door number one, and just let 'em believe I'm crazy or mean or both. I'll be that mean old lady, that don't care about her son, that they call crazy. She didn't even want to visit her son in prison before he's executed. So, I can't tell the pastor and them busybodies. I know what they think. And now, you can't tell 'em either.

"That phobia stuff, as you call it, is real to me, and it means I can't leave here. I looked it up when Meliss tried to take me shopping once, and I had to get out of the car before she could even get by the water processing plant. I told her I was carsick, but I never got back in her car again, and that was twenty years ago. The encyclopedia said it was *Ho-do-pho-bia*, a unreasonable fear of travelin' someplace new. But to me it ain't unreasonable, it's real. I start to sweat, and I can't breathe if I even think hard about getting' outta this town. I don't know how to explain it." She was sounding frustrated but continued, "Do you remember when you and Juney was bout twelve and yawl was playing down by the water treatment plant, an' it got dark before you knowed it? Me and yo' mama went out looking and found you down there scared to walk by the plant. The bullfrogs was so loud Juney claimed they was aliens? Yawl never went back down there, did you?"

"I still don't go down there," I said, seeing the opportunity to inject some levity.

"So, you see what might seem strange to me and yo' mama was perfectly understandable to you and Juney."

"I get your point, I guess." I said, knowing she had

given me real insight.

"What about Meliss, does she know by now? I mean, you got to tell her, right?"

"No, I don't. All I got to do is stay black and in my few little blocks from here. All I got to do is be suspected of being crazy, know who sayin' what about me, and not confirm that shit to the whole world. That's all I got to do! See, right now, I'm just the mother of a killer and he 'bout to be put to death. But if word gets out that I got this other thing, then the TV people'll be down here in front of the house wantin' me to talk crazy for them 'cause that makes good TV. You know that stuff!"

Then things got quiet, by country standards. We got quiet. We could hear the breeze in the treetops. That neighborhood dog was barking in the distance. Other dogs barked too. And my daddy was hammering on that screen door. We looked towards my parents' house and saw Daddy had taken down the door and had it laying across a couple of makeshift sawhorses out in the yard.

I smiled. "He's fixed that door a hundred times, and if it's right when he puts it back up, it'll be back sagging again in a day," I said. "What do they call that? Doing the same ol' thing over and over and expecting different results? Means you're crazy, right? Everybody's a little crazy. I don't know about this phobia you got, but what happens if your doctor moves or if the new Wal-Mart that's coming finally puts the grocery store, or the whole town, out of business? Eventually you'll have to go farther than a few blocks or a couple of miles. What then?"

"You know I was good in school." She appeared to be talking to the pine trees standing firm at the edge of her yard and then to the gravestones across the red-clay street. "My grades made me number two, and I had a full scholarship offer to Tux College—*Tux College*, but I gave it up. I dreamed of finishing Tux nursing school back then and maybe even going on to medical school in a couple of years to be a real doctor. Now... well now I have to pretend not to be above my station while I clean a doctor's house and struggle to keep his hands off me. Oh, he don't mean no harm and he wouldn't know what to do with me even if he had me, but it still irks the hell outta me. I headed off to school with my daddy, and I was scared, but I just thought it was, you know, leaving home for the first time. By the time I got towards the edge of town, I was in a panic and 'bout to jump outta the car. I passed out and woke up back home on the couch with Mama and Daddy looking down on me. They never really ever said a word about it, and I never tried to go to school again, or anywhere else, for that matter. I'm sure they knew something was wrong, but they wouldn't 've known where to start to get me help."

As I looked down to my parents' house again, Daddy was holding the door upright and planning how to finish his work. The screen was still in patches, but once he secured it back in the frame, his work would be done until the next time.

"Guess I better go and help Daddy put that door back up," I said into the breeze. "I'll stop back by if Meliss makes it back. I be here till Friday at least." The morning had passed into the afternoon.

We both stood and I was feeling what a coward I had been by not doing what I needed to do or saying what I needed to say. But then I noticed two dark figures crossing the road in front of my house and heading towards Daddy. I could see them only in silhouette. They appeared to be dressed the same and walked one behind the other with their heads down and arms folded behind their backs, as though they were monks going to prayer. Without realizing it, I sat back down as I watched. Apparently, a wave of confusion passed over my forehead and I pursed my lips.

Mrs. Cora said, "You know them two. That's them twins. You know, the go-n-tell-it-sisters, Stacy and Lacy. I'll tell Melissa you come by."

"You need to tell Melissa more than that."

Mrs. Cora looked at the ground. "Yeah, I know," and then she stood and added, "excuse me."

There was thunder in the distance, and clouds were rolling in between us and a pale blue heavenly sky.

I heard Mrs. Cora's screen door slam, and moments later a record-player echoed through the house from rooms away. A male's soulful voice was singing, "A change is gonna come." I cannot truly express the feeling that fell upon that house and me at that moment. The heat became buoyant, and the distant thunderstorm welcome. Each word of the singer hypnotized me. I admit I wanted to go in that house and throw a sixty-something-year-old woman over her bed. The breeze and sounds became the music of cooling sweat that had formed in the crooks of my neck and elbows. I started to stand up and act on this acute feeling but closed my eyes and sat—no lay—back in the steel chair. I was considering: if God created a heaven better than this, I would not find it in this life.

"It's afternoon. You want a beer?" I heard Mrs. Cora say from what sounded like another life—another time and place—maybe like 1965, when I played with Juney and we were both just teenage boys. Sometimes we raided Mrs. Cora's refrigerator for Budweiser's, knowing we would get in trouble, but she wouldn't tell my mama. We were exploring our notions of adulthood.

"Yeah. I'll take one. Daddy and that door can wait," I said, thinking I was only putting off something I knew I had to do, something I knew I had to tell. My message was no secret confession of love or passion, but it was intimate to both Mrs. Cora and Melissa.

By then, I could see the twins were talking with Daddy, and I remembered those two from school, when Juney and me ran these streets and country roads together. They were two years behind us, and I hadn't seen the twins in twenty or more years, but I laughed, and Mrs. Cora saw me.

"What's so funny?" she asked. "You remembering that ass-beating them twins gave you an' Juney when yawl trash-talked 'em about whatever it was?"

"Yeah, I was thinking about that, but I don't quite remember it the way you do. I do remember when me and

Juney tangled wit' Stacy."

I had forgotten the twins and their real names until Mrs. Cora mentioned them. I remembered Juney had said, "Lacy must've been born first because she was always a little ahead of Stacy when they walked, and Lacy always talked first when they said something." And Juney was right about how they stood and how they talked. They got their nicknames, "the-go-n-tell-it-sisters," for obvious reasons. In school, they told everything, and, I guess because they tattled on their classmates so much, the two had to know how to fight.

Several records had dropped, and the music had changed to blues songs by the time the twins got to Mrs. Cora's porch. The singer was a woman by then, and the lyrics were in cadences of moans and words of "Crazy Blues." I felt something cold touch my arm, and there was Mrs. Cora leaning from her chair and offering me another beer. I nodded in gratitude.

"How you ladies doing today?" Mrs. Cora said to the twins.

"We good," Lacy stood on the first step of Mrs. Cora's porch. "We would be better wit' come cold water or a beer."

"Yeah!" exclaimed Stacy, nodding her head from her usual position, behind. "It's hot as a bear out here today!"

"Well, them dark clothes ain't helpin'," said Mrs. Cora.

The sisters had changed since we were in school. Lacy was still dark cream coffee, but it looked like someone had taken a charcoal marker and drawn dark splotches around her eyes. Both women were heavier, and that was to be expected, so was I. However, Stacy looked the same from the waist up but had enormous hips that didn't match her normal-size top. It seemed weird, because in school, they had been very shapely, with strong, athletic legs. I remembered that we had gotten into the fight with them because Juney called Stacey "horse legs." That was the only name he could think to call her, and of course, everybody in high school had to have a nickname. He was being rude because he liked her.

"What you ladies got for me today?" Mrs. Cora asked, getting down to business and not moving to get the water or beers.

They both looked at me the way a pair of black Siamese cats might look at a bird—as though with one brain. They didn't smile but blinked in a creepy, synchronized motion.

Mrs. Cora nodded in my direction and said, "He al' right. You know him, anyway."

Stacy said, "Yeah we know him. We beat his ass in ninth grade."

I smiled. "That was the tenth grade," I said. Then Lacy gave a shy smile. That made me think about how they had also screwed Juney and me silly one night in the twelfth grade after a football game. We had a parking place out behind the trash ditch. *I bet you won't tell that,* I thought.

Lacy turned her attention back to Mrs. Cora but kept her eyes on me. "Mrs. Taylor said yo' son finally gonna die far that stuff he did, but she pray he still go to heaven." Then I could have sworn she winked at me.

Stacy, looking at Lacy, said, "And you said to Mrs. Taylor, 'What did he ever do to get to heaven?'" Stacy laughed, and then, remembering she was talking to Mrs. Cora and tattling on own her own sister. Stacy put her hand over her mouth as though to stop a vomit but stifled a smile.

That was the way of Lacy and Stacy. They had a reputation of telling everything, even on themselves.

Mrs. Cora just reached in her apron pocket and started to hand over a folded bill. It looked like a five or a ten, but I couldn't really tell.

"Anything else?" Mrs. Cora asked with a gesture before letting go of the money.

"No," said Stacy, "But we'll be at the grocery store and two churches this week, so we'll have more next week. What about that cold water?"

"Then good day, ladies. My refrigerator is broke down. The hose is over there for your water, though."

They let the hose run to make sure the water was cool, if not cold, and took turns bending over and gulping, while trying to keep the overflow from splashing their shoes.

Their eyes started to show the signs of where they would go next, but before they left, Stacy looked straight at me and said, "Your daddy said he don't know why you sniffin' around up here. Melissa still too fast for you."

Then Lacy added, "He said you gonna kill that dog

that's been around here, too. And that information is for free."

As they walked away, I thought of the days I had chased Melissa around the pool without ever catching her. I realized the twins were right, she was—no is—too fast for me. But that was the furthest thing from my mind. I smiled, because I also remembered that me and Juney had caught them sisters so many years ago.

I said, "What was that money about?"

"Didn't you know?" said Mrs. Cora, "Them two is the biggest and best snitches in the quarters. They better than the newspaper. I treat 'em like snitches, too. I give 'em about ten dollars a month, and they tell me all the news I want to know 'bout. Hmm! They reliable, too! Anytime somebody say something about me, Juney, or Meliss, I get it straight out. They tell everything and they don't lie. Kinda lets me know where I stand wit' folks."

"What you know about snitches?" I laughed.

"Baretta!" she said with emphasis. "Him and that parrot get all the info from the one young, black snitch. He fine, too. I think maybe the snitch should be the police and cut out the middleman." She laughed, and her brown eyes came back to life then.

"So why would anybody tell them anything? I mean, anybody that knows them?" I asked. I paused to consider her equation, then added, "I work with snitches all the time. They can be some of the most loathsome creatures in this world, and I wouldn't trust them if I were you."

"You would be surprised how it works. Just like your

daddy knew they would probably tell you what he said, but now he don't have to say it directly to you. So, some people just like to talk, and they stop by and talk. But some other folks want to pass along information without looking like they're gossipin' or somethin'. You know, so that's how they do it. People say they loanin' them money or just givin' them a few dollars to help 'em get by, but it's all about information."

Then conditions in the atmosphere became still. I could hear no sounds—no birds in the distance or crickets close by or other insects that were usually loud in the afternoon. The sound of a tractor in some faraway field, probably at the edge of town, broke the quiet first. I was wondering if Stacy or Lacy had told my father about that double date they had once gone on with Juney and me. I smiled.

Mrs. Cora rose up in her chair. "Gonna be a thunderstorm, looks like," she said into the pregnant air. "When it gets quiet like this, gonna be a big one." There came a faint rumble of distant thunder.

"That's it for me," Mrs. Cora said to me and to the man in the background music playing a guitar and singing: "He's just a man who plays the blues."

We sat there not speaking through that song and the next. Then, a yellow convertible, with the top down, followed by a trail of red dust, pulled off the dirt street into Mrs. Cora's yard. The driver, a beautiful, golden-brown, woman with a big Afro, hoop earrings, and large sunglasses, raised her glasses, squinted, smiled, and waved to her mother and me.

"Meliss," her mother exclaimed, "I thought you was gone to Mexico!"

"My plane never got off the ground because of bad weather in Texas. I ran out of hours—can only work fifteen on that run—so I asked for a day off and came back home." She smiled directly at me, pushed the button to put up the top on her car, and asked, "What are you doing home? Everything all right with your mom and dad?"

"Yeah. Just checking on 'em. Me and your mom was just enjoying the day."

"So, I just heard that you been sniffing around after me," Melissa laughed. "The twins didn't tell me you were here, though. But I wondered why they wanted to flag me down and 'borrow' five dollars. Don't worry about it. I know what your daddy meant, and I am too fast for you."

"You think so, huh? I was wondering why that storm was coming so fast. You brought it with you!"

"Well, maybe. You were a little slow when you was chasing me around the pool, growing up. Anyway, how them kids of yours doing? They come with you?"

"Naw, they in school, so I just ran down by myself."

"Did you fly? I don't see no car up there."

"Yeah. I had to make a quick trip. Be going back day after tomorrow—maybe Thursday or Friday."

Melissa's thoughts seem to fade from summers so many years ago and move to today and her worries. She went over and kissed her mother on the cheek. Mrs. Cora teared up once again, stood, and walked back into the house. The blues music stopped and was immediately followed by a gospel song. This time it was a loud and brash woman's voice singing Alto about the troubles of the world:

>Soon it will be done
>Trouble of the world
>Trouble of the world
>Trouble of the world

Melissa, making sure she could be heard, yelled out, "Oh, Mama!" Her voice showed exasperation with the mood her mother was setting.

I whispered to Melissa, "Your mother is holding up well. Better than I could."

"So, you know about Juney then?"

"Yeah, 'bout three weeks, huh?"

"You know Mama won't go and cook for 'im. She say why?"

"Naw, but I suspect it's her disappointment in him. He's my brother, but he was always a pill, especially after he got back from Nam. He went out that same night after they killed that guy in the store, and he was in a bad mood. He'd been that way all afternoon. I just happened to be home that day, and Mama caught him in the back room playing that game with a gun. The one you see on TV."

"What game?" I interrupted, already knowing the answer.

"You know," she continued. "The one where you point a pistol at your head and pull the trigger. He did that in front of Mama; then he pointed it at her and pulled the trigger again. Well, my kind, little mama beat on him till he got out the door. Told 'im he'd better never come back in here."

Melissa looked out across the road, then towards the church, but really at nothing in particular—just like her mother had. She wiped her eyes and nose on her wrist.

"Well," I said, "don't be so hard on your mom. Talk to her, and she may just surprise you."

"Oh, I don't think she'll surprise me, but I might surprise her. I know Mama's got a problem riding in cars. She gets sick. But I believe if we maybe take a bus or something like that—ride in something big—she might be alright."

"Well, talk to her about it," I said, getting up. "I've got to go down and help Daddy with that door he's been working on."

"You going to stop back?" she asked. "Tell you mama and daddy that fast Melissa said hello."

"Yeah, right!" We both laughed.

"You leavin'? We havin' po'k chops." Mrs. Cora's voice boomed from the kitchen.

"Yeah, I got to go. Mama is cooking, too—think it's fried chicken. But I might be back, if that's okay."

Melissa gave a shy, mischievous, smile and quietly said, "It's okay."

Mrs. Cora came to the door then to see me off and said, "I hope you kill that dog." She smiled and turned to go back in the house.

But before her back was turned, a big, white four-door car with a whip antenna on the back bumper glided into the yard as though appearing from the dust it brought with it—red dust and a cloud of red wind. Everyone in town knew this was the sheriff's car though it was plain and had no markings that identified it as a police car. Strangely, Pastor Jame was sitting on the passenger side in the front seat. Expectantly, sheriff Ed Holly was driving.

It was clear that the thunderstorm would start any minute. I had stepped to the ground and made up my mind to make that long dash back to my house when Melissa looked at me and silently mouthed the words, *"Don't go."*

I replied to Mrs. Cora's comment. "And I hope you tell the go-n-tell-it twins sisters what you need to tell 'em before I do it."

Melissa gave me a puzzled look, confused from knowing she had missed an earlier conversation.

I stepped back up onto Mrs. Cora's front porch, looked down towards home, and saw Mama and Daddy standing on their side porch, backlit from the kitchen light, looking in my direction, which was to be expected with the sheriff's car just feet away from me. I realized the cloudy sky had darkened the day.

No doubt Mama and Daddy were wondering, just like everybody else in sight, what the high and mighty Sheriff Holly, himself, was doing in the quarters when it wasn't even election time. Election week was the only time he came into any of the black sections of our county unless it was to make an arrest. More darkness was coming with the storm. But I noted the time was also late and I wandered where the time had gone.

Ed Holly was a big specimen of a Caucasian male. He had sun-freckled skin, tobacco-stained teeth, and stains from the tobacco juice on his chest. An ivory-handled, nickel-plated, forty-five revolver hung on his hip. This seemed odd because his hips appeared too slim to support his massive belly, though they did.

I remembered my daddy once telling me as clear as a bell, "Colored people in the quarters don't believe a black gun can kill ya. These folks still live in old times." He shook his head in disgust. "Here it is the eighties, and these people still don't believe a gun without a hammer can kill you." Daddy was talking about a semi-automatic pistol. Of course, this is the same man that didn't believe men had walked on the moon.

Holly was the embodiment of those who perpetuated these beliefs. That's why he carried that revolver knowing that belief about a gun's hammer would make his job easier. The fact he had killed his share of men, both African American and Anglo, and one African American woman, reinforced the fear in the community. He would let anyone, who dared to ask, know that his nickel revolver always brought death. And personally, I thought he even smelled like death cooked down and warmed over, along with tobacco, onions, and baloney, even in high school.

He'd been a bully in high school, and we'd had our share of run-ins. Unlike Juney and me, he was always too heavy to get into the military, but his daddy got him a job as a prison guard at the county work camp. That was where his life of death and destruction actually began. We heard that two prisoners died under his care in seventy-one. This occasioned his move over to the sheriff's office, first as a dispatcher then a road deputy. He finally won an election as the High Sheriff after his father died.

I had not talked to Holly since Juney and I went off to the marines, though I had seen him around on one or two occasions. Now here he was, squeezing out of the front seat of his sheriff's car, white cowboy hat and all. My mind went to all those days we had squared off under the bleachers in the ninth and tenth grades.

Holly un-hunched his large frame after he got out. He gave everyone on the porch a brief glance up and down but showed no recognition of me or anyone else accept Mrs. Cora, to whom he smiled and tipped his hat. I guess he figured he was the only one of any consequence because everyone always greeted him first, at least everyone in the quarters. But not me.

Just as I was forming a thought on this perception, a voice on my left said, "Hi, Sheriff, Pastor Jame!" Mrs. Cora nodded as she spoke, giving confirmation to my unformed thought.

As I was about to sit back down, Holly lifted his sunglasses with his left hand and quickly drew his pistol with his right. He swung the pistol toward me, then on past me, in one quick motion. The crack of an igniting bullet and the sudden smell of fresh smoke and powder hung on the stirring breeze for a few seconds that seemed like minutes. I stumbled back over my chair as anger caught me off guard. I had heard the bullet whiz by my head and land near the well, and then came a dog's yelp.

The sheriff re-holstered the pistol, pulled a red bandana from his back pocket, and cleaned his sunglasses while looking at me. "Been tryin' t' kill that dog for a week. It's been all over town. Thought I had 'im then," he said.

He removed his hat and held it high in the air as he casually turned all the way around, waving it at the angry sky as though he had just ridden a killer bull at the rodeo.

"Don't think me foolish, Cora," he said. "Whenever I come in the quarters, people are always watching whether I see 'em or not. They spectin' a show. Hot damn, I giv' 'em one. Feels almost like it's election time."

"Well, don't be given' no show at this house," Mrs. Cora snapped in frustration.

Holly laughed and looked at me again. "You Moony's good friend, ain't you, from down the street there? I recon we went at it a time or two in school, didn't we? Had you in my sights there for a second with my pistol, didn't I?"

"Y-yeah." My voice unintentionally cracked, still rebounding from the shot he'd just taken. This also confirmed he knew good and well where he had pointed his revolver.

Holly grinned.

"Wha-what the hell you think you doin', Fat Boy?" I said, reverting to the crudest name the kids had for him in high school.

Before Holly could speak, Pastor Jame said, "Now! Now! Gentlemen, no cause for guns and name-calling." The pastor had added a navy-blue sports jacket with brass buttons to what he'd been wearing earlier. I supposed he was dressing for the sheriff.

"People been on me for the last week to kill that dog, an' I almos' had 'im this time," Holly said, still jovial.

I was sure he meant Anglo people because nothing else would have brought his personal actions to a dog problem.

I know he had heard me call him Fat Boy, and he had chosen to ignore this insult to him and his office. I found this incredibly funny and started to laugh out loud. "I thought you were shootin' at me for a minute Fat... I mean, Holly."

He opened his mouth to reply, but just as he did, the sky gave up water in big droplets and, sudden, heavy showers in waves. Mrs. Cora invited everyone out of the rain and into the house.

In my mama's house, a picture of Jesus—eyes turned upward in prayer—hung in the living room over a bookcase, as sort of an altar. The family Bible, open to the Ten Commandments, was on top. The picture was laminated and varnished onto an oblong cross-section of a two-inch thickness of southern pinewood, bark and all. It had hung there since I could remember. It was a place of honor in our house. The companion to it was the picture The Last Supper, made in the same fashion. It hung over the dining room table along the window wall.

In Mrs. Cora's house, the same likenesses appeared in reverse order: The Last Supper in the living room, and Jesus praying in the kitchen next to the dining-room table. I was thinking about the position of the pictures—just a random thought—when I noticed Holly had taken a seat at the head of the dinner table just under the picture of Jesus. For some reason, I became incensed that Holly would even consider he belonged in a seat of honor in any house but his own, but my respect for Mrs. Cora kept my bottom lip pinned shut. It took some effort. I guess Pastor Jame saw my inner struggle, though I doubt he recognized the cause. He leapt into the conversation with Mrs. Cora.

"Me and the sheriff is got some good news for ya," he told her.

But Mrs. Cora wasn't having it. She seemed to think for half a beat before she asked, "Yawl staying for dinner?" Obviously, she wanted to keep the topic off Juney.

"What yawl havin'?" Holly spoke up before Jame could offer the polite "no thanks" perched on his moist lips.

Thunder clattered outside, and lighting lit darkening sky all around the house and neighborhood in flickers. Mrs. Cora said, "Good, then. We havin' po'k chops, and I think I got a jar of applesauce."

I suspected the grease was already hot, because soon the smell of fried, flour-battered pork wafted through the house. Mrs. Cora moved among her visitors as we inhabited her combination sitting room, dining room, and kitchen. It was then I reacquainted myself with the small picture of Mrs. Cora's great-grandmother occupying a spot next to Jesus. Unframed, the paper image was merely pinned to the wall, and the bottom curled upward. It had always been there, but it was like I was noticing it afresh. Meliss had told me the picture was a copy from a museum collection held by a family near Macon, Georgia. This young woman, her grandmother, had be the property of this family.

In high school, any depictions of my unknown ancestors intentionally showed a defeated people under the yoke of colonial and antebellum slave master. But the picture on Mrs. Cora's wall showed a woman in astounding dimension and stature. I learned from one of my college instructors, Professor Eric Grayson, that there were few, if any, pictures of enslaved people showing any dignity. Grayson was a short black man, light in complexion with a narrow face and rat-like green eyes. He said, "It's because portraying enslaved people as anything but work animals defeated the justification for treating them like animals. There were few exceptions. Wealthy owners included slaves in their photographs as decorations and status symbols. You know, to show they owned other people."

The picture on Mrs. Cora's wall showed a smiling, young black woman, maybe twenty years old, balancing a bundle of some sort on her scarfed head. She was tall, apparently strong, and even regal.

Melissa had said, "My aunt got a copy of the picture from a genealogy place in Savannah, and they copied it from the Shine Family Archives. I've not seen it, but there is supposedly a picture just like this in the Shine Museum."

As Mrs. Cora moved around the room preparing the supper, I clearly saw her great-grandmother's waistline, hips, lips, and brow reflected in her. Mrs. Cora's features, of course, were modified with European and even Native American touches, and she had brown skin with a yellowish tinge, the result of interethnic relations in her bloodline. Even if you pushed the term voluntary to mean submitting to one's owners by the women in her bloodline, you still came up with a perverse power dynamic. Mrs. Cora had the same looks as her great-grandmother, but there was something missing in the modern-day woman—perhaps the grandness and dignity of the African people I had seen in the magazine photos of the Congo's Bantu people. Even after the colonial Belgians had ravaged them, they were a people of great strength. Maybe it was their knowing they were survivors and would be there long after their oppressors were gone.

Just like that, I knew what it was. Mrs. Cora's ancestor was smiling in the photo. The young woman was outside, perhaps in a garden, but she was smiling. That's what was off, despite the generational resemblances. Mrs. Cora herself had not smiled since the sheriff had arrived. The grace to smile for a photo taken by your oppressor, and maybe rapist—and to mean that smile because there is still joy in your soul—is exceptional. Yes, Mrs. Cora had told me that her great-grandmother had come directly from Africa at twelve years of age—before the Civil War—and had been owned by a wealthy, Jewish mill owner near

Savannah. He used her as a nanny, housemaid, cook, and caretaker of his family's vegetable garden.

I was considering the power dynamic behind women being owned by men, even men who considered themselves good, when I heard Holly ask, "What you lookin' at me like that fa'?"

I had not realized it, but I was no longer looking at the picture but through Holly and into another life. Now he brought me back to this one.

"Nothing," I said, but I doubted Holly caught my true meaning that I was referring to him.

Pastor Jame, catching my meaning, cleared his throat.

Mrs. Cora had finished dressing the table and sat down at its foot. Holly was still seated at the head, and the pastor pulled up a chair at the corner next to him. I sat next to Pastor Jame, and Melissa sat next to me. One side of the table was against the wall and that is why we three ended up on the same side.

"Pastor Jame, why don't you do the honors?" Mrs. Cora suggested.

The freckled preacher responded in a deeper than usual baritone voice, that was official to Baptist preachers all over the South. "Please bow your heads, he said. Dear Heavenly Father, please grant Sister Cora and Sister Melissa and Brother Mooney Jr. an extra modicum of Your grace and mercy as they travel through difficult times. Please bless this food for the nourishment of our bodies and bless us all to Thy service. Amen!" And everyone said, "Amen!"

Flour, lard, and milk had become hot, flaky biscuits, and the pork chops that had been raw just minutes earlier were now golden brown; their smell filled the whole house. A cold jar of applesauce had become a warm bowl of nutmeg-seasoned confection that smelled like apple pie. Green beans had been flavored with pork. It was all on the table, and Holly had placed a whole biscuit in his mouth by the time Pastor Jame said amen.

There was a farm scene printed on the beige, vinyl tablecloth. It depicted a chicken pecking near my plate and a cow looking well-fed near Pastor Jame's right hand. The butt of a pig protruded from beneath the plate of biscuits. Melissa moved her left hand and revealed a woman and girl standing in silhouette with bonnets covering their heads. They appeared to be standing on the tablecloth maker's label: Atlas. She put her hand under the table and onto my knee. I casually looked at her, and she smiled. I looked at Mrs. Cora, and her brown eyes glared at the sheriff with full fury. At that moment, I thought how the tablecloth represented the ideal America and we poor wretches around the table represented the real America—privilege and poverty all in one setting.

Holly was talking with his mouth full. "Cora, these some good 'o biscuits, hmmm, hmmm!"

"So how can I help you gentlemen?" Mrs. Cora asked the other two men as the platters of food moved around the table accompanied by murmurs of, "Yes, let me have some of that," and "I haven't had beans like this in a long time." This went on for some time before an answer came to Mrs. Cora's question.

Finally, Pastor Jame said, "Mrs. Cora, we need to talk to you about this thing that's gonna happen with Moony Jr. You see…

Holly, displaying the nauseating contents of his full mouth—chewed meat and green beans—interrupted Pastor Jame: "How would you feel if I could get you the chance to visit Moony Jr. and cook 'im a meal? And before you say no out of hand, what if this was Moony Jr.'s request?"

Mrs. Cora thought for a moment and then asked disgustedly, "Sheriff Holly, why do you even care?"

This question hung like humid air between claps of thunder. Everyone knew an explosion was coming, but nobody knew when.

Pastor Jame added coaxingly, "Don't you think it might be a good thing? You could make peace with Moony Jr. I know he would enjoy a visit."

"You new here, Pastor, so I must tell you I don't have a need to make peace with Moony Jr. I talk with him every first Tuesday night at 9:35 p.m. when he calls. It's you an' Sheriff Holly that needs to make peace wit' Juney, maybe?"

At that moment, all eyes fell on Holly, but he had kicked off his shoes, bobbed his head, and nodded off at the table.

I yelled out of frustration, "Holly!"

Melissa's hand on my leg tightened its' grip but did not move, and that both calmed and excited me at the same time. My mind quickly moved to a vision of Melissa across the bed instead of her mother. But then the certain knowledge of that not happening doubt of that happening brought me back to reality.

The sheriff jerked awake and yawned while stretching his arms out wide and twisting his wrists. "I'm sorry, but them biscuits put the sleep mojo on me. Always do."

"Mrs. Cora asked you a question," I said.

"I know. She wanna know why I want to see this thing happen wit' her and Mooney, right?"

"No," Mrs. Cora said.

Melissa jumped into the conversation from my side. "Mama want to know why you care what happens to Juney, since you help put him in the death house in the first place." The slight movements of her hand on my knee made me stir in my seat.

Pastor Jame cleared his throat again, but before he could speak, I said, "Pastor, let's just let the good ol' sheriff answer that. Is it that you figured out you might finally need those votes you lost back from when you railroaded Juney in the first place? You think you can take some of that guilt off yourself for what yawl did to him? I knew Juney long before we all ended up in the integrated high school. Do you even know why everybody calls Clarence Moony Jr., Juney? Me! That's why! I started calling him Juney when we were six years old. It was short for Moony Jr. People liked it so much that everybody started calling him that, and by the time I was eight, it had stuck. You don't name a man and then not do all you can to help him.

"I mean, everybody knows that Juney didn't kill nobody. I'm not even sure Juney was a get-away driver. I heard it was the Stenson brothers that did all of it, and they brought Juney into it to keep themselves off death row. You made a deal with them devils, and you knew them boys would say anything—do anything—to save themselves. You petty, Holly! And you know it! You'd been trying to get Juney on something serious for years, just cause of how we treated you in school. You finally got your chance, and you took it. Now the politics in the county has changed and you want to make amends for it."

Holly looked hard at me then, and I could see a boil of fury in his eyes. I had to give him credit, though. He held himself in check and said to me, "You work for the FBI, right?"

"You know I don't, Holly. No! It's the Postal Inspection Service, U-S-P-I. Been there over fifteen years. What about it?"

"What? You work at P-I?'

I could tell he intentionally left the U-S off in what he thought was a clever dig.

"I work armed robbery from the mail. Been there five years. I was in employee theft before that and theft from the mail before that. Again Holly, what's your point!"

"In all that time, did you ever make a deal wit' the devil? Did you ever threaten to take kids from they mama if she didn't tell on they man? Did you ever give the best deal to the criminal that got to you first, even if you knew they was the ringleader or the triggerman? Did you ever play wit' the evidence just a little bit to git the right conviction? Did you ever play God just a little bit?"

Holly knew I had, because, as quiet as it was kept, that's how police departments all over America at that time did business. You would sometimes lose sight of humanity just to get that conviction, especially when you were on the way up or when you were dealing with a smart suspect. I found myself experiencing self-reflection then, and I was not proud of some of my career choices at that moment. I wanted to yell back at Holly. I wanted to tell him I never played with evidence or suborned perjury, but I realized he wouldn't even know what that meant. I thought to myself, I don't even really know what that means. It's really just another way of getting evidence and maybe making someone tell the truth. But by then, I was thinking am I really no better than Holly.

I stayed quiet, but when I looked up, I saw Holly was in his own moment. He had that big, nasty, red-paisley bandana in his right hand, and he was wiping his eyes before blowing his nose. His left hand was outstretched, as though he was holding his life in it. His face was raw-red with blood vessels popping from beneath his skin.

He said, "I didn't mean for Moony—I mean Juney—to get caught up in this the way he did. It wasn't my intention, but Juney got to take some credit, too. After all, I offered him a chance."

"Take credit for what?" I asked back, coming on the offensive again. "Take credit for being Juney? Everybody knows Juney was a easy target, low-hanging fruit, as they say. He was high half the time and lying around some alley trying to figure out where to get some more money and drugs the rest of the time. I heard he was trying to pull his life back together for a while, but this town don't allow of that. But you needed to be tough, get some more votes in, so why not Juney? The mood of the county about crime has changed now. People know the truth and more black folks vote. Now my good friend's gonna be killed. Juney got twenty-two years for the armed robbery 'cause it was a second offence. Hell, on his first offense, the gun wasn't even loaded. He got put in the death house for what he did after he got to prison, but you're the one who put him in there in the first place. Yeah, he killed another prisoner, but he wouldn't have been there to do that if you hadn't put him in prison in the first place!" I was wiping my own tears by the time I finished my little speech. I casually pushed Melissa's hand away.

Mrs. Cora shouted, "Stop!" I thought she had seen my actions under the tablecloth. The shout was enough to bring silence to the entire house. Even the radio went silent, and the lights went out, though we soon realized it was a coincidence of the storm. The power had gone out.

Melissa was walking from further back in the house with a lit candle before I even realized she had gone.

Things remained quiet, except for the noise of the storm. It was like nobody wanted to talk in a sinister darkness lit only by lightning strikes and two small, wavering candle flames. The sounds of distant thunder only added to the surreal atmosphere of an arrogant sheriff, a well-meaning preacher, a grieving mother, and an angry daughter, each with leery eyes glowering at each other and at me. I wanted to leave—my leg was impatiently jumping—but there was Melissa's calming hand again, back in place. I knew I couldn't go, not because of the weather, but because of what I had to tell Mrs. Cora and Melissa.

Melissa said, "I know Juney better than anybody in this room, except maybe Mama, and he wouldn't hold grudges against anybody here, so don't go thinkin' you can somehow help your standing with him by coming in here claiming to help him, or me and Mama, for that matter."

"What do you want!" Mrs. Cora demanded again, emphatically. "Yawl come in here, and you don't tell me what you want. Both yawl got blood on yo' hands if'n you ask me. No tellin' how many lives you changed for the worse up in Atlanta." She was talking in my direction then but changed her gaze to Holly.

I knew she was referring to Holly's comment about all cops doing the same job, the same way. She then continued, "You know goddamn well you changed my life, but somebody please tell me what you want."

Pastor Jame gave a slight caught and calmly said, "We want to know if you want to cook a meal for Moony Jr. Sheriff Holly arranged for you to take in a meal or cook it on the premises."

"I thought that's what yawl wanted. I heard about it."

Holly and Jame looked at each other, and both

mouthed the same soundless names at the same moment, "Lacy and Stacy."

The candle flickered, and the air in the room turned suddenly heavy and still. A clap of lighting and loud boom of thunder shook the whole house. Apparently, we were directly under a thundercloud. Heavy rain slanted down in heavy winds that manhandled the environment outside the house. I looked down towards home and saw a dark house with the porch light on and realized the power was back. Mama and Daddy's porch was being pelted in the wind and rain, and I could just make out the small body of a dog, a puppy really, curled up and cowering at the kitchen door. I smiled.

"Now what you grinnin' at?" Holly asked.

It crossed my mind to say nothin' again, but I said, "The last time I saw Juney was at your big mama's funeral." I was looking at Melissa as I spoke and referring to Mrs. Cora's mother and, of course, Juney and Melissa's grandmother. "It was right over there," I continued. "It was in that graveyard, and there were thunderstorms passing through that day, too, only it was in the middle of the day." Melissa and Mrs. Cora both nodded, more out of politeness, I believe, than conformation, though what I said was true.

That day, Juney had to sit in the second row by himself, behind the family, except for the two big prison guards that escorted him. I guess they figured we should have been grateful that the warden let him come. Of course, this was before Juney did what he did to get on

299

death row.

All me and Juney's friends, the people he went to school with, were there. And I felt so bad for Juney 'cause they wouldn't let anybody get close to him to shake his hand, tell 'im how sorry they were or anything. I showed one of the guards my badge in the palm of my hand kinda underhanded-like, and he waved me over in the same way. I asked him if I could speak with Juney privately, and he just shook his head, but he said I could talk to him right there. 'No touching,' he whispered. Standing near that crowd, all I could think to say was, "How you doin', Juney?" He shot me a look and never said a word. I felt like a fool just standing there, so I walked away. I guess that was because I could, and he couldn't.

"I haven't spoken to him since that funeral," I said.

It was not long after that that he killed that other prisoner. I remember thinking at that funeral that Juney was a little scuffed up around the edges, but I had no idea if he was going through something in prison at that time. I felt like a damn fool for asking him that. *How you doing Juney?*

"About five years before the funeral, I had visited him in prison—had us set up in a lawyers' room since I was the police, you know, thought I was doing him a favor. But he told me I was gonna get him killed, 'cause everybody knew I was the police."

I asked Juney, if they knew me and him were supposed to be friends, that we were in Vietnam together? But he just started talking about mutual acquaintances after that, and I believe that's what he thought I came there for.

"So, I just put money in his prison account after that. He's never thanked me or even acknowledged it—at least for a long time—not that I wanted him to. But two weeks ago, I got a letter from 'im."

Melissa seemed confused, and I believed she was about to ask me what I had gone there for, but Mrs. Cora was more interested in what he'd had to say in his letter.

"What did he want?" she quietly asked.

"Want? He didn't want anything. At least not from me." I answered back quietly, as though it were only she and I in the room. "First off, he told me he was sorry for how he had treated me at the funeral and at the prison. He thanked me for sending him money over the years, and he told me he was better off on death row than in the general population at the prison. He said he had taken out one of the most brutal people in prison to get on death row and he would have killed more without that change.

"He told me to tell Meliss that he appreciated all that she had done and that he wanted her to do one more thing. He asked that you be patient with your mother and make sure she is always all right. He said you would know what he means"

Mrs. Cora started to murmur and cry then but nobody moved to console her, not even Melissa. I thought that was strange, but it seemed to fit the mood.

"Nevertheless," I started again. "He said he loved you, Melissa, something I know you already knew. He said he understood if you didn't want to come see him at the prison anymore—I took that to mean since his death date had been set—and that was all right with him.

"Mrs. Cora, he said it was hard for him to ask you to come, but he would love to see you one more time. He knows you don't like to travel but he also he knows you love him, and he was sorry for all the heartache he caused you. He knew that someone would ask you to cook for him because his death row sergeant had asked him if he wanted that to happen. He told me he gets to call you the first Tuesday of each month and that he didn't want those calls to change because of what he put in my letter. He loves the way yawl laugh and talk about nothing in particular and he doesn't want to lose that."

Mrs. Cora said, "I thought that was our little secret, Juney's an' mine, an' I can't understand why he couldn't tell me them things his self."

"I believe you answered your own question buy the way you talked about Stacy and Lacy earlier today," I said.

Melissa's expression changed to brilliance, as though a light bulb had popped on in her brain. Then she immediately looked sad again.

Mrs. Cora and Melissa started to sob then, and I looked away outside, trying hold back my own tears. I was unsuccessful. Holly and Pastor Jame were astonished at my sudden disclosure but they also seemed to know there was no place for them in this conversation.

Mrs. Cora asked, "Did you bring the letter?"

"No, mam." I answered, the child in me speaking. "Frankly he gave me some messages for other friends of ours, too, and he asked that I not show it you or Melissa. There was silence.

Dogs howled somewhere to the south of town. I could hear bullfrogs croaking all the way from the water-treatment pond, two miles away. The thunderstorm had passed. The air was fresh after the storm and there was a crescent moon with a corona of haze around it hanging over my parents' house. Suddenly the phone began to ring from its base somewhere back in the house. Everyone but Mrs. Cora looked at his or her watch. It was 9:30 p.m. on the dot, and it was the first Tuesday.

THE CHILDREN OF ATLAS

"Today, I bring you the truth about our situation—about your situation! Give me your complete attention for the last time because examples will be made, and some of you may not walk from this sanctuary today. Others of you will be re-educated. Maybe?

"This is my fault! This is all my fault, but you young'uns will suffer the consequences. Some of you will most likely die simply because you came here to get away from the sterility of your life here at the Institute and not because you really wanted to hear what I had to say about God, or anything else.

"And, it is all my doing. I stand here, as the corporate police are surrounding us—this institute and my church. I proclaim, in this pulpit of familiar ground, as a prophet might! But I am no prophet. I am just a disfigured man. Deny me as you see fit, for I am no Messiah neither. I have the ordained human privilege to speak the truth to you but earlier today, I denied you! I denied you all. I am more like Aristotle, who dared to corrupt the minds of the youth, than Peter, that rock of a church and later disclaimer. I will pay for my sins, just as Aristotle paid for his—with a poison death, no doubt—but so will you, one way or the other, and that's my fault, too."

Those were the beginning words of the self-anointed Most Right Reverend Calvin Jones-Stray at the regular Saturday evening gathering of his congregants—young congregants—who usually seemed somehow mesmerized by his words even if they didn't show it. More aptly though, the grip was by his rhythm and vocal inflections that were somehow captivating, yet soothing, to their young minds. They would stare at each other blankly and then at him while he went on for hours at a time. They seemed to love the way he chewed on words and thoughts, and picked at themes, both religious and secular. They watched as he made exaggerated movements with his body to make his points. It was better than watching the usual Institute propaganda on the campus big screens or studying. In short, he was the best show in town.

"Hear me on this!" His big black hands went wide. His color favored fruitwood down to the minor striations. "The corporate not only owns your labor for the next sixty years, it owns your souls, your intelligence, your feelings—

to be used as generals, chiefs, educators, administrators, and so forth!" His sermon was different this time, but this time the situation was also different. It was real and dire. Though he wore the same tie dyed, multicolored, dashiki, this time it was blood stained as well. The color red did not match the blue, green, and brown.

"And oh yes, you are also their modern-day versions of concu- bines, and in the same breath, their innovators and industrialists and inventors. They have big plans for you! You are seedstock for the coming order in America—I dare say, the world!

"While their children play in the garden of Adam and Eve—the world you create—you will learn and they will inherit your know- ledge, your time, and your talents. While you fight their wars—they gather your medals of valor and put them on their walls! You will shed your blood! And your DNA will seed them in their efforts to become immortal—these people you don't even know! Yet, they can say you are not slaves. You will have freewill—you think! But they owned shares in your productivity even before you make a single innovation."

When Reverend Stray had preached to his congregation of prison inmates, he would have received an "amen" or a shout with his last pronouncement; the shout of voices signifying a vision of glory or the "amen" just recognition of a phrase well turned. But he knew not to expect that kind of feedback from this group.

"I stand before you as a broken, toothless, ol' half-blind fool, but hear me on this, for it is truer than the numbers in your eyes—their way of keeping account of you—you are the beginning of the next wave of what will come. I was the beginning of the first wave. I was found in prison, tested and acquired. I have the numbers in my eyes too. I am double-zero!"

He removed his dark glasses, took a small round flashlight with a blue lens from his podium, and illuminated his own face. The number zero revealed itself in his one available eye. For the first time, he revealed himself to be one of them. They had never seen him without his dark glasses—what he called "shades." When asked about his constant use of dark eyewear he would only say, "My shades protect me from you and you from me."

He had one bandaged eye that day of his last sermon—the bandaged eye they could see even under the dark glasses, but the other eye bore a zero, as revealed by the light. He opened his mouth and pointed to a blank space in his gum at his lower jaw. The space was where teeth were firmly planted the day before. He shouted, "Look what they did to me!"

"This Atlas Institute—this place they have brought you, so they can train your minds—is no more or less a brainwashing place on a magnificent order. They tell you, 'you are special.' They tell you, 'you are the children of Atlas!'—Atlas, that brother of Prometheus, who dare give the world the gift of fire and suffered horribly for that present. Atlas! —who is doomed to carry, not the world, but the universe on his shoulders. They tell you that one day you will carry the world! That is why your labor, your intelligence, your time and talents were bought by the corporate founders and placed here to be trained. But what they don't tell you is that you will carry it for them—the universe I mean—not for the betterment of humankind, but for them! They, the investors, shareholders, and owners have all the rights of exploitation. Not you!"

There was loud banging at the wall to the right of Reverend Stray as though the little structure would fall at any minute. It held because the reverend had secretly reinforced the walls and doors with rebar and concrete. This small whitewashed, rickety, wooden church, as it appeared from the outside, was actually of saferoom and storm shelter quality on the inside. It faced an alley on the backwater of a multimillion-dollar campus. He had his living quarters in the basement and had secretly, over the years, constructed escape tunnels to the outside because he knew this day would come.

"Let me explain *time* and *risk*, while there is still *time* left!" He began again, "I wish I had time to pick at this more, but the risk is too great. Though it is the year twenty-thirty, there was a time when you would have been raised in the homes of loving parents, maybe. You would have lived off what your parents earned in their work and you would have been raised by them in *their* value systems. You would have gone to college, or not; found a mate, or not; loved or been loved, or not; but the choices and experiences would have been yours and your parents'. But you will not experience any of that. What better way to increase the efficiency of time and destroy the risk of your freewill asserting itself, or you becoming contaminated with knowledge or your own purpose, than to collect you here in their sterile petri dish. In this place they control your environment, risk, and time. But time is coming due and I will explain the real risk. They had not counted on me, the contaminant.

"In a short ten years from now you will see such a change in the world. And it is you who will usher in that change, though you, the individual, will not know it! They will know because they own the masterplan. They created the formula. They proved the concept. It was proven ten years ago that they could buy anything, including you.

"Your labor will carry the universe much like some believed the industrialists of the Twentieth Century carried it for your great ancestors. I give you Ayn Rand, for example, an author who three-quarters of a century ago wrote what some believed to be an obscure text extoling the virtues of unchecked free enterprise and the greatness of industrialists and innovators."

Reverend Stray stood six-foot-six, and when he exaggerated the use of his outstretched arms in the pulpit, he appeared even larger to his charges of ten to twelve-year-old's. He could usually tell he had lost their attention after the first fifteen minutes but, on this day, his self-possessed divinity, conferred over his natural charisma, was in overdrive and even the youngest ones were paying close attention. Or, maybe it was the noises emanating from outside that helped them focus. They were afraid of the noises of power tools, but he had their attention.

"The hero of her story is John Galt! It is no accident that you are owned by a corporation controlled by John Gault, spelled different: G-a-u-l-t. The Gault Companies own your intellect, your mussel, your gristle, your agility, and even your charisma. I know from where I speak because my soul too was purchased from my prison cell and the state received an income for my life. In exchange, the Institute owes my future potential, as they called it. They said it was a business proposition. They trained me in their image. And I, in turn, was supposed to train you. They sold stock in me, as a conglomerate. It was not enough that they owned stock in the prison industrial complex, therefore receiving a dividend on my incarceration, they now owned stock directly in me. I believe at worst; they knew they could sell me for parts if I displeased them. They said they invest in the risk that I could be trained and educated to suit their needs. That need was ultimately for me to become your caretaker and confidant. They said I was not bound to them. But for me, it was here or back to prison where I still remained their property. I am first generation you! And if you seek to withhold that which they believe is theirs, they will destroy you. Remember what I tell you today!

"Just a few short hours ago they removed my shades and sought to destroy me because of what they thought I told you! Rand, in her story, fashioned a world where Atlas—he became indifferent—and the universe was almost lost because the industrialists, architects, and entreprencurs chose to withhold themselves from the world. She showed a world where the greed of politicians—hungry for more power and corrupt—destroyed the spirit of American democracy and independence. Atlas, this son of a god, who carried the universe on his shoulders was indifferent to the America they had created.

"I tell you today that the pendulum that supported this belief has traversed so far in that direction that Atlas is dead. Money and greed have gone uncheck to the point that you exist, and you are here! They have purchased Atlas by purchasing you. But you *are* the children of Atlas, just not in the way they tell you. It is in the way you will become. Your labor was purchased from your guardians by the Gault Companies in exchange of a lifetime of income to those same people. You are to be the next generation of workers in their plan to own everything—all the institutions in our country—political, religious, legal, media, capitalist, medical! —. Why run for President of the United States when you can buy the presidency and all its powers? Why seek to influence the institutions of power—like the Congress—when you can simply buy them through the corporate structure of stocks and dividends, then mold them to your will? This is not the first time in our history this has been done, but it is the first time it's been done so completely by one person or one family.

"You are the pride of the Atlas Institute and that alone will save most of you! But they must make examples of some.

"It will be up to you to carry the universe! The

question is, will you carry it for them, or will you carry it for yourselves and the betterment of humankind? Think hard on this my young charges before they come in here."

A hand goes up from one of the youngest in the pews. His name is Renaldo. He has thick black, curly hair. His labor was purchased even before he was conceived and placed in a womb. His genetic attributes had been arranged to please his makers.

"How will we know what to do, or when to do it.?" He asked.

"You all are among the brightest they could find or make. And especially you Renaldo, you have a charisma that will make you a servant leader. The expectation is that you will please them. But you, and those others like you, must make your pack while you can, here and now! I cannot tell you anything beyond why you are here at Atlas and your intended purpose. I have seen these things, not in visions but in files stored in data streams. I have cared for you as your servant. Now I care for you as your sentinel."

There was a banging on the steel bars of the outer door to the side entrance. It was louder than the old man expected but he suspected that was because of the words he had just uttered. He knew they were probably listening through the walls as they tried to break in. He had constructed his little church well, so he knew it could take a beating. He was sure his persecutors had torn the wooden slats down and found the reinforced concrete. But then, he heard a mechanical grinder that cuts steel like butter and that worried him. He knew that dynamite would be out of the question as long as he had the young charges in his pews because they represented a great investment to the Institute and the payout would be even greater in the future. The Institute could only afford to sacrifice a few.

The licks were ferocious, and the sweat ran down into his eyes and stung. He sat straight mainly because the ropes were so tight. He somehow convinced himself that his cause was noble and worth of the pain, but that conviction didn't last long.

One of his tormentors was a thin-faced black man who seemed to enjoy his role too much. He knocked another tooth out—from the space Reverend Stray would show his congregants later—picked it up from the floor, shoved it in old Stray's mouth, held Stray's nose, and made Stray swallow it. His thin face laughed while he did this.

The other one was vicious, too, but he would sit with his legs crossed and sip coffee or tea—Stray couldn't tell which—from a porcine cup while his partner hammered away. This second one was the inquisitors. He asked the questions. He slapped with a synthetic leather glove when it was his turn.

Stray held his piece when he could and cried out when it hurt. He would breath hard to prepare for the next barrage and he stuck with his story mainly because it was mostly true. He wondered why they had a caged bird in the room, a little thing that flitted around its cage while they beat on him. *What perversion was this?* He thought.

They wanted to know the extent of his "infection,"

they called it. They wanted to know everyone involved. They called out names of others at the Institute and in the town, but Stray resisted. Stray was the only one involved, but he didn't want to give his torturers the satisfaction of knowing that for certain. So, he resisted and appeared to hold back as best he could.

"I set that place up to help this institute, not to hurt it!" he begged. "Those young minds needed a place where they could just rest!" he shouted over and over again. And that was true. "They came on their own and I preached a little gospel! That's all." He pleaded, and that was mostly true.

But his two tormentors weren't listening. They didn't seem to really care what he said. They seemed to be possessed, as far as he was concerned. That was why he considered it a trap when they left him alone, still tied in his torture chamber. They left the birdcage door open while they went to lunch, laughing. But his struggle was only beginning.

Stray scanned over his young audience and some of them look puzzled at him. "My eye? They made me fight a bird—with only my teeth and tong! It wanted to take my eye. They took me to Hell and tormented me and the beast picked at my bones!"

This simple statement was all he said on the subject then, but the truth was that every time he fought the small, winged creature by shaking his head and biting at it, the bird would fly back into its' cage to rest. It would look at him the way birds do—turning its head one way or the other while sizing up the situation—then come again with another attack, flapping and squawking. He struggled for what seemed like hours. He finally caught a foot only to feel a talon ripping his lower lip as he bit down. Then he simply freed himself, the way desperate men do, and walked out.

He considered it was too easy, even with his battle with the bird. *Was it they wanted to make sure that the place they knew about, my church, was the only place? Or, they wanted to know how many children would show up at my chapel and therefore know how many had been infected by my words,* he thought at the time. Though logic told him they had been watching him and his church for some time, he was still puzzled by it all. So maybe they just enjoyed beating the hell out of an old man was an angle he also considered. In any case, he had overcome, and the children had come to their weekly meeting. He had no way to warn them not to come that day. That was that. There was nothing he could change.

"I won my battle with the bird," he said, calmly. "And now I ask you to fight—not today, but when the time is right for you to win.

"There are tunnels leading from the basement of our church. I don't know if our persecutors know of their existences, but I am sure they are, at this moment, listening in and initiating a frantic search for where those tunnels exit. So, go! This is all you need to know!"

Then he shouted loud and clear: "You have been warned!"

ABOUT THE AUTHOR

Wallace Shields had a 30-year career in criminal and intelligence investigations (Georgia Bureau of Investigations, Customs and Border Protection Office of Internal Affairs, and U.S. Secret Service). He also taught law enforcement and criminal justice courses at Seattle University and the University of North Carolina at Charlotte. Wallace holds a bachelor's degree from Georgia Southern University in Criminal Justice and a master's degree from the Joint Military Intelligence College (Defense Intelligence University) in Strategic Intelligence. Wallace has a passion for social justice and explores that passion in his writing.

www.ingramcontent.com/pod-product-compliance
Lightning Source LLC
Chambersburg PA
CBHW061642180626
46818CB00010B/112